still the one

Symbols of Love
Book Two

dylan allen

D1519616

Proofreading by
virginia tesi carey

Proofreading by
chloe kill trivelpiece

V-DA08052021

foreword

Dear reader,

I am a huge believer in making the most of second chances.

I've seen, first hand, how rare and fleeting they can be and think they are a special kind of magic.

Rewriting this series has reinforced that magical quality for me. I'm so grateful for the opportunity to give Milly and Dean the story they deserve.

I hope you enjoy it!

Thank you for reading.

All my best,

Dylan

also by dylan allen

Also By Dylan Allen

Then Came You

Set in London this is a workplace romance that features two people who are trying to outrun their pasts and protect their cynical hearts from more pain. But when their lives collide and their hearts and bodies yearn for each other, they'll have to decide if they are brave enough to fight for their love.

Still The One

This second chance romance features high school sweethearts who were torn apart by tragedy and treachery. Years later, when they realize that their feelings haven't changed, they embark on a mission to unravel the mystery surrounding her father's disappearance. But what they discover about their past might make a future together impossible.

STANDALONES

The Sun and Her Star

A friends to lovers, second chance at story. Angsty, emotional, sexy, and unforgettable. Graham and Apollo are two people who find each other just when they need to. What starts as a deep, abiding friendship grows into the kind of love that can move mountains. This story is a reader favorite.

Thicker Than Water

A friends to lovers and workplace romance that follows the love story between an undocumented writer and the movie executive who changes her life. This story is hopeful, honest, and achingly relevant. Go in with an open mind and prepare to fall in love.

The Sound of Temptation

A second chance forbidden romance that follows star-crossed lovers, a talented musician and the artist who becomes his muse. It spans nearly ten years and is a turbulent, exhilarating, heart pounding, and deeply intimate love story you will never forget.

Find all of them here.

If you've read my books and haven't already, please leave a review. Nothing fancy, but a line or two helps so much!

I love to hear from readers! Stay in touch with me everywhere using this link.

To my sisters, Mia and Alma.
You are my constants, and I am yours. I wouldn't be me without you. I
love you both so much. Thank you.

fifteen years earlier

Houston, TX

dean's prologue

fertile soil

My biggest fear has always been that the only fruit tainted trees could bear was the rotten kind. Then, I met Milly and saw a reflection of myself in her eyes that proved me wrong.

I was nothing like the miserable man and the cruel woman who'd made me.

From her, I've also learned that love doesn't hurt. Family can be found and is never, truly, lost.

Over the last three years, her home has become mine.

In this house, love made room for a boy who needed it.

In this house, I found that love is a strength when it's got fertile soil to take root in.

I thought nothing could change this.

But tonight, the tranquility of this home had been fractured along with the rest of my life.

The girl I love is right in front of me. Our fingers are intertwined, our foreheads pressed together.

Yet, I can feel her slipping away.

"Do you think they are going to arrest us? If they can't find him? I mean?" she whispers after a prolonged silence.

My heart twists at the fear in her voice and in anticipation of how little anything I say will do to soothe it.

"You haven't done anything wrong. We both know there's no way he'd leave you or your mom. Not for all the money in the world."

She nods, but her lips are pressed together the way she does when she's trying not to cry.

"Red, you've got to have some faith."

"I'm trying. I don't know how you can be so calm." Her voice is quiet, but the accusation in it is loud and clear.

I unlink our fingers and lean away from the frantic energy coming from her. "Let's give them a few days before we start panicking."

She pushes out of my arms and leans away from me, her face pinched with disbelief. "Listen to what they are saying on the news about my father. This house was a crime scene. We're getting death threats. You had to sneak in here tonight." She paces the small carpet beside her bed.

I grab her wrist and pull her back to the bed and put my arms around her as much to comfort her as to ease the ache of helplessness building inside of me.

"My dad will be back tomorrow and whatever is going on, he'll clear it up."

"But…why hasn't he called? He must have heard the news." The accusation is gone but what's replaced it is harder to take - doubt.

I break our eye contact. "I don't know," I admit, my eyes on the cornflower blue bedspread.

"What if… he can't and what they're saying is true?"

"It's not," I say with as much certainty as I can. "I ignore the small lump of worry that's growing in the pit of my stomach at the mention of the new theory that the blood found in the back of Mr. Hassan's abandoned vehicle was my father's. "My mom spoke to him. She said he sounded fine. He'll be here tomorrow, you'll see."

"That your dad wouldn't leave you guys for all the money in the world."

She sighs a long, deflating exhale and her eyes fill tears. "I'm so scared, D. Where's my dad? And if he didn't take it, where'd all that money go?"

The "it's going to be okay" that should be on the tip of my tongue is lodged in my throat. "Come here." I pull her toward me until she's curled onto my lap.

"Oh God, what are we going to do?" she asks in a hushed, teary voice.

"I don't know. But whatever it is, we're going to do it together."

She lays her head on my shoulder. "I don't know what I'd do without you."

"You won't have to find out."

"Promise?" she asks and holds up her hand with her pinky crooked.

I link mine to it and nod. "Promise."

A thread of guilt knots itself around my gut. I rub small circles over her back and fight back the voice of doubt telling me to stop making promises I can't keep.

I muster a tender smile for her and make a promise I know I'll keep. "If you need me, all you have to do is call. Nothing will keep me from coming to you. Everyone's on edge right now. Saying and doing things they'll regret. Let's not fall into that trap, okay, baby?"

I urge her to look up at me by putting two fingers under her chin. "Red, promise me that this," I put my other hand on her chest, over her heart, "won't change. Please."

"Never," she whispers earnestly, her eyes full of an aching, urgent love I recognize because I feel it too.

Our friends and parents think we're too young to feel this way. I don't care.

Not even a little.

I know right from wrong and Milly's been "right" since that first "hello."

She's my person. She was meant to be my best friend, my partner, my co-conspirator and I was meant to be hers.

"Dean? Are you in there?" Her sister Lilly's voice carries through the door and I get to my feet.

"Come in," Milly calls.

The door opens just enough for Lilly's head to poke through. "You didn't hear it from me. But Dean, your mom called and she knows you're here. She's on her way to get you." She presses a finger to her lips with a warning glare and then disappears again.

"Shit." My stomach falls to the floor. "I told her I was going to the gym. How does she know I'm here?"

"Why did you lie about where you were going?" Milly asks.

I curse under my breath and look away.

"Why, Dean?" Milly repeats with a steel in her voice that forces my gaze back to hers.

"I promised her I wouldn't see you."

Hurt blooms in her eyes and she looks down at the floor. "I see."

The disappointment and heartbreak in those two words makes me sick to my stomach and I wish I'd lied. "It doesn't matter what my mother thinks. It never has."

She gives a dry laugh. "Yeah. She has always hated me. But your father... if my father did the things they're saying —"

I cut her off with a firm hand on each of her shoulders. "Our fathers have been best friends longer than either of them have been married. No matter what happens, he loves you all like family. And families don't turn their backs on each other."

It's what I've always thought to be true. But as the fallout from what looks very much like her father's embezzlement continues, I'm less sure of their relationship surviving. That company is the only thing my father loves more than me. No matter why her father left and no matter what really happened to the money, there's no denying the total collapse of the company and what that means for his future and mine.

She nods but doesn't look up. "You should go meet her outside. The last thing we need is her making a scene."

She's right, but I'm torn. "I hate leaving you like this."

"It's okay. It's just for now." She looks up at me then and gives me a brave smile even as tears roll down her face.

I pull her into a hug.

She wraps her arms around me and buries her face in my chest. "I love you, too," she whispers.

"We're Reddy, remember?"

She smiles up at me and I wish my eyes were a camera to capture the happiness budding in her eyes. "I'll never forget. No matter what."

———

"I can't believe you came here after I told you not to." My mother's eyes flash with anger as soon as I climb into the car.

I buckle my seatbelt and meet her gaze, unflinching and unapologetic. "I needed to see her."

"Damn it, Dean." She slaps the steering wheel and glares at it like it's a proxy for my face. "Your father taught you better than this. You know that a good son puts his family above his whims."

I scoff and shake my head. "She's so much more than a whim."

"And, you're not a good son." She presses the car's ignition button and throws the car into drive.

I don't reply. There's nothing to say.

We've never gotten along. And I'm *not* a good son.

I once told my father that I hated my mother. He'd said, "You may not like her all the time, but you *can't* hate half of what makes you whole."

He was right.

But it's been a very long time since I liked her.

The feeling has always been mutual. We used to avoid each other. I'd been counting down the days until I could put real distance between us.

Now…everything is up in the air.

"Her father *stole* from us." My stomach clenches with dread and doubt, but I don't let any of it show in my voice.

"We don't know that. They're *both* missing. And Mr. Hassan may have been the face of it, but it's dad's company too."

Her hands grip the steering wheel so tight, her knuckles look like they might break the skin. "You're *so* disloyal," she snaps. "Your father would *never* willingly leave me."

The truth strains against the back of my throat, I want so badly to tell her just how wrong she is.

When he told me a few months ago that he was planning to ask her for a divorce as soon as I left for college, I was relieved. No more suffering through family meals where he put on a brave face, she put on a kind one, and I pretended to believe them.

I asked him why now and his reply had been simple. "Once you're gone to college, I'll have no reason to stay. And that feels like a really good reason to go."

I was happy for him. He talked about moving to Palo Alto so that when I started at Stanford next year, we'd be in the same place.

Keeping his confidence was the last promise I made to him. I bite my tongue so hard I taste blood and stew in silence for the rest of the ride home.

"Dean, wake up." My mother wakes me up with a rough shake of my shoulder.

I blink, bleary-eyed and confused. She's standing beside the car. "Are we home?" I sit up and blink at the wall of flashing lights in front of our house. "

"What's going on?" I ask, my eyes darting around the swarm of police cars before I look up at her.

Her expression is grim and pale, her eyes are red-rimmed and glassy with tears.

Fear prickles my scalp. "What's wrong? Tell me."

She releases a shuddering breath and her stricken eyes fill with fresh tears. "They found your father."

.

milly's prologue

rotten roots

My father used to say I had nerves of steel.

But like the rest of what my father said, that was a lie. In the two weeks since he left, I've learned that my nerves are as tender and fragile as everyone else's and that my judgment is no good.

I was sure my father was a good man and certain that my family was unbreakable.

My father is now on the FBI's most wanted list and the pillars that my life balanced on are gone and for the first time in my life, I'm on my knees, helpless and suddenly very alone.

I texted Dean the day after he left here, asking if we could meet up. He wrote back to say, "I need some space. I'll call you when I can talk."

The rejection hurt, but I understood. We were in a pressure cooker that had no release valve.

I pick up my phone and struggle with what to do next.

I should leave him be, but time isn't on my side. We've been offered a new start and decided to take it.

We're not supposed to tell anyone, but I can't disappear without so much as a goodbye to the boy who planted a flag in my heart so deep I'm not sure I can ever wedge it loose. Who I promised I'd be here for whenever he needed me.

I take several deep breaths to force my racing heart to calm itself.

He loves me. I know that for certain. No matter what else is happening, I can count on that.

I quit stalling and hit the call button.

The phone rings so many times, I'm afraid it's going to voice-mail again. Anticipation makes my stomach drop and I think I might be sick. Finally, he picks up and I sit up straight with a gasp and hold my breath until he speaks.

"Hello?" He sounds like he's sleeping but his voice is still smooth as honey.

I release my relief in a long exhale and let my worry spill over.

"Dean. It's me. I know you said you needed space but they're moving us."

"Millicent Hassan, is that you?" His mother's smoke rough-ened voice is made even more guttural by the disdain in her voice. My name sounds like a curse.

I pull the phone away from my ear and peer at the screen to confirm it's Dean's number I dialed. This can't be good.

"Milly?" she asks again, her voice is an impatient whip coming down on a horse's side. I almost hang up.

But, I *need* to speak to Dean. I swallow my fear. "Yes, it's me, Mrs. Orleans." My voice comes out in a croak.

"Where is your father? Are you helping him hide?" Her voice is a snarl that makes me rear away from the phone.

"No...of course we're not," I gasp, shocked that she's repeating the accusations the public has thrown at us. I know she's never warmed to me, but we're all in the same boat, we sink or swim together. "You *know* us."

"What I know is that you and your family have picked our bones clean and left us with nothing. He's gone forever and I know your father is why." Her tone is caustic, her words razor-sharp, but dread at what she *hasn't* said is what sends my heart into my throat.

The phone trembles in my hand. "What do you mean?"

"His father is dead. *Dead.* All because he trusted your father...that *stupid* man." I don't know if she's talking about my father or Dean's, but it doesn't matter.

I shake my head in disbelief. "Can I please, *please* talk to Dean?" My voice cracks on his name and tears sting my eyes and blur my vision. My worst fear is coming true.

"Are you crazy? He doesn't want to speak to you. He hates you. We both do. Do you hear me?" Her voice breaks on a sob but keeps going. "It's your father who should be dead. It should be *your* family suffering. Don't call this number. Not *ever* again. If you do, I'll find a way to make sure you never know a moment of peace again."

The line goes dead. The phone slips from my hand and clatters onto the floor.

Numb with shock and moving on pure muscle memory, I bend over to pick it up and put it back in its cradle.

I lie down on my bed and close my eyes. I can't escape the turmoil, sadness, loss, and pain that have been my constant companion since this nightmare started a week ago.

Dean's father is dead.

My father might be too. As much as it hurts to believe he stole that money and ran off the way they're saying, I'd rather that be true than imagine him lost to me forever.

"My gems." He called us that and treated us that way, too.

Now, I wonder if he ever really loved us. If he did, would he have left us this way?

I fall back on my bed with a groan and curl my body in on itself, hugging my knees to my chest, making myself as small as I can.

What if...someone found them and hurt them? We can't go to school, all of our communication is being monitored, we're moving away and changing our names because we've gotten plenty of credible death threats.

I reach out for the framed picture of my father I keep next to my bed and gaze down at his face until my tears blur my sight.

"Daddy, what did you do?" I hug it to my chest and squeeze my eyes shut.

My father was a big, powerful man, but he was so gentle, he couldn't swat a fly, much less hurt his best friend.

The Omar Hassan I know is an honorable man who taught us that shortcuts were a waste of time and that lying to someone was the worst thing you could do.

I can't reconcile him with the man who's been accused of terrible things.

I put his picture down and pick up the other framed photo on my bedside and my heart breaks all over again.

We took this the night Dean was crowned homecoming king. He jumped off the stage before they could announce who would be the homecoming queen, ran out to the sidelines and kissed me until we were both breathless.

I was deliriously happy, but I was acutely aware that everyone was watching us and waiting for him to get back on stage.

"Let them wait. I want my first picture as king to be with *my* queen," he'd said.

I trace the outline of his face through the glass of the frame.

He's grinning straight at the camera with his crown askew on top of his head of shiny dark blond hair. His startling green eyes are dancing. His arm is around my waist, pulling me into his side, both of my arms loop his hips. I'm smiling up at him, my face in profile, but the adoration I felt for him was impossible to miss.

I used to look at this picture and marvel that this beautiful boy who had been every girl's crush freshman year had only ever had eyes for me.

We'd been together since the first week of school. And three years later, he was so much more than my boyfriend. He was my best friend, my sounding board, and my study partner.

I thought he'd be my forever.

His mother's angry insults echo in my head and I pick up the picture, press a kiss to it, and put it at the bottom of my bedside drawer.

It had been my solace and hope until today.

Now, it's another painful reminder of everything I've lost.

present day

chasing highs

"I DON'T UNDERSTAND why you're cleaning when you have Jenn." Like the scratch on a record, my fiancée's question brings my thoughts to a screeching halt and annoyance flares, like it does far too often these days, at the sound of her voice.

"It's the day after Christmas." It's an effort to keep my voice neutral. I keep my eyes on the dishwasher I'm emptying because I know, if I look up and she's got that smug, bored, disdainful look on her face, I'll say something I shouldn't.

"Exactly, so *you* should be relaxing." She stands next to me, one hip resting on the counter and trails a hand down my arm.

"The dishes won't do themselves." I shake her hand off and step around her to put the silverware away.

She sighs loudly and trudges over to the sink and leans a hip against the counter. I glance at her out of the corner of my eyes. "What's up, Nic?" I ask.

She touches my jaw with the tip of her finger and traces the outline of it. "Are you sure you don't want to come with me to Houston?"

My stomach tightens and I cast her a sideways glance. "Very."

Dylan Allen

"But Dean, how can I choose a wedding planner without you?"

I scoff and turn back to the dishes. "The same way you picked out the ring, decided we'd be getting married in Houston, picked the date, and took out an announcement in the Times without me."

She sighs. "Are you still upset with me? I thought you'd moved past that…"

I drop the sponge and turn to face her fully. "I'm not upset with you. I just…I have a lot on my mind. Work is crazy right now."

She squeezes my hand. "Are you sure?"

I'm not, but I don't know what to do about it. I muster the most sincere smile I'm capable of. "I'm almost done here, why don't you go have a bath, relax."

Her entire face lights up and she nods. "That's not a bad idea. It *has* been a long day."

She had that fucking right. "Go ahead."

"Thank you, babe." She squeezes my hand but her eyes are already drifting to the door of the kitchen and she doesn't notice, or maybe just doesn't care that I didn't respond.

As soon as she's gone, muscles I hadn't realized were tense, relax. I take a deep breath and exhale, relieved to be alone again.

I shouldn't have let her move back in.

Nicola is an actress, not a particularly successful one, but she likes nice things. I never minded them for her. But apparently, I wasn't generous enough because I found out three months ago she had opened several lines of credit in my name and had racked up almost one hundred thousand dollars in debt on clothes, shoes, and makeup.

I find it obscene she could spend that amount of money on anything in such a short amount of time - but that's not the part that I can't look past. It's the deception and the lying she did to try and cover it up when it all started to come apart.

2

I found myself engaged to a woman who was not only capable of lying to me, but stealing from me, too.

I called off the engagement and asked her to move out.

The day she called to ask me if she could move back in and have a second chance, was on a day when my guard was down and nostalgia had a grip on me - Thanksgiving.   The Hassan family was back in the news with a story of Addie, the youngest being spotted in London. There was no news of Milly. But, it was enough to open up wounds I'd stitched closed a long time ago. The longing for things I'd lost or never had was acute and keen. When Nicola called and asked if she could come over to talk about us trying again, I said yes.   In that moment, I was sure nothing could feel worse than being alone.

When she kissed me and asked me to fuck her, I did.

I wanted to escape the hard edges of my reality in the soft-ness of her body. I said yes to everything she asked of me while I fucked her and tried to feel something other than a cloying reminder of my lost dream.   I tried until I was too tired to keep going and collapsed - exhausted but far from satisfied.

In the morning light when nostalgia no longer clouded my vision, my regret was instant and ran deep. But certain that nature would take its course and we'd reach another breaking point soon, I chose the path of least resistance and let her stay.

She's been back a month and our pantomime of a happy couple is still intact.

She's been on her best behavior. So much so that I've had moments where I've thought we could make it work. I want a family, and at least with Nicola, I know what I'm getting. It should be enough.   But it's not.

Her trip to Houston is a step toward something I don't want anymore. I need to tell her.

I walk into the bedroom, practicing what I'll say, bracing for the shitshow that will certainly follow.

Nicola is wrapped in one of my white terry cloth robes and

sprawled across the bed, eyes riveted to her phone. "We need to talk."

She holds up a finger but doesn't look up from her phone. "One sec."

Glad I don't have to make small talk, I drop onto the steel blue sectional in front of the bay window, put my feet up and close my eyes to contemplate my next move.

"How old were you in 2008?" Nicola asks suddenly.

My eyes open, but just enough for me to see her out of the corner of one. "Eighteen." My chest tightens as the rest of the answer unfurls in my mind.

It was the year I lost everyone who really loved me.

"Did you hear a story about a company in Houston that went under and the guy at the top who disappeared with like, a gazillion dollars?"

The morbid excitement in her voice is grating and I force myself to relax. She doesn't know anything about that time in my life and that's the way I'd like to keep it.

I close my eyes again. "Yeah, I didn't live under a rock. But that story is hardly the news, it's been a long time." I try to keep my voice neutral. "Why are you asking?"

"They found his family."

An alarm goes off in my head. Fully alert, I sit up, swing my feet back on to the floor and lean forward. "Whose family?"

"Look." She scrambles off the bed and strides over to hand me her phone.

The video she's watching is on mute, but I don't need to hear it to understand what I'm seeing. Milly, her mother, and two sisters stand next to the woman who's speaking at the podium with the FBI's emblem on the front of it.

I hit the button on her phone so I can hear.

"The family has come forward at great personal risk to themselves. We would like to state, formally, that these women are not persons of interest in our ongoing investigation into the whereabouts of Omar Hassan. They are assisting us in efforts to locate him. They will not be

taking any questions today and do not want to be contacted by the press."

Holy shit.

Holy shit.

"Wait. I need to check something," Nicola says. But I barely notice. I can't take my eyes off the screen.

My heart has been thrust back in time and is beating so hard I can hear it.

Milly.

She looks like she's been frozen in time. Nothing about her has changed. Her hair is the same burnished bronze pulled back into a ponytail at the nape of her neck, her skin the is still that beautiful cafe au lait. She's wearing makeup now, but I can still see the small freckle that dots the end of her left eyebrow. I'd forgotten how effortless and traffic stopping her beauty is. I can't look away.

Nicola sits back down with an iPad on her lap. "Oh my God. I knew it. That's her alright. But her name isn't Hassan."

I glance at her sharply. "Who are you talking about?"

She looks over her shoulder at me with a coy smile. "Ask me nicely, first."

Annoyance makes me grit my teeth. I narrow my eyes at her. "That *was* nice, Nicola," I warn.

She rolls her eyes. "Gosh, you're such a grump. Hold on."

She scrolls the screen of her tablet. "Here, on her website, it says her name is Milly Bishop."

My heart stops. Or at least, feels like it does. "How did you find her website?" I ask even though I'm not sure I want to know.

"She's one of the wedding planners we're meeting with when we get to Houston. She's my top choice."

My whole body lights up, blood rushes to keep pace with my pounding heart. "We're meeting with *her?*"

She grimaces. "I know...I mean, it says here her dad stole

like, two hundred and fifty million dollars from his business partner."

I sit up at full attention. My earlier resolve is forgotten. My mind is back on the one track it has no business even looking at. "No. If she's the best, what does it matter what her dad did?"

She furrows her eyebrows. "I thought you'd say it would be terrible PR if we were associated with her."

"What harm is there in a meeting? When did you say it was?" I ask, my heart pounding.

"Day after tomorrow."

My mind starts moving before I can think better of it.

"No. Don't cancel. Let's meet her first before we decide?"

Her eyes widen in surprise. "We?"

"Yeah, I'll come with -"

She squeals and lunges for me, wrapping her arms around me. "Oh this is going to be so perfect. I can finally meet Val, and your mom."

I disentangle her arms from my neck. "My mom is in Arizona and Val...we'll have to see."

"Oh my God, it's totally going to happen. Thank you." She presses a kiss to my cheek and I have to suppress the urge to wipe the slightly damp imprint off my face.

"Sure, we'll see." I disentangle myself from her arms and stand. "I've got to make some calls. I'll be in my office." I leave the bedroom as quickly as I can without running.

My head is pounding and my heart is beating too fast when I enter the cool, dark retreat of my office. I sit down without turning the lights on. The hard rich leather back of the chair has no give. Val bought it for me because he said it was a metaphor for me as a human being - uncompromising and sturdy but peel away the leather and you'll find something much easier to wrap your arms around.

It's been a long time since I've let anyone see behind this thick skin... I'd almost forgotten what lays behind it.

The shock of laying eyes on her, two decades after she left me, has given my vulnerability an unwelcome jumpstart.

Emotions I've long thought dead - *love*, it's cunt of a sister-hope, and resentment - surge in through the fractures she made that never healed.

I pull out my phone and google Milly Bishop. The first hit is a business called Ready Events.

Red-D. That had been our motto and our posture.

It has been five years since I gave up on that idea that Milly was out there somewhere trying to find a way back to me.

Five years since I graced the cover of *Rolling Stone*, wrote a book that was an instant #1 NYT Bestseller and became a regular commentator on a broad variety of television shows. Even if you don't follow sports and entertainment, I spent a decade building a career and making myself easy to find. And when she didn't make contact, I had to swallow the bitter truth I'd been holding in my mouth- she didn't want to find me.

And now I know why.

"Milly Bishop is an award-winning event planner with an eye for detail and a passion for making other people's fairytales a reality. She lives in Houston with her husband and their son."

The ice cream I had for dessert curdles in my stomach.

She's married.

She has a *child*.

A quick name search shows that they got married three years after the last time I saw her and that her son was born less than a year later.

I was stuck in neutral for ten years.

God, and now I've just committed to going to Houston. My stomach clenches again. I didn't avoid the city because of her - I didn't know until now that she was still there. It's everything else that happened, all the reminders of things lost forever, and the questions I can't ignore when I'm there.

My father's cause of death was ruled a suicide a week after he was found. It made sense - he'd lost everything. There were no signs of foul play, no indication that anyone but him had handled the cup holding tea laced with cyanide found next to the bed where he'd laid down to die.

And yet…I'd never been able to believe it. My father may have lost everything, but he had plans and someone he cared about and a fresh start he was determined to make. I wish I'd asked him for more details. I wish…so many things.

I log onto Southwest's website and book a flight for the next day. Then I email my realtor to let her know I'll be in town and that I'm finally ready to talk about selling my parents' house.

I want to see Milly, to look her in the eye and ask her why she gave up on us.

Then, I'm closing that chapter in my life for good.

dodging lows

"HE'S GONE. You can come out now," I call to my sister through the closed door of my closet.

The lock disengages and she opens the door just a crack at first, and a few seconds later, wide enough for her head to pop out. She cranes her neck to survey my bedroom before she steps out completely.

I used to take it personally that she never took my word for anything. But now, I understand it's a defense mechanism.

My dad's disappearance hurt us all equally, but the scars we bear from that period in our lives look different on each of us.

"Your closet is bigger than my entire bedroom," she remarks as she strolls through the door. "I've been playing dress-up." Lilly turns to face the full-length mirror on the inside of my closet door.

"Those both look great on you," I remark.

She fingers the black and gold silk scarf around her neck and positions the camel-colored fedora on her head at a rakish angle.

"I think so, too." She gives a little twirl and my heartstrings give a wistful stretch at the look on her face. She looks almost lighthearted.

"You should keep them."

She whirls to face me, her eyebrows raised in surprise. "*What*? Why?"

I smile and nod. "Yeah, I want you to have them."

She tugs the scarf off and holds it out to me. "No. I couldn't. They're both so beautiful." She brings the scarf to her nose and shakes her head. "I can smell your perfume on it, you must have *just* worn it."

I stand, taking the piece of silk from her hands and draping it over her shoulders. "It looks *so* good on you, it matches your hair." I step back and give her an appreciative appraisal. "I've never worn that hat."

She narrows one eye and purses her lips. "Are you *sure*?"

"Absolutely." I nod. "It would make me happy," I add.

She sighs as if she's resigning herself to something. But as she turns back to the mirror and admires her reflection, a small smile tugs the corners of her heart-shaped mouth. Tears sting my eyes. She looks like the Lilly she'd been before. That sixteen-year-old girl had the sweetest, easiest smile I'd ever seen. Now, it's a rare sight. I hold up my phone and snap a picture before she can stop me.

"Delete that," she orders me with a wag of her finger.

"No way, I love it."

"You do? Let me see it."

I hold out the phone and pat the cushion next to me.

She plops down next to me, smile gone, but her eyes are still bright and happy. She glances at the picture and her breath leaves her in a rush. Her jaw tightens and she swipes her thumb across my screen. "I hate it."

"Hey. You can't delete my pictures." I snatch my phone from her with a glare.

"It's *my* picture. I didn't like it." She shrugs and then fixes me with a glare. "And are we *really* not going to talk about the fact that I ran into the closet to avoid seeing your husband?" She raises an eyebrow in challenge.

"Ugh..." I groan and roll my eyes. "What is there to talk about?" I throw my hands up in frustration. "I know you don't like him. You avoid him as much as you can. End of story."

She doesn't say anything, just keeps that level, far too discerning gaze on mine.

"Milly, are *you* okay?" She volleys the question back with a disgruntled frown that draws her dark brows so close they nearly touch.

I look down and fold my hands in my lap. A reflexive, "I'm fine," is on the tip of my tongue. But it's so far from the truth, I can't bring myself to say it. She puts her hands on each of my shoulders when I don't respond. "Milly, look at me."

I shake my head.

I can't.

I'm miserable. And yet, so afraid to break apart the thing that has kept me safe all these years.

There's a ball of tears in my throat.

She gives my shoulders a gentle shake.

"Milly, tell me what is going on."

"I don't know what's wrong," I lie with a miserable shake of my head.

"Yes you do. You just don't want to say it."

I snort a mirthless laugh. "How do you know me so well?"

She shrugs. "Easy. We're eighteen months apart, shared a room for ten years, and we're best friends."

I cast her a sidelong look. "Then how come *I* never know when you're keeping something from me until it reaches crisis level and you have to tell me?"

She grins. "I'm *much* better at pretending than you are."

"Shut up, Lilly," I snap and jerk away from her. "Seriously, I wish you'd talk to me."

"Don't deflect. We're talking about you. What is going on with you and Kevin?"

I sigh and shake my head. "He's been impossible since the

press conference. I've lost a lot of clients and he's worried about money."

She scoffs in disgust. "Of course he's worried about money. Who's going to pay for his three-hundred-dollar haircuts and week-long boys' trips if his golden goose stops laying eggs?"

I rear back. The force of her words are slap in the face.

I set my jaw and cross my arms over my chest. "That was a low blow."

"The truth hurts." She shrugs, not a hint of apology on her face. "Am I lying?"

"Why *do* you stay with him?" My sister's cadence is uncharacteristically hesitant and like she's bracing herself for whatever I'm going to say.

"Because unlike you, I don't want to be alone," I say with a small lift of my eyebrow.

She wrinkles her nose like she smells something foul and looks at me like I've grown another head.

"What?"

She shakes her head and laughs humorlessly. "So, he can just fuck around, sleep where he wants, spend your money, and you prefer that to being alone."

I stiffen at the judgment in her voice. "I never said it was okay. He's not perfect. But he's a good dad, he doesn't get in the way of my work, and..." I sigh a deep sigh, close my eyes, and try to think of one more good thing to say about my husband.

"Do you love him?" Lilly asks in a soft, almost compassionate voice.

Startled, I open my eyes and sit up straight and frown at her. "Are you *serious*?" My heart is racing and my throat is heavy with something like fear.

She gives a slow blink and nods. "It's not a trick question. Do you *love* your husband?"

"Of course." Should be on the tip of my tongue, but it's not. It's in the back of my throat either.

I look away from her penetrating stare. "I've never thought about it."

"Say what?" She gives me a hard side-eye. "You've *never* thought about it? You've been married for like...ever."

"Thirteen years," I correct her.

"That's a long fucking time, Mil to be married and to *never* thought about whether or not you love your husband." Her voice escalates in volume with each word.

"Anthony's sleeping," I remind her.

"That kid would sleep through an air raid. And you are entirely too calm for..." Her phone trills and vibrates on the small table next to her. "Shit, I think that's my Uber."

I stand. "Oh what a shame. I do *wish* we could keep talking about this."

She gives me a reproachful chuck on the chin. "You're not off the hook. I'll be gone, but you can't escape yourself."

"Gee, thanks," I grumble.

She grabs my hand and stands so we're face to face. We're exactly the same height and have never been able to avoid each other's eyes. "I love you. I want you to be happy."

My eyes burn with tears and because it's her, I don't hold them back. I pull her into a tight hug. "I love you more. And *I want* you to be happy, too."

She hugs me back and we stay in that temporary shelter until her phone dings again.

"Thank you for coming."

"I'm glad she's moving out of there. I hate that house."

"I know you do." I wish I also knew why. But I know better than to ask. "Come on, let me help you take your things down."

I didn't say it, but I'm glad my mother is moving out of that house, too. I only lived there for a year, but it was the longest, hardest year of my life. The house holds even worse memories for Lilly, she hasn't stayed there since I got married.

I only asked her why the first time, and I'll never forget how she shrank away from me. She told me she'd explain when she was ready. That was more than ten years ago. And, I understand having parts of your life you don't want to share with anyone.

———

I toss my phone onto the bed and step into the small ensuite bathroom, slip my glasses off and without turning the lights on splash water on my face to get rid of any telltale tear tracks and signs of sleep. I retie the bun of hair at the nape of my neck and smooth a hand over my clothes.

Satisfied that my outward appearance doesn't betray the turmoil inside me, I go tuck my son in.

He's fallen asleep already and even though I love our night-time routine, tonight, I'm relieved.

The lights that decorate the outside of the bedroom's window cast jewel toned shadows over his sleeping face. He's not a baby anymore, but his cheeks and parted mouth have the soft plumpness of childhood that make him look impossibly vulnerable. My heart constricts in my chest as I gaze at him, and I'm overcome with a sense of helplessness at how unfair it is that he has to live with the consequences of choices people made before he was even a twinkle in my eye.

I tried to break what felt like a generational curse on my family and not only have I failed, I've made everyone miserable. The only people fooled by the appearances I work so hard to keep up are me, myself, and I.

Anthony sighs and turns from his back onto his side. I press a kiss to his cool forehead and turn away before I'm tempted to lay back down.

I want to wrap him up in cotton wool and keep him far away from all the things and people that might hurt him. The hardest part of being a parent is knowing I can't protect him from anything. I wish I'd at least been able to give him a happy childhood with parents who showed him what love can be when it's right.

When I was a little girl, my parents would dance around the living room late at night when they thought we were all in bed. I'd sit at the top of the stairs, watching them swaying, chest to chest, sometimes with no music. They looked at each other like the sun rose and set in their eyes. Our house was *full* of love and they were the source of it. The first eighteen years of my life were something out of a fairytale. Our house was where all of our friends hung out after school.

We had it all, I couldn't wait to grow up and replicate it.

My father leaving was just the first domino to fall. My entire life collapsed in on itself. I had to leave my school, my home, my name, my love. My life for months was about lying, hiding, being afraid, hurting. Our disappearance was headline news for less than a week. But our lives would never be the same again.

All of that loss didn't make me afraid of relationships, the way it had for my sisters. If anything, it made me desperate for that same sense of certainty and belonging that had been the bedrock of my existence. I was waiting, giving Dean time, hoping that once his grief wasn't so fresh, he might forgive.

I was still waiting when I started my freshman year at LSU, so far away from Stanford and the future I used to take for granted. I scoured social media for his name, holding my breath every time I hit "return" on my keyboard. I would have waited forever.

But, three months was all it took for me to realize, what I was waiting for wasn't looking for me.

One night, I put his name in the search bar on Facebook and got a hit. He'd scored a touchdown and his arm was slung around a girl and they were both grinning at the camera. I was so happy to see his face, so glad that he was smiling, that it took me a full minute to actually read the caption. "Dean Orleans poses with his girlfriend Heidi after he clinches a win for the Cardinals."

I closed the browser and threw up. Then, I took a shower, got dressed, and walked with my roommate to the fraternity row and got drunk for the first time in my life.

I met Kevin that night. He was a perfect gentleman from the word go. He walked me home, didn't try to do more than hold my hand, and called to check on me the next day.

He was a law student at LSU with beautiful brown eyes, dark hair, and an infectious smile. He was handsome, thoughtful, and did his best to sweep me off my feet. He came really close a few times, and for a girl whose heart was shattered, that felt like enough. And when I told him the truth about my past, he said I could leave it behind and focus on a future with him.

I said yes because I wanted to. But also because despite everything, my heart was still stuck in neutral. I wanted to move forward.

I married him and tried to make peace with my past. But *it* has never made peace with me.

trapped

"GOOD MORNING, ZEN," I call out to my assistant as I sail the office and showroom that's my pride and joy.

"A good morning indeed, boss lady." Zenobia holds up a small, white cup of coffee from my favorite bakery, Sweet and Lois and hands it to me with an excited grin.

"Oooh, you splurged," I say with an appreciative waggle of my eyebrows after I take a sip of the delicious steaming cardamom flavored latte.

"I have a really good feeling about today."

"Me, too. Wait till I tell you who else I'm meeting with today." I shimmy my shoulders.

"Whoever it is, it can't be anyone more exciting than the groom of the bride you're meeting with today."

"How do you know who the groom is?" I shake out of my jacket and fling it onto the back of my chair. When I realized that plenty of women seek me out in anticipation of a proposal, I stopped asking for the name of the groom until I'm sure there is one. Even then, I've planned weddings where I didn't meet the groom until the rehearsal dinner. It's always a bit of a red flag, but I'm the last person to question someone's relationship.

"She called this morning to let you know that the meeting room is reserved under his name and that you should reference it when you arrive."

"So…" I lift my eyebrows and cock my head to one side with an expectant smile. "What's his name?"

Her smile turns coy. "I doubt you'd recognize his name, because you literally don't know who *anyone* is."

"That's not true," I protest with a chuckle, because it is.

"But…I *think* you'll recognize his face." She reaches into the massive tote bag on the floor beside her desk. "After I stopped at Sweet and Lo's, I went to CVS and bought this." She sits up and raises her hand with a dramatic flourish and holds up a small stack of magazines.

I hold my arm outstretched and she hops up with an uncharacteristic giggle and practically skips to my desk.

"Why are you being so weird?" I'm amused and quietly relieved to see her upbeat. "If it's not George Clooney, I'll be disappointed," I quip and take the magazines from her.

My humor is snuffed out in an instant and my stomach falls to my toes. I drop the magazine like it's on fire. "Oh my God." It lands face up and it's like seeing a ghost. My whole body is covered in goose pimples. I cover my mouth with my hand to hold back a scream.

"Milly? What's wrong?" Zenobia put a hand on my shoulder but I can't take my eyes off the magazine.

It's this month's *Esquire* magazine and on the cover is a man who was a boy I used to know.

His unsmiling face is still as stunning as it had been fifteen years ago. His wide set, heavy lidded, lushly lashed eyes are a clear, startling green. His skin is tan, more rugged, and his blond hair is swept completely off his forehead, revealing a broad, heavy brow that is perfectly proportioned to his high cheekbones and full mouth.

The caption right below his chin—his perfect, with the dimple in the middle, chin—reads "Winning. How Dean Orleans

Does It Without Breaking a Sweat."

All at once, I feel dizzy, despondent, thrilled, hyperaware, terrified. This can't be happening.

"You're scaring me." Zen stoops to pick the magazine off the floor. I follow her hand and then look up into her face, dazed.

"What did he do to you?"

"Nothing," I whisper. Except throw me away weeks after he promised he'd love me forever.

"I...I know him from a long time ago. It's ancient history. I was just...I didn't know he was getting married." I give her a weak smile.

She returns it, but it's halfhearted. "I'm sorry. I wouldn't have...if I'd known." She walks slowly back to her desk.

"You couldn't have known. I've never talked about him. It's fine." I reach for the bottle of water on my desk and drink half of it in a handful of gulps.

I sit back in my chair and try to catch my breath. My heart is racing still, but my mind is absolutely clear. There is no way I can plan this wedding.

I can't cancel less than two hours before the meeting. She's in town from New York, and if I cancel on her now, I'm sure she'll leave a negative Yelp review and tag me in a social media rant. I can't afford to lose any more clients.

I'm trapped.

My stomach tightens on a horrible thought and I brace before I ask Zenobia, "Did she say he'd be there?"

She shakes her head. "No."

I exhale in relief. "Okay."

She frowns. "You look like you've seen a ghost."

How do I even begin to answer her? "He might as well be. It was so long ago. And I'm sure he doesn't remember me at all."

None of that is true, but it's all I can give her.

"Okay, whew. Cause that would be awkward, right?" She chuckles and drops the magazine back into the bag.

"I've updated the sample book with our new colors and

fabrics. The venues are in alphabetical order and the new packets are gorgeous."

"Thank you. I know they'll be impressed," I say with all sincerity.

She beams at the praise. "I hope so, this is going to be a high-profile wedding, it's going to be so good for business."

Guilt nibbles at my conscience. She worked hard on this and I hate that my baggage is going to ruin it for her.

"Wait, you said you had news too, right?"

It takes me a second to remember, but the bubble of excitement I had earlier has dimmed, but I don't have to fake my smile. "I got a call from Sebastian Hayford's office today."

Her jaw drops and her mouth hangs slack. "You are *lying*." Her eyes are comically wide.

I chuckle and am grateful for the release of tension. "I had the same reaction."

"Holy shit. What did he want?"

"A meeting in two weeks to discuss something that he needs to send an NDA over before he can tell me."

She claps her hands together repeatedly. "I *knew* it was going to be a good day. We're about to book two high-profile weddings in one month. The tide is turning."

Excitement leaps in my chest, but I hold up a hand. "I don't know…I haven't heard he's engaged. Let's not get ahead of ourselves. But…I think you might be right."

She giggles. "You *have* to let me go with you."

I cross my legs and lean back in my seat with a wide smile. "I was *just* about to ask you if you would."

She covers her mouth with both hands. "Oh my God, really? You think I'm ready?"

I nod. "Absolutely."

I also feel like I need to give her this so she won't quit when I tell her I didn't land Nicola and Dean.

Just thinking their names together makes my stomach hurt.

I've moved on. But I haven't healed from the hurt he caused me.

"I'm supposed to be at his office at 1:30 p.m. next Monday. There's a place called Claudia's in the building next door, meet me there at 12:30 and we'll get on the same page and go over the presentation."

"Sounds great," she beams.

She works so hard, I love being able to help her reach her goal of being a full-fledged planner herself. "Okay, let me get ready for this meeting. What's on your calendar today?"

She switches from playful colleague to serious assistant and grabs her planner. "I have a tasting at the St. Regis at eleven and then I'm taking the Patterson wedding's bridesmaids dress shopping at three."

I groan at the prospect. "I'll give you a Xanax to take when you get there."

She snickers and shakes her head. "No way. You know I love that stuff. The bitchier the bridesmaids, the more entertaining." Her eyes light up with glee.

I'm amazed at how sincerely she loves that part of the job. I'm the ideas person, she's the executer. I land the clients, she keeps them happy. We're a good team.

I glance at my watch. I've got an hour before my meeting with the woman who Dean is going to marry. I have time to do some admin work before I go. I sit down at my large tempered glass desk and let myself enjoy the view.

The small building is a glorified "she-shed". The space is split into two rooms. This smaller one is our office. It's simply decorated and clutter-free. We saved all of our glam and window dressing for the showroom. If a client is on the fence after our initial consultation, a visit to our showroom always seals the deal.

The day we broke ground was one of the proudest days of my life.

I'd been event planning on the side since Anthony was a

baby. I was great at it. I loved being home with him, but I was ready to have my days back so I could finally give event planning a real go. As I've grown, I've considered renting more space so I can have a bigger showroom, but no amount of extra space can outweigh the benefits of having an office in my backyard.

I've put so much into this business. In just a few years, I went from planning events for the local school district, to small business launches, to large corporate fundraisers. Two years ago, I hit the holy grail of event planning- weddings.

It's a crazy amount of work and no matter how meticulous the planning, something *always* goes wrong.

Despite all of that, I love it.

It's lucrative, rewarding, and an evergreen industry. The vicarious joy that comes from being present for a couple's "Big Bang" is a special kind of high I hadn't known I needed until the first wedding I planned.

But as I head out to meet with the future Mrs. Orleans, joy is nowhere to be found.

fifteen years earlier

butterflies

"MILLY, WAIT UP!"

I glance over my shoulder and my heart skips a beat. Dean is rushing down the hall and moving much faster than I am. I walked the long way to class to avoid him — how did he find me?

I hunch my shoulders and pick up the pace, my irritation growing with every step.

I wish he'd just leave me alone.

"Milly, wait." He's close enough that he doesn't need to raise his voice for me to hear him. I resign myself. There's no avoiding this confrontation. I stop so suddenly he crashes into me and sends me stumbling forward.

"Shit. Sorry, Red." He grabs my arms and steadies me.

I jerk myself free and glare up at him, my eyes blazing with anger. "What do you want?" I snap.

His frown brings his already furrowed brows together to form a unibrow. "What do I *want*?"

He shakes his head. "Are you serious?"

I tip my chin up and set my jaw. "Yes, I am very serious."

He folds his arms over his chest and leans away. "You left my game without speaking to me, you haven't answered your phone all weekend, and you didn't call me back. You missed our Monday breakfast. And now you're asking me what I want? What the hell is going on?" His voice rises with each accusation he makes and a few people stop and watch us.

"Jesus," I hiss and grab his arm.

He lets me pull him down the hallway, toward the deserted lunchroom but yanks out of my grasp as soon as we're inside and alone. "Tell me what's wrong."

I turn to face and let him have it. "I saw you after the game. With Amanda."

He straightens and something like guilt flashes in his eyes. "You did?"

My stomach heaves and tears prick my eyes.

"Yes. And if you hadn't been all tangled up together, you might have noticed me."

He pales. "Milly, no. That's not what – "

"The day after I gave you my virginity. I told myself it was in my head when you were acting all funny before the game." I brush away the hot traitorous tears that spill from the corners of my eyes.

"Red, listen to me." He takes a step toward me.

I take a step back and shake my head. "I thought… You were hugging like you were the ones in love," I end on a sob.

Dean takes advantage of the break in my voice to speak. "Red. Stop and listen, please. Yes, I was hugging Amanda. She hugged me too. And yes, I was on edge before the game. But I was nervous about seeing you later. I bought you something. I wanted to surprise you. So, I had Amanda hold on to it for me during the game and she was only giving it back to me and saying how excited she was for you to see it." He is talking so fast that it takes my brain a minute to register what he is saying.

"You bought me a gift?" I look up at him, my tears clearing and dread and regret quickly replacing my anger and sorrow.

He glowers at me. "Yes. I can't believe you thought I'd cheat on you. With one of your best friends. At a game that I knew you were watching. After the night before when I gave you my virginity. Is that really what you think of me?"

I groan and look away, unable to meet his eyes. I feel like such a jerk.

"Dean, I don't know what to say. I'm sorry. I just . . ." I trail off.

"You just don't trust me," he says, his voice flat, devoid of its ire. I reach out for his arm.

"No, it's not that, Dean. You wouldn't understand. I'm . . ."

"Help me understand, please. Whatever it is, it can't be worse than you thinking I am a lying, cheating asshole," he says, leaning against the wall of the hallway, looking away from me. I grab his arm to implore him to understand.

"Dean, you're Mr. Popular. Everyone wants you. And I know half the school is wondering what you're doing with me. Ms. Nobody," I say, feeling small and vulnerable. I never wanted him to know I felt this way.

He turns his body to face me and grabs my chin, forcing my eyes up to his.

"Milly, anyone who's wondering that doesn't have eyes. And since when have you cared what people say or think? You're the prettiest girl I've ever met. And the smartest and the funniest. And the kindest."

His eyes search mine, the anger in them gone and replaced with tenderness.

"I've never told anyone I loved them before you, Red. I've never known anyone like you. I never want to lose you."

He pulls me into him and hugs me to his chest.

Relief rushes through me and I burrow my nose into his sweater. Smelling that familiar comforting smell of soap, fabric softener, and Dean.

"I'm sorry, D," I mumble into his chest.

He pushes me back away from him. "What was that? I didn't hear you." A teasing grin covers his face.

I roll my eyes and smile in self-deprecation. I know I deserve that. I am just so relieved that what I saw wasn't what I thought and that he's forgiving me so easily for treating him shabbily over the weekend.

"I'm sorry, D. Very sorry," I say again, louder this time.

"Buy me a burger at Fuddruckers and all will be forgiven."

I wrap my arm around his waist and steer us back down the hall. "You're a cheap date. You've got yourself a deal," I quip.

He stops us in our tracks. "Aren't you forgetting something?" he asks, peering down at me.

"You're the best lacrosse player in Houston?" I say, not sure what he's getting at.

He rolls his eyes and reaches into his pocket. "I told you I bought you a present, Red."

I smile sheepishly. "You still want to give it to me?" I feel bad taking it now.

"Of course." He pulls out a little piece of tissue paper, like the kind that comes in gift bags, but it's the size of a quarter and hands it to me.

I smile at him shyly as I unwrap it.

I gasp when I get it open and look up at him. "It's so beautiful." It's a ring, a simple silver ring. Its thin band interrupted by a hollow heart right in the middle.

"Oh, thank you, Dean," I breathe out as I stare at it.

He grabs my hand and says, "It gives me butterflies every time I remember that you chose me, too. And fuck if I don't love the way that feels. I want the whole world to know my heart is yours."

I look up at him, and my tears are back, but this time, they are happy tears.

"I love you." It's the first time I've ever felt like those words weren't enough to express how I feel.

"I love you, too," he says simply. He presses a kiss to my cheek and takes the ring from me and slips it onto the third finger of my right hand. "I promise," he whispers.

present day

5 /
dean

consequences

"SHE'S LATE," I mutter under my breath and glance at my watch.

All the time I knew her, Millicent Hassan was a stickler for time. My stomach feels like it's eating itself and my whole body is vibrating with anticipation.

"Are you okay? You're *sweating*." Nicola gazes at me wide-eyed. "You never sweat. Are you sick?"

I pull a handkerchief from the inside pocket of my blazer and wipe my brow. "I'm not sick. I'm hot."

She casts a skeptical eye up to the air-conditioning vent above our heads and then back at me. "Are you sure?" She leans over to place a hand on my brow.

"Yes." I lean back and out of her reach.

I don't know why—she's fucking married. *I'm* engaged—but I don't want Milly to see her touching me.

Next to me, Nicola's attention is back on her phone and the Pinterest board of table settings, flowers, and venues that she's been building since long before she met me.

Maybe she's not coming.

Instead of relief, the thought fills me with dread.

30

I glance at my watch again, but before I can check the time, there's a sharp rap at the door a second before it swings open.

Millicent Hassan walks into the room and in as long as it takes me to blink, completely obliterates every expectation I had for what this moment would feel like.

Jesus, this was a terrible idea.

I don't know why I thought I could do this. Or that catching her off guard would give me the upper hand. I feel like a spider caught in my own web.

"I'm so sorry I'm late, the parking was..." She stops mid-stride, one foot ahead of the other, her fingers curled around the shoulder strap of her bag.

My head is spinning but years of bluffing my way through make-or-break moments have left me with a poker face that falls into place on reflex.

I'm also *very* aware of Nicola next to me and how, for reasons I don't want to think too hard about, I don't want her to know who and what Milly was to me.

So I force a smile, fix my eyes on a spot right over her shoulder and rise to my feet, intent on greeting her with complete indifference.

But my eyes, like darkness in to light, are drawn to her face. Her mouth hangs open slightly and her eyes are wide and glassy and stuck on mine. And what I see in them makes my heart stop. Her hair seemed a more vivid shade of red. Her eyes, the gold that could cut me down with a single glance, seemed to burn even brighter on her face.

She was always pretty. But the years have been very kind to her and now she's impossibly beautiful.

The years have also done nothing to dampen the effect she has on me. Even after all this time, all of the things she made me feel - love, anger, fear, relief, sadness - are so close to the surface, I can almost taste them.

"Oh my God, Dean, where are your manners?" Nicola

stands, nudging me with her elbow and giving me a quizzical look as she circles the table to shake Milly's hand.

I sit. My heart is lodged in my throat, my head is spinning. This is not what I expected.

"I'm Nicola and this is my fiancé, Dean. I promise he's normally much nicer than this. We've been here a whole week and this is the first time I've even seen him. He's been working so much." She puts a hand on my arm.

Milly's eyes follow her movement and close for a second before she smiles and nods. "It's fine."

The breathless catch in her voice tugs at me, like I know what her fear sounds like. The last time we spoke, I heard it for the first time and I'll never forget it.

Then, I'd put my arm around her and told her it was okay. Now, I have to pretend I don't even know her.

"We're so glad you had time to see us, aren't we?" Nicola says and I can feel her eyes on me. Nicola is an asshole, but she's not dumb. She'll know something is up and once she does, she won't have to dig far to connect the dots.

"Yes, we are," I echo Nic and force myself to look up and brace for impact.

But it doesn't come. "It's my pleasure." She's twisted in her seat, hands in her large tote bag, rifling through.

She pulls out her laptop and a huge binder and busies herself getting it set up, her head bent to her task.

"I'm so excited to see what you've got to show us," Nicola gushes.

A small tight smile crosses her face and she swallows hard enough that I hear it. Her eyes dart to my face for half a second but it's long enough for me to see that she's reeling.

She turns her full attention back to Nicola and gives her a warm smile. "I've got some ideas, but let me check something," she says and looks back at her computer screen. Her eyes narrow and her lips pucker into a frown.

"Your wedding is set for September 6th?" she asks.

"Yes. Right after Labor Day, so I'll be the only one wearing white," Nicola says with a conspiratorial grin that Milly doesn't return.

Instead she sighs and closes her laptop. "I'm so sorry. I have a conflict, the timing doesn't work."

Nicola goes still, her cheery demeanor cools and she sits back in her chair like she's been pushed. "What do you mean, a conflict?" She puts the last word in air quotes and shoots daggers with her eyes.

Milly doesn't flinch or back down. "I *mean* I have several events already booked and I can't commit to planning yours."

"So then why did you agree to meet us and have us come all this way?" Nicola's voice takes on an edge.

"Because, I didn't realize I had the conflict until now. I *am* very sorry." She drops her laptop and the binder back into her bag. She gets to her feet in one swift motion.

"Wait." Nicola gapes and leans forward in her seat, both of her hands are palms down on the table. "You can't just *leave.* You owe us a consultation."

Milly's eyes narrow and flash with irritation before she softens her expression and smiles. "You've had your *free* consultation. If I'd realized I had this conflict, I wouldn't have come all the way here. The last thing I'd ever do is waste someone's time."

She slides a glance in my direction, but rather than the anger I'm expecting, her eyes are full of hurt and disappointment.

Shame punches me straight in the chest and I look down at my hands.

This is hurting her.

I'm hurting her.

I may be angry at her and she still owes me answers, but the realization makes me feel like shit.

"I can give you the names of event planners that I've hired myself."

"As *if* we'd trust your word again," Nicola hisses.

Milly ignores the venom in her eyes and smiles as if they're having a pleasant conversation. "That's your right, unfortunately that's the most I can offer."

"Dean, say something," Nicola pleads.

I shake my head. I can't help her.

Fuck, I can't help *myself*.

She's leaving. And just like all those years ago, I can't make her stay.

"It's too late to change your mind. You couldn't pay me to hire you now." Nicola surges forward and I put a hand on her shoulder to stop her from getting out of her seat.

"It's fine, Nic."

"It's not," she snarls at me.

"It was nice to meet you both. I wish you every happiness." Then she walks out of the room.

I sit there, head spinning, trying to think fast about what to do next.

"What a bitch," Nicola hisses.

I surge to my feet before I know I'm going to.

Nicola's hand circles my wrist, bringing my feet back down to the earth. "What are you doing?"

I look down at her, and in an instant, my mind is made up. I don't care what it costs me, I'm not letting her walk out of my life again.

6 /
milly

so cold

I RACE out of the room and head for the stairs instead of waiting for the elevator. I slip my shoes off my feet so they don't slow me down and ignore the stares of the people I pass as I race down the stairs. By the time I reach the valet, I'm out of breath.

"Please, I'm in a hurry," I say with a pleading smile and hand him my ticket wrapped in a twenty-dollar bill.

"I'll be like the wind," he says with a grin and then takes off down the driveway.

I slip my shoes back on and lean against one of the stone pillars and try to regain my composure.

My soul left my body when I walked in and saw Dean sitting at that table.

I have often imagined our paths crossing. I wondered how I would feel, and I wondered how Dean would react. Nothing could have prepared me for the riot of emotions which started to gallop, like unbroken mustangs, through my chest.

He still looks like a cross between James Dean and Achilles. His green laser beam like gaze still sweeps the room before they settle on their target.

Those few seconds when I entered the room were the only

time we made eye contact, but that brief collision transported me at the speed of light back to the last time we saw each other.

The last time we kissed.

The night he made promises he'd break a week later.

I saw *that* boy and nearly came undone on the spot.

I don't even remember what we said until the end when the bride snapped on me.

My mind was frantically trying to figure out the fastest way to get the hell out of there without making an ass of myself.

Nothing could have prepared me for how much it hurt to see the man I never stopped loving sitting next to someone else.

But what was even more startling was how angry I still am at him. I didn't *think* I was lying when I told Lilly time had healed me. But I was.

Time hasn't done a thing *but* passed. The night he asked me to stop calling him could have been yesterday for how close to the surface that old hurt is simmering. It doesn't help that I'm in the place where I used to daydream about *us* getting married. Or that he seemed completely unfazed by seeing me.

But for the first few seconds of that encounter where I saw the shock in his eyes when I walked in, there was nothing to indicate that my presence was of any consequence to him at all.

"Milly."

My pulse had started to slow but takes off at sprint again and my insides turn to liquid. I can feel his eyes burning into my back and I want to dissolve into a puddle at his feet. I steel myself and turn around to face him.

making up

"DEAN?" She gasps and her jaw drops. Her eyes are wide with surprise and a hint of panic. She's never had a good poker face, there's something reassuring about seeing that hasn't changed.

What's also the same is how easily she rattles me. Being close enough to touch to the one person I've ever *really* needed has my entire nervous system overheating and leaves me struggling to find the right words to say.

"It's a surprise…"

"I can't believe…"

We speak at the same time.

Back then, when we were us - Best friends, confidantes, and fledgling, but enthusiastic lovers who thought we had a future ahead of us - we'd laugh when it happened.

Now, she turns her stricken expression downward and I'm glad she's not bearing witness to my pain, either.

After all these years and the way we parted, this wariness between us shouldn't come as a surprise. And yet…it makes my chest ache as acutely as it did when everything fell apart.

Without distance as a buffer, I feel the loss of our physical connection so keenly, I can barely breathe. I never thought we'd be anything but together.

"You go ahead," she says quietly, her gaze still downcast, her hands linked in a white-knuckle grip.

"No, you first, I insist." I still can't find words beyond the ones I won't allow myself to say aloud.

"Did you know I was going to be here?"

"No," I reply, quickly and vehemently.

Her gaze rises to meet mine and there's so much in it at once - anger, hope, trepidation - and I want to wipe it all away and tell her whatever she's worried about is going to be okay. This woman brought me to my knees and kept me there for a decade, and yet…all I want is to make her feel better.

She nods but purses her lips and narrows her eyes. "Did you know I was the wedding planner you'd be meeting with?"

I look away and respond with an uncomfortably tight, "Yes."

She sighs. "Why?"

"I don't know. I needed to see you. I couldn't pass up the opportunity," I answer honestly, unable to meet her eye.

"To do what? To rub it in my face that you're thriving without me?"

My eyes snap back to hers, surprised by the frost and accusation in her tone. "Why would I do that?"

"I don't know, Dean. Why *would* you do that?" she retorts, her mouth pinched tight.

She glares at me and I flinch at the heat of anger in her eyes, but I meet it with one of my own. "I wouldn't. And you know it. So, are you saying if you'd known I was going to be here you wouldn't have come?"

She makes a sound halfway between a laugh and a sigh and with eyes full of hurt that quickly turns to scorn. "No fucking way." Her voice is so cold.

I cross my arms over my chest as if I can protect my heart from the frost in it. "Why not? You've moved on a long time ago."

She scoffs and looks at me like she's trying to piece a puzzle together. "That doesn't make it hurt any less, Dean. You broke every promise you'd ever made me at the very same time my world fell out from under me."

My anger starts to simmer. She's the one who disappeared on me. She's the one who got fucking married and had a child with someone else. "Your memory is certainly selective."

She narrows her eyes at me. "Are you kidding me right now?"

"No. I'm not."

She shakes her head at me and then her shoulders straighten and her jaw sets. And any emotion that had been in her eyes is banked. "I'm not so petty that I can't say that there's a part of me that's glad I saw you. I've missed you, so much." Her hand comes up to the base of her throat and for a moment, there's a break in the dark cloud in her eyes.

"I missed you, too," I admit before I can think better of it.

Her expression softens and when I take a step toward her, she doesn't move away. I'm close enough to touch her and my pulse is going wild.

"Dean?" A man stops next to us and the spell is broken. Milly blinks and takes a step back.

"I thought that was you. What are you doing here, son?" He claps me on the back and then seems to notice Milly. His eyes narrow. "Have we met before?"

Milly shakes her head and her eyes fill with something akin to panic and my instinct kicks in.

I turn so my body blocks his view of her. "Mr. Woolier, long time no see. I was just headed back inside."

I turn back to face her with my hand out to shake hers. "Nice to see you, Mrs. Bishop. Here's my card. Call me if you change your mind."

And then, I walk away and pray like hell she'll call.

remember

I WATCH Dean until he disappears around the corner. Then I look at my hand. It's still tingling in the places where he'd held it. I feel the stiff edge of the small white card he placed in my hand. It's blank. I frown and flip it over and my breath catches. I'd forgotten how neat and precise his handwriting was.

Below the embossed type with his name and phone is a small note.

Call me, please. I'll be in town for the rest of the month.

I gaze down at it and turmoil rolls in my gut.

I'd imagined that moment for years, but nothing could have prepared me for the onslaught of emotions breathing the same air again brought on.

I glance up at the grand facade of the Rivers Wilde Country Club and tears fill my eyes. I used to dream of us getting married here. I could see it clearly, down to the last detail. But the girl who used to dream about things like that is long gone. **Now,** all I see are the happy memories I made for everyone else here.

Whatever might have been is water under the bridge.

Dean is engaged to be married.

I'm married - even if I wish I wasn't.

The time for conversation is long gone.

Nothing good could come out of talking and rehashing the past.

"Your car," the valet calls from behind me.

I walk over to the driver's side and climb into the door he's holding open and slide him a folded twenty-dollar bill.

I'm putting on my seatbelt when he knocks on the window.

I roll it down and he holds out the small white card I wrapped his tip in.

"I think this is yours."

I smile at him but shake my head. "Could you throw it away for me, please? It's trash."

dean

face the music

I EXTRACT myself from the conversation with my dad's old golf partner with a smile and an excuse.

I'm still shaken from that interaction with Milly. So, I make my way to the office space I've rented instead of the conference room I left Nicola in.

I see a few familiar faces, most of them old friends of my father. I stop to say hello but excuse myself before they can draw me into a conversation.

By the time I reach my office, I'm sweating from the effort it took to act like I'm not coming out of my skin.

I lock the door behind me and rush to my private ensuite bathroom and splash water on my face.

I thought I would see her; she would look guilty or angry, and I would feel vindicated at showing her that I'd moved on.

Finally get her out of my system and out from under my skin.

I rinse my mouth and splash water on my face and stare at myself in the mirror. It's been a long time since I've been so wrong about anything.

Seeing *my* Red standing there was like being hurled back in time to when I was a boy and she could tie me in knots with one smile. And who would have set the world on fire to erase hurt, pain, or sadness from her eyes.

Why did she look at me like I was the one who ripped her young heart to shreds?

She was the one who disappeared when I needed her the most.

She's the one who got married and had a child in the same decade I spent trying to get over her.

My phone buzzes. Nicola's name pops up on my screen and drags me back to the present.

NICOLA

Where are you?

How could you just leave me like that?

ME

Had to check on a few things. I'll be back soon.

Guilt presses heavy on my shoulders.

I'm her fiancé, I *should* have stayed.

I should be comforting her and giving her space to vent.

I should be holding her hand and telling her that all we needed to make our wedding day perfect was each other.

I know it.

I just... don't *feel* it.

Seeing Milly was like a lightning strike on a moonless, starless, and stormy night over the lies I've been telling myself for years. And now that I've seen the truth so clearly, I can't keep denying it.

I need to end things with Nicola before they go any further.

She may not be the great love of my life, but I care for her deeply. I wouldn't have asked her to marry me otherwise.

But caring deeply hasn't been enough to get me over the hurdles that we've come up against in the course of our relationship. We've been over since the minute I learned about her dishonesty.

The only reason I didn't pull the plug as planned on Thanksgiving is because I wanted to have this face to face with Milly. I wince as a jagged edged truth breaks the surface.

Since the moment I learned where she was, my mind has been fixated on the woman I have spent all my adult life trying to forget. Nicola deserves a man who can comfort her the way, even after all these years, I wanted to comfort Milly.

I take a deep breath and open the door to the office where Nicola is waiting.

"It's about time." She gives me a withering look. "Where have you been?"

I step inside and shut the door behind me. "We need to talk."

Her expression goes from annoyed to wary. "Why?"

"This isn't working."

Her gasp is followed by a whimper that turns into a sob. Before she sees it coming, I've got the tip of her chin between my fingers and force her eyes up to mine.

They're as dry as her heart. I let go of her face and take a step back. "I should have let it stay dead the first time, but I can't do this."

"Dean, why are you doing this?" She presses a hand to her chest and gapes at me. A shimmer of unshed tears makes her dark eyes luminous, but the calculation in them is clear as day.

I wish I'd never met her.

The thought comes unbidden, and my stomach tightens when I catch a glint of light from the ring I put on her finger.

"I know you're still upset with me."

I scoff. "I'm not upset with you. I don't trust you and right now, I don't see how I ever will."

"If this is about the money, I'll pay you back. I promise I'll never keep anything from you again." Her eyes are wide and wet with desperation.

"Nic, it's not the money. I've got plenty and I would have

spent five times that amount on you without thinking twice. I'm a generous man and you know it. This is about trust, your greed, and your dishonesty."

I want to tell her the rest - that I don't love her. That my heart belongs to someone else.

But the last thing I want is for her to get wind of anything to do with Milly.

"I'm not giving up on us, Dean," she says.

I sigh, suddenly exhausted. I stand, hands in my pockets and rip the Band-Aid off, quick and clean. "You'll have to do your "not giving up" somewhere else. I'll be back and forth for a few weeks. But you should go back to New York and start looking for a place to live."

She shakes her head, desperation ratcheting up to panic. "You can't get rid of me like this. You made me a promise."

"I'm following your lead and breaking it. And I am sorry. But it's better this way."

Her eyes narrow, darken, and glitter with malice. "You tight fisted asshole. No wonder your mother can't stand you."

I flinch at the below the belt hit. She's been on her best behavior for so long I'd almost forgotten that a snake doesn't become less poisonous just because they shed a skin. "The two of you can form a club and hate me together."

A scowl twists her face. "I'm going to make you pay through the nose for this. I'll take you for everything."

I give her a cold smile. "Do your worst. Just do it away from me."

She picks up her phone with a growl and hurls it at me. She misses by a mile and it lands on the floor with a loud clatter as I walk out of the room.

enough

MY EMOTIONS WERE SWINGING on a pendulum between anger and anguish, and I could barely breathe by the time I walked through the door of my house.

My mother took one look at my face and announced that she was taking Anthony to dinner at Twist and then to a late screening of his favorite Disney film down on the Wilde Green.

I could have cried with gratitude. I *loved* living with other people, even when everyone was tucked into whatever corner of the house they called their own, I loved knowing everyone I loved was under my roof where I could protect them. But tonight, I was desperate to be alone so I could unravel.

As soon as they were gone, I stripped and ran a bath with the luxury bath salts I bought when we were visiting Addie last summer and soaked until my bones felt a little less weighed down and weary.

Drenched in my favorite shea butter body balm and dressed in my favorite pajamas, I grab the silk eye mask from the small cosmetics fridge in my bathroom and drag my sorry ass into bed.

I plug in my sleep earbuds, slip into the cool comfort of my bed, and lay right in the middle of it.

The Xanax I took when I got out of the shower is finally doing its job. My anxiety eases its grip on me and when my mind drifts to Dean instead of panic or hurt, the other thing I'd been feeling all day finally has room to breathe and joy bubbles up until I'm smiling.

I thought I'd never see him in the flesh again. I didn't realize how much that grieved me until today.

It's what I imagined I'd feel the day my father's whereabouts were finally known.

I wrap my arms around my pillow, hugging it to my chest and trying to imagine what it would feel like to be held by him now.

The door to my room creaks open and I pull one eye of my mask up and peer in the dark.

"Kevin?" I reach over to turn the light next to my bed and sit up.

"Oh good, you're awake." My husband strides across the room and sits down in front of me, his body shedding nervous energy.

He hasn't stepped into our bedroom since the night we argued about the press conference.

He's been traveling for work and when he's here he's never home before I fall asleep. Instantly on my guard, I pull the sheet up to my neck.

"I thought you were in LA until next week." I'm confused and irritated at the same time.

"I was. But I have something to tell you."

The first time he said those words to me, less than two years into our marriage, it struck the fear of God into me.

Over the course of our ten-year union, I've come to think of them the same way I thought of that three-minute warning bell before the final one. I was in danger, but all was not yet lost, I had time to fix whatever was wrong. But tonight, I find I don't have the desire to.

"Milly, please look at me," he pleads in a gravelly voice full of emotion I know he spent hours honing.

I look up slowly, bracing for the bite of betrayal and the stricken, guilt-ridden expression he wears when he tells me he's done it again. My eyes move up his flat blue Oxford encased torso, over his broad chest, up the corded neck I used to love nuzzling.

His mother's Puerto Rican and Haitian parentage blessed him with perpetually tan olive skin and thickly lashed, dark-brown eyes. He works out and is as trim at thirty-three as he was at twenty-one. But for the head he's shaved bald to hide the thinning hair at its crown - he still looks like the man I married. Yet, there's no trace of the kind, patient, generous man I hoped would make a good partner for me and a good father to my children.

"Milly," he croaks, adding desperation to his voice by raising it an octave. He's a good actor, but I've seen this play too many times.

"Kevin, just say it. I'm tired." I sigh with resignation and annoyance and close my book. It's been a long week, and I don't have the energy for the drama this too familiar scene always creates. I don't even care what he's done, or who he's done it with, I don't want him to apologize. I just want him to leave me alone.

"Please look at me," he repeats, holding that pose of sorrow - wrinkles in the corner of his eyes, his heavy lids drawn down to half-mast.

His thoughts are dry and flat and betray his lack of sincerity. He's going through the motions. But in truth, so am I. I have been for so long, I'd forgotten that apathy isn't normal in a marriage.

Or maybe I've always known, but wanted the safety of my

status as a married woman, a stable person more than I wanted to feel anything.

But after Dean blew the crust right off my heart this afternoon, I can feel *everything.*

Including anger at my husband for being such a piece of shit and an absolute refusal to take it for one more minute.

Adrenaline is pumping through my veins. God, I am so sick of these *fucking* men who think my life is a game that they make the rules for as they go along.

"I've had enough," I say to myself.

"What?" Kevin asks.

I meet his eyes. They used to make me feel safe. Now, they make me feel nothing.

"I said, I've had enough." My legs are over the side of the bed and the plush pile of the carpet tickles my bare toes, grounding me. I stand resolute and buoyed by the courage of my sudden conviction.

"I want you to leave. I want a divorce"

My words shatter the atmosphere of our marriage with a finality that should scare me.

His head snaps back like I spat in his face and his jaw slackens with surprise. There is fear in his eyes as he watches me, like he's waiting for me to say something more.

I have said everything I'm going to. I fold my arms across my chest and hold his disoriented gaze with my steady one.

It takes him half a minute to finds his voice.

"But you don't even know what I was going to say," he sputters.

I shrug. "Does it really matter? You're going to tell me you fucked someone else, you're in love with someone else, you borrowed money from my trust, you totaled your car again. Then you'll say you're sorry. But you're not. And I'm not either. In fact, I'm glad you gave me a reason to be done."

"You don't mean that. Come on." His dark brows furrow and he reaches a hand out toward me.

Dylan Allen

I take a step back and shake my head in disdain. "I mean it more than I've meant anything else I've *ever* said to you."

"What's changed?" I snort a laugh in ironic disbelief at how earnest he *finally* sounds.

"Nothing. And it never will."

He shakes his head, his eyes unfocused as he stares at me like he's never seen me before. "This is us. This is what we do."

He isn't wrong. A pattern has developed over the course of our marriage that began with those four words and ended with my forgiveness and his gratitude and empty promises of "this is the last time, I swear."

I'd come to accept that there would never be a last time - and told myself that was fine. I had the one thing I needed in life from him and so, I could live with it…nothing was perfect and this thing… His infidelity was just my cross to bear.

We'd reset and then, we'd be fine again.

A month ago, that's how this would have gone.

Hell, maybe even a day ago. But I can't take this shit one more fucking second.

I look into his eyes again. The dark depths of them used to make me smile, but now I feel nothing. The illusion I'd created shattered it into pieces so fractured that even if I wanted to, I could never put it back together again. "It's dead. Has been for a long time."

His chest heaves and he drops his head into his hands and rubs the heels of his palms into his eyes. Then he stands, lip curled in disdain and his eyes glittering with contempt he used to try and hide. "You know what, fuck this. And fuck you."

He marches to his closet, pulls out a suitcase and tosses it on the bed. He starts filling it with clothes from his chest of drawers.

He stops packing and glances over his shoulder at me. His expression darkens and he turns to face me fully. "Why wasn't this enough?" He flings a hand around the room. "We had our problems, but we've built a life. Why did you have to ruin it?"

It's a question with a dozen different answers. I give him the one that covers them all. "I want more."

"More what?"

"Of everything."

This is the moment I've worked my entire adult life to avoid, and yet as I meet it, my heart feels lighter than it has in a decade.

"What the hell are you talking about? You're the one who created this model home where nothing feels right. I didn't want to live like . . . *this*."

I sputter an indignant laugh, my eyes wide with incredulity. "Are you *kidding?* When we got married, this—" I sweep my arms out mimicking his earlier movement, "is all you wanted. A wife who looked the part, kept this house pristine, your son is happy, smart, and loving," I remind him.

He looks me up and down with the apathy he might show a door to door salesman and shrugs. "Maybe if I had a wife who didn't bore me to death. Or a wife who still turned me on so I don't have to pretend I'm with someone else just to get hard enough to fuck her dry, wooden body."

I gasp, shocked by his crude words and their callous delivery. "How would you know what my body is like, you stopped touching me as soon as I got pregnant."

His responding chuckle is dry and without humor. "Oh please. I'm sure your frigid little cunt has been rejoicing."

I flush, hot and hard not just at his language, but at the truth of it.

Sex has never been my favorite part of our relationship. I'd never had an orgasm with him inside me, and he doesn't like oral—giving or receiving—so it was over once he was done. I haven't missed it and I thought he didn't either.

He grabs the last of his underwear from the drawer and slams it shut. "I only married you because my mother liked you and was desperate for grand babies."

Ouch.

I forgot how dirty he fights. It's not the death blow he intends it to be, but it stings. "Your mother has been dead for five years. Why are you still here?"

He snaps his suitcase closed and gives me a cold smile. "Divorce is expensive. And I felt sorry for you."

"*Sorry* for me?" I sputter.

"You may hate it now, but you were *so damn* desperate to be married, Milly. And you just wait. I know you hate being alone because you're as bored by your own company as everyone else is." He watches me with a gleeful, anticipatory sneer on his face, expecting me to crumble under the weight of his cruel words.

Kevin didn't know the Milly before.

He wouldn't know that I've been in fights worse than this. I've had my heart sliced in two. It's healed and the scar tissue is even stronger than what was there before. But, he couldn't truly hurt me if he tried.

I stand straighter than I have in years to look him straight in the eye and tell him the truth of things. "I married you because I needed someone too self-absorbed to see through all the lies I would have to tell."

His eyes narrow and his head jerks back. That surprise on his face puts a smile on mine - it's nice to have the upper hand. But my satisfaction only lasts for the few seconds it takes for him to dismiss my words. "What lies?"

For the first time in more than a decade, the truth I never thought I'd speak dances on the tip of my tongue. "*Every single time I said I love you, too.*"

There's enough hurt between us to last a lifetime and I'm tired of trafficking in it just to score points. There are no winners in this game. "I thought you were leaving."

His sneer deepens. "Wild horses couldn't keep me in this pristine prison you've created."

I don't say another word as I hear him pick up his suitcase and start toward the door.

His footsteps falter just as he starts to open our bedroom door. "Oh, and Milly?"

I cast my weary gaze on him. "What?"

"I'm fucking someone else. Happy New Year." With a flip of his middle finger, he's gone.

The thud of his heavy footfalls down the stairs are followed by the slam of the front door and then, the roar of his car engine.

I don't move for a long time. I'm numb.

He's gone.

He's not coming back.

This life I've built with so much intention and purpose has, in the space of a day, completely unraveled.

I lie down, my mind spins with the implications of my impulsive decision making.

I meant everything I said to Kevin. All of it.

But what now?

What am I going to tell Anthony? He *loves* his dad.

What am *I* going to do? This is all I've known, all I've been for so long.

What will my mother say? She's always liked Kevin.

What will my *sisters* say? They'll probably be thrilled.

Maybe I shouldn't tell them. Not yet.

Kevin and I could work this out. All marriages go through hard times.

You never loved him.

The words sound like an alarm inside my head and I know for sure that this time, it's truly over.

I open my bedside drawer and dig to the bottom of it. I pull out the picture I haven't looked at in years and stare at it.

It's Dean's junior year picture for the yearbook. He's unsmiling, his jaw set, his green eyes piercing like he could see me.

When I framed this photo, I couldn't have imagined it would be the last one of him I'd ever have.

I close my eyes, overwhelmed by how much it hurt to see him today.

That should have been me next to him. Planning our wedding and our lives.

The space in my heart he occupied is still his.

Oh, God. Why is this happening?

Why does it hurt so fucking much?

I press his picture to my chest and without warning, the dam drops.

Emotions I've kept stored away they had the power to overwhelm me, come rushing out and I surrender to them.

I'm tired of fighting and pretending and being alone.

I cry until I finally fall asleep.

In the middle of the night, I wake myself up, calling out for my father. I call my mother.

When she gets here, she doesn't ask me what's wrong.

She crawls into bed with me, wraps her arms around me, and holds me all night.

my funny valentine

THE SHOWER IS where I go when I need to clear my head. The water had a rhythm that could melt away anything that still clung to me at the end of even the most stressful day.

Tonight, not even a shower can make me forget that I'm leaving Houston for a whole week tomorrow without accomplishing the only thing I really wanted from this trip – I haven't heard from Milly.

I climb out of the shower with my mind set on getting lost in the mountain of work I've let pile up.

I glance at my phone and my heart gives an annoyingly hopeful leap when I see there's a text from a number I don't recognize.

That foolish hope fizzles as soon as I start reading.

VAL

Heard you're in Houston.

From who?

Nicola.

55

…How did she get your number?

She called my office. She was pissed. Asked me if I knew how to reach your mother when I told her I didn't know where you were.

Jesus.

Praying this means you finally ended things.

Yes. She didn't take it well.

Tell me about it over dinner?

You're here?

Yeah, we're opening a campaign office. We just bought a house.

We?

Heidi and me. Dinner? I'll pick you up.

I glance at my watch, it's been nearly two hours since I started working and I've spent more than half that time thinking about Milly.

What time?

Where are you staying?

4 Seasons.

Thirty minutes?

I'll be ready.

I'm down in the lobby in less than twenty minutes and step outside to get some fresh air while I wait for Val.

Known to most of the world as Sebastian V. Hayford, he's been my best friend since he and his father moved into the house next door to ours.

We were both six-years-old and in the same first grade class.

His father and my mother *hated* each other.

It started with a dispute over the wall Mr. Hayford built between the houses and ended when Mr. Hayford dropped dead on the last day of middle school. We'd been walking home, thinking about all the girls we were going to make out with and the movies we were going to see.

It's ironic that when I think back on that day, what still I remember most about is how happy we were.

His parents had been divorced since he was a baby. His mother married his father's ex- best friend. When he died, Valentine left to go live with them in Arkansas. We didn't see each other again until he came to Houston for my father's funeral, but there wasn't a moment we weren't in touch or anything about each other's lives that we didn't know.

We managed to attend college and law school together. But after that, our lives took very different paths. He became a *real* lawyer, joining the Justice Department's Antitrust division as a litigator.

I joined a powerful entertainment firm in Los Angeles that represented every major film and television studio on the planet and discovered I was better at making deals than writing contracts and soon, signed on as a junior agent.

We were on opposite coasts and living polar opposite existences. But he's been my constant and I've been his. He's the only person who knows, intimately, how badly I dealt with losing my dad and Milly at the same time.

I spot his sleek silver Aston Martin at the end of the driveway. The completely blacked out windows make it impossible to see inside, but it's the only one of his cars no one else is allowed to drive so I know he's in the driver's seat.

I open the door and climb in. "I can't believe you drove yourself."

"I told you I needed to talk." He lifts his dark glossy Tom Ford sunglasses off his nose and gives me a once-over. "You look like shit."

I curl my lip and shrug. "I've had a hell of a week."

He slaps me on the shoulder and throws the car into drive. "Well, things can only go up from here, right?"

"Don't tempt fate," I mutter and put my seatbelt on.

"I owe you a glass of champagne. It's about fucking time. I never liked Nicola."

"You never met her."

"Exactly. Because, even from afar, I didn't like her. I could tell she was a fraud."

"Thanks for telling me."

"Oh please, you see what you want to see. And...I hoped I was wrong."

"I'm kind of glad you weren't. She's not the one."

He groans. "You've got to stop thinking like you don't know what real life looks like. The *one* isn't a thing."

"I know," I mutter, but I don't really mean it.

"Let's eat, and talk, just the two of us. That always makes everything better."

I nod in silent agreement. Less than ten minutes later, he maneuvers the car into a narrow driveway and stops in front of a huge modern monstrosity of a gate that slides open on a remarkably quiet track to reveal a two-story structure of stucco and glass and dark wood that is so stunning I can't hide my awe.

"This is your *house*?"

"Yup, closed last week." The pride in his voice is unmistakable and really good to hear.

"It's amazing."

"Heidi found it."

"Wait, we're eating here? With her?"

"She's not here."

"Thank fuck," I mutter.

He snickers. "What have you got against her? She likes you so much."

"I like her too…kinda." I chuckle when he gives me the finger. "She's an exhibitionist and I'm not in the mood for one of her shows tonight."

He snickers. "Fair enough."

We sit idling while the gate comes down behind us. "What are we waiting for?"

"Since I started leaking that I'm considering a run, I've had reporters strolling up to my front door. I don't open the garage until the gate is closed. Make sure no one can follow me in, you know?"

"Yeah," I say, even though I don't really know what it's like to worry for your safety, but I know Val has very good reason, more than just nosy reporters, to be hyper vigilant about his security. Long before he had the aspirations of being a politician, his stepfather was murdered and they've never solved the case. It's not something that is public knowledge and he does his best to keep it that way.

His garage door opens to reveal a huge elevator that lowers his car down a level.

We climb out and the man who parks his cars appears from the small cottage to the right of the main house. "Evening, boss," he calls and runs forward, catching the keys Val tosses with a practiced ease that I know Val likes. He's had the same staff working for him since we graduated from law school and I follow him up the steps and inside.

He locks the door and engages his alarm and gives a command that turns on all the lights at once and even though I've known him for so long, I'm always struck by how starkly he lives for a man with more money than he can spend.

I'm not a spendthrift, but Val's outsized lavish interior makes my penthouse in LA look like a starter unit.

"This house is straight up Bruce Wayne level shit," I say with a low whistle of approval.

"I'm going to ask Heidi to marry me."

Surprise stops me mid-stride and I turn to face him. "Uh, I thought she was your campaign manager with benefits."

He rolls his eyes. "She's been my girlfriend since law school, Dean."

I narrow my eyes. "Okay, but do you love her?"

He shrugs. "In my own way."

I raise my eyebrows in surprise. "What way is that?"

He nods to the sofa and takes a seat, leaning back and crossing his legs at the angle as he appears to ponder my question.

I sit next to him. "That wasn't a trick question."

He shoots me an irritated glance. "I love her in the way you love someone you want to marry and spend your life with."

"So…what about Rey?"

He gives me a dark look. "Her father was married to my mother."

"That doesn't make her your sister. And you're in love with – "

"Dean, please, it's not a starter, leave it alone." His expression is without its trademark nonchalance and I back off.

I lean back in my chair and force my back to relax into it. "So, Heidi's your choice for First Lady, then?"

He gives me a grateful half smile and walks over to the small drink cart. "She's perfect. She looks the part, has the pedigree and the money, and she's got political ambition on her own. We have a plan and we're going all the way with it." He hands me a short glass with a splash of amber liquid in it.

I take a sip and smile in appreciation. "You've always got the best scotch." I raise my glass. "To you and Heidi."

We clink glasses.

I'm not convinced. But, he's wanted to be a lawmaker as long as I've known him. He's an adult. He's one of the smartest people I know and if he wants to marry Heidi, who am I to stop him.

"So how long are you in town?"

"I'm leaving tomorrow. I have to go to New York for a few days, but I'll be back. Got business to put in order and shit."

"Business like...patching things up with Nicola?"

I huff a humorless laugh. "We're done."

He frowns but nods his head in approval. "You mean it."

I nod and let out a deep breath. "I saw Milly."

He whistles and throws back the rest of the drink and gets to his feet. "Woah. You need to start that story at the beginning. Let me get the whole bottle."

punchline

IT'S BEEN NEARLY a week since my life turned to shit, but it feels like a year has passed.

I woke up sure I'd just made the biggest mistake of my life and since then, regret has morphed into numb disbelief, stuttering confusion, and now has settled on grief.

My mother told me to stay in bed, let the feelings run their course. She made sure Anthony got to school every morning and spent the day sitting beside me knitting or reading. She didn't ask me how I was feeling and she didn't tell me everything would be alright.

If it was just me, I could have stayed in bed for a month. But I've got a little boy to look after and there's no punching out on being a mom.

I don't care that Kevin hasn't been in touch since he left, but Anthony misses his dad.

I steel myself for whatever is coming next and dial his number.

"Are you fucking serious, Milly?" he demands by way of greeting, his voice rough with sleep.

I glance at the clock. "It's seven thirty." He's usually at the office by now.

"I don't give a shit what time it is. I can't believe you're fucking calling me after what you did."

The hostility in his voice sets my teeth on edge. "Believe me, I wish I didn't have to call and remind you that you have a son."

"Oh, I haven't forgotten. I hoped you'd get tired of the bullshit and stop, but after yesterday, I'm done."

"Kevin, what the hell are you talking about?"

"Oh please. Save it for someone else. Better yet, get yourself a lawyer because I'm suing for joint custody and if you don't stop what you've been doing, I'll ask for full custody."

I almost retch at his threat.

"Did you understand me? You need to stop." His voice isn't as loud, but his tone is sinister.

"Stop what?" I sputter, confused and terrified.

"Fine. If you want to play dumb, I'll spell it out. Stop sending Rachael dead flowers. Stop leaving those stupid notes on my car, just stop."

I feel like I've stepped into the twilight zone."Kevin, I don't know what you are talking about. I—"

He cuts me off before I can finish. "Yeah, sure you don't know," he mocks, his voice full of venom. "But, *I* know. Stop it. Or I'm going to take him away from you. Do. You. Fucking. Understand. Me?"

Then he hangs up. I sit there, staring at my phone, shaking, my confusion blooming into full on panic as I replay the conversation I just had with him.

A knot of fear and anxiety settles in my stomach as I replay that absurd conversation.

He must be making it up. Nothing else makes sense.

I haven't sent her flowers; I haven't left notes on his car. What in the world is going on? I put on my jeans and run down to Anthony's room. I feel a wild sense of relief that he's still lying in bed. He has twenty more minutes before he needs to get up for school.

I'm downstairs making breakfast for Anthony when I hear my mother come down the stairs. For the last month, she's come down while I stayed in bed. So, when she walks into my kitchen, she's startled to see me standing at the center island, drinking a cup of coffee while making Anthony pancakes.

"Milly! What are you doing here?" Her question would be absurd, but I've been acting like a hermit for a whole month.

"Ummm, I *live* here," I return wryly.

"You know what I mean. Did something happen? Are you okay?" She fires these questions at me as she hurries into the kitchen.

"I do. Yes, and maybe. That should answer all of your questions," I return dryly, struggling to hide my smile.

She looks at me, clearly puzzled, but sits down across from me at one of the stools which line the other side of my massive marble island.

"Tell me. What's going on?" she says, her eyes grave.

So, I tell her about my call from Kevin. Her eyes turn from grave to stricken. When I finish she bursts into tears.

My mother doesn't cry. I rush around the counter and wrap an arm around her. "It's okay. He's got to be making it up, Mom. Even though he sounded genuinely pissed off."

"He's not," she whispers.

"He's not what?"

She shakes her head and drops it into her hands.

"Mom, it doesn't matter. *I* didn't do any of those things. So he can't use them to get the court to let Anthony live with him. Whoever's it is has nothing to do with me. I don't even know who Rachael is."

"I do." She says it so quietly that I'm not sure she's spoken until she repeats herself.

"You know who Rachael is?" I am completely confused.

"She's his girlfriend."

64

"His...girlfriend?" I quirk my brows. "I didn't even know she existed. He can't pin something on me that I haven't done."

"He's been seeing her for a couple of months."

"And you know this, *how*?" I look at her expectantly when she doesn't answer.

She sighs and closes her eyes. "Rabea and I.." she trails off on a sigh and stares at her clasped hands.

My stomach drops at the mention of her best friend. My mom and Rabea met in the international food aisle of our local grocery store. They fought over the last jar of tahini paste and ended up trading hummus recipes and phone numbers. She's my mother's only friend from our life before. They have a lot of fun together and I have been so grateful my mother has had her as a companion all these years.

But, Rabea is terribly mischievous and has a *very* strange sense of humor.

"Start talking," I demand.

When she looks at me finally, her eyes are full of regret.

"Millicent, I'm sorry. I broke your confidence. I told Rabea about Kevin." She doesn't look up as she continues talking.

I drop my forehead into my hand. This cannot be good.

"She loves you...And, you know her. She said she was going to 'haunt' them."

I gasp and cover my mouth with my hand.

"Milly, she never signed your name, she never let herself be seen. She was taking the weeds she pulled out from her yard and putting them on that idiot's doorstep once a week. And then she would type these notes to Kevin." She looks up at me then, gauging my reaction. I'm livid as I listen to this crazy story unfold.

"What do the notes say?" I demand.

"Oh, different things every time." She glances down and clears her throat. "Mainly dick jokes she found online. She would type them up and put them on his windshield while his car was parked at work."

I stare at her, unable to believe what I'm hearing. *"Dick* jokes?" I sputter.

"Yes. You know. Your dick's so small you could screw a pasta strainer. Your dick's so small you could get head from a crease in my lip. Your dick's so ugly it looks like a pimple with a pulse."

"Mother! I get the gist," I yell.

She goes on like she hasn't heard me, smiling fondly now. "Oh, and a week ago she sent him a doozy. Your dick's so small, satisfying a woman is Mission Impossible."

Her smile brims at this last one.

I can't help it, that ridiculous joke, added to the ludicrous scheme of Rabea's, and to just how crazy it all is, I burst out laughing.

She joins me in the laughter and when we catch our breath, we stand there and look at each other.

"Milly, I'm sorry. I figured he would never be able to make the connection. And he can tell the judge whatever he likes, but he won't be able to prove it."

"Is that your legal opinion?" I ask dryly.

"No. But I'm right. And he's bluffing."

"I hope so."

"And I hope you're going to let him go, finally."

"I thought you liked him." I chuckle.

She sighs and grasps my hands before she responds. "He's your husband. I live in your house. Of course you think I like him because that's how I act."

"We had a good life," I say weakly, defending my marriage more out of reflex than real passion.

"Why have good when you can have great?"

"It was better than nothing."

"You've never had nothing," she says.

"Do you remember the heart shaped Adinkra pendant we gave you?"

My hand goes up to my bare throat. I couldn't bear to look at it after my father left, so I took it off. But I still have it. It's sitting in my jewelry box right next to the ring Dean gave me. They were reminders of everything I'd lost. "Yes, it's called Sankofa, right?"

She nods. "It's one of the most meaningful of the symbols. We chose it for you, our firstborn, because you were born with an old soul. I hoped you'd call on the wisdom in your eyes and never forget the lessons you'd already learned. You are powerful, but you've forgotten that. And... I know it's been a while, but I also *know* you've had great, you know it's possible. You just have to be willing to try."

I sigh. I don't have a response to my mother's advice.

My mind is swirling with so many conflicting thoughts.

Maybe the end of my relationship with Kevin is a good thing. Do I have it in me to find out what life lived with less caution holds? I'm not sure.

I sigh and close my eyes.

She pats my hand and hops off the stool.

"I'll go get Anthony up." She starts to leave the kitchen, but then stops to say, "He's bluffing, Milly. I'll get Rabea to stop the notes and flowers, and then he will leave you alone. He won't take Anthony from you, he won't even try."

don't call it a comeback

A FEW DAYS after our disastrous phone call and my mother's confession, I got Kevin's petition for sole custody of Anthony.

The trust funds were set up with my mother's money and remained intact when my father left. I don't live on it and plan on leaving as much of it as I can for Anthony, but for this fight, I wasn't taking any chances especially when I saw that he'd hired one of the best divorce lawyers in Houston.

So I splurged and got the *very* best. And she's been worth every penny. This mediation was set up at lightning speed. We only had a week to get ready, but that was more than enough.

Whatever sadness, pain, wistfulness, or regret I was feeling over the demise of my marriage disappeared when I got the letter. They were replaced with one, white-hot rage.

In this, there are no shades of gray.

He *cannot* have my son.

My lawyer told me she'd be ready and told me to focus on making the right impression.

I've spent years dressing for comfort. But a few days ago, I walked into Saks Fifth Avenue, intent on buying one thing that made me look the way I hoped I'd feel one day - in charge, unafraid, and smoking hot.

As soon as I tried on the first dress the shopping assistant brought and felt the soft finely milled cotton against my skin, and saw the way I looked in the mirror - like a woman with choices, power, and a plan - I changed my mind. I didn't want *one* thing that made me feel like this. I wanted *everything* I wore to make me feel this way.

I made up for lost time and left with the start of an entirely new wardrobe.

I pulled some strings and got an appointment with the world-famous hairstylist who makes her home in a sleek salon in Rivers Wilde, Tanaka, to color and cut my hair.

She blew it straight and feathered the layers. When she was done, recognized myself in the mirror again.

Gone was the Milly who put everyone else's needs above her own - I the woman knew I couldn't take care of anyone if I didn't take care of myself first was back.

I give myself a once-over in the full-length mirror of the elevator with ruthless scrutiny.

I smooth my hands over the white wool Carolina Herrera sheath that fits me like a bespoke glove.

The gold chain around my neck is strung with a pendant and the heart shaped ring Dean gave me.

Something about wearing these things, given to me out of love, feels like a source of strength.

Kevin hated it when I wore heels because it made us the same height and for years, I yielded to his ego.

Today, I slipped on a pair of cognac patent leather Jimmy Choo stilettos because I love them.

I'm done making myself small for him.

I'm not confident about many things and I haven't always made the best decisions in my personal life. But I'm a damn good parent and Anthony is a well-adjusted, fearless, and thoughtful child. I won't let him be a pawn in Kevin's play to hurt me.

My lawyer is already waiting when I step off the elevator and into the firm's reception area.

"Abby?' I call and wave when she turns around and sees me.

"Millicent, good afternoon," she greets me as I approach her.

"I hope it will be." We shake hands.

"I'll do my best." We share a small smile and step into the mediator's suite.

It's late afternoon and we're the last appointment of the day.

Kevin and Rachael are already there with their attorney. It's galling he brought her to this meeting, but Abby advised me not to make an issue of it. The mediator would find it odd and petty as well. Any protest I made would just have me getting into the mud with him.

So, I ignore them.

Abby Quan is a stunning woman in her late forties. With her sleek fall of black hair cut into a chin length bob, immaculately applied makeup, and expertly tailored suit, she looks every inch the high-priced lawyer she is.

She told me she has faced Kevin's lawyer in court before and that he plays dirty.

Thankfully, I don't have any skeletons in my closet. My one secret is now public fodder and so, I'm ready for whatever Kevin tries to throw at me.

We are called into a conference room and Kevin and Rachael make a show of rushing to walk in ahead of me. I get my first good glimpse at the woman my husband left me for. She is everything I'm not. She's short, curvy, blonde, and young.

She glances at me and smirks as they walk past us into the room. It stings to see them holding hands. Not because *I* want to be the one holding his hand, but because right now, I hate to see visual proof of his ability to move on.

As I walk into the room with Abby at my side, I push this feeling aside and focus on why I'm here.

When we are seated across the table from each other, I fight my initial inclination to look away when Kevin makes eye contact. I know he wants to intimidate me by trying to appear confident. Well, I'm confident, too.

Our gazes lock and I find myself staring into the eyes of a stranger; someone I don't know. Maybe I never did. But this cruel, cold man is a far cry from the warm, loving person I married.

I see his stare turn from one of challenge to one of surprise and then discomfort. He looks away abruptly, and Rachael grabs his hand on top of the table.

The mediator comes in, and the meeting begins. Abby has advised me to let her do all the talking and so I do.

It's infuriating to sit here and listen to his lawyer lie about the "environment" in my home. He calls it distracting and disconcerting for Anthony. He talks about the resurgence of interest in my father's criminality and says the chaos it has created will negatively impact Anthony.

He argues Anthony needs to be with his father who has a partner who can help create some "balance" in the home. I almost lose my cool at those words. But I hold my tongue. I know what is at stake here.

When Abby begins to present her points, I immediately feel better. She makes a very clear case for Anthony remaining with me. She cites Kevin's frequent absences even before we were separated and his lack of contact since. She doesn't mention my father or the recent blow up that surrounds his actions all those years ago. It's true the press camping outside our house for a few days was stressful for Anthony, but I was there for him and talked him through his confusion.

It becomes clear I'm not willing to concede any points in this matter. And neither is he. He may not be able to look me in the eye any longer, but on this issue, he's standing firm.

No resolution will be reached today and the mediator asks us to submit our individual proposals to him in writing. He'll make a recommendation we can accept or reject. If we reject it, we'll be cleared to pursue a custody arrangement in court.

Even though this is the outcome I expected, it's not what I wanted and I feel defeated and tired as we walk out of the office.

Abby and I say our goodbyes and I head to the restroom before I go to my car.

Rachael is there, at the counter reapplying her lipstick, when I walk in. I'm immediately on edge but walk into a stall without acknowledging her even as she watches me in the mirror.

"He's going to win, you know," she calls out in a singsong mocking tone as my stall door closes.

I don't respond.

"And we are going to have your son and you'll have nothing," she continues in that same tone.

I still don't respond, but I'm nearly trembling with anger. Who is this odious woman Kevin wants to have his son live with?

"Are you too scared to come out? He told me you were a doormat."

Disgusted, I finish my business and she continues her hateful taunt. "You're so pathetic. He told me *all* about you. How frigid you are. How boring you are. How needy you are."

I step out of the stall quickly and step directly in front of her, taking her by surprise. In my heels, I'm over six feet tall. I tower over her and look down into her eyes, my eyes boring into hers, which go from creased in glee to wide with shock. The rapidity of the change is almost comical.

"Pathetic? Frigid? Needy? Boring?" I laugh dryly. "He's a liar, Rachael. And if you think for even one second you will have *anything* when he's done with you, you're even dumber than you look."

With that, I face the mirror, turn on the faucet and wash my hands, but keep my eyes locked on hers in the mirror and let her see the steel in my eyes. She thinks she's going to raise my son? Over my dead body.

I tell her, "And if I find out that you are putting any of your hateful ideas in my son's head, you can forget lawyers, courts, and whatever else Kevin promised you. I will fucking *kill* you."

I smile coldly at her and reach for a paper towel. Her face drains of color as she stands there watching me for a beat. Then, she grabs her purse and rushes out of the bathroom. She gives me a wide berth as she slinks into the hallway.

I wait two minutes and then follow her out. My legs are trembling and threatening to give out on me. But, I make it to my car without collapsing. I've never spoken to anyone like this before in my life. I have never used the "f" word in such a manner. But, I'm done living my life with my back on the ropes.

When Kevin left me, I was sure I wouldn't be able to get over the pain. But this stunt he has pulled is just the kick in the ass I needed. I thought I'd lost my whole future. When really, I have been spared. Spared a lifetime of making myself small so that he could look big. Putting any desires I had on the back burner so that my *husband* could have whatever he wanted. But with this flaming arrow, shot directly at my heart with an aim to kill, he has shown me exactly who he really is.

Sitting in my car, I pull my vanity mirror down and look at myself. I look like the same person, but I feel as if something has come loose. And not in a bad way.

I'm starting to remember who I am. I'm not powerless, I'm not small, and I'm certainly not afraid.

set up

"I THINK I'm going to be sick," Zenobia whispers through lips that barely move. "I can't believe we're here."

"And, feeling very much the same way. "We're ready, we're going to nail it." The reassurance is for me as much as it is for her.

If I can land this gig, for one of the most visible and popular politicians of our time, it'll help me regain some of the professional credibility I've lost since my father's identity came to light.

This is do or die for my passion project that turned into a business.

"Ladies, Mr. Hayford is ready for you," the young man who had greeted me when I walked into the office building called from behind the reception desk.

We glance at each other and exchange "here we go" smiles and stand in unison.

"Please, come this way." He waves us over with a warm smile and we follow him down a hallway of glass walled offices.

The entire office is decorated in white leather and stainless steel. The only color in the entire space comes from the bold, abstract paintings on the walls. I barely notice them. I'm laser focused on what comes next.

The young man stops at the open door of an office where Sebastian V. Hayford sits behind a desk that's so large I suspect it was designed to be a dining table. His office is expensively decorated and smells like a spa.

"Mrs. Bishop and Ms. Rice, please, come in." The man himself stands and rounds the desk. He's a tall, lean man and I have to look up to meet his eyes. They're warm and friendly as is his smile. I've seen him on television plenty of times, but I'm still struck by how good-looking he is. He moves with a confident grace that immediately puts me at ease and makes me want this job even more. He's going to win. One look at him is all it'll take to convince a lot of people to vote for him.

He's not in his trademark three-piece suit but he's still dressed in all black and everything about him says, "power".

"Mr. Hayford, we're thrilled to have the opportunity to meet you."

"Please, call me Val," he says and takes my hand in a firm, very reassuring handshake. My nerves ease their feet off the gas a little.

"Then you must call me Milly."

His grin is a devilish flash of his teeth that is outrageously charming. "Milly, a pleasure to meet you."

I smile at him and gesture to my right. "This is my associate planner, Zenobia Rice."

Zen's smile is wide and enthusiastic. "It's Zen," she offers as they shake hands.

"Please, have a seat."

He strides back to sit behind his desk and get right down to business.

"I had you sign that NDA before you came back because I'm about to share something that isn't public knowledge yet."

I nod in understanding as excitement starts to simmer inside of me. "I'm going to propose to my girlfriend at a surprise engagement party and I'd love you to plan it."

Zen was right, I catch her eye for a split second before I turn to Val. "That's incredible and we would be honored to make it as special an evening as possible."

He leans back in his seat with a satisfied smile. "Excellent. I'm very glad to hear that. I'd like to get started as soon as possible."

He presses a button under his desk. "Send the food in, please."

"Oh you didn't have to go to the trouble," I say as a caravan of people come into the room, each pushing a silver service tray.

He waves away my protest with a flick of the wrist. "It's just a few snacks. Although…" He leans forward. "I did wait to see if you'd say yes before I had them set up. I don't feed people who say no to me." He winks and signals the servers with a raised hand. "Please make your plates and we'll talk."

The servers lay everything out in front of us. What he calls snacks are actually huge cheese Danishes, an assortment of sandwiches cut in geometric shapes, bowls of fruit, a charcuterie board, and a tray of chocolate covered strawberries.

"This will be an engagement party - but it's also a photo op for my campaign. I'll have a camera crew on site and I want to make sure it sets the tone for the rest of the campaign events we plan. Elegant, luxurious, inclusive without a hint of gaudiness. Do you understand what I mean?"

"So it's a dual purpose event?" I ask for clarity as I start revising the plans I put together as soon as I got their call.

"Yes. And if it goes well and Heidi agrees, I'd like you to plan the wedding as well."

My spirits rebound. "We'll do our best to wow you."

He leans back again, arms folded across his abdomen. "Great. So, tell me how you are going to blow our minds."

It takes superhuman strength not to gulp. I reach into my briefcase and pull out my party planner and the design sheet

I've already created. I lay it on the table between us and say, "I can do even better than that. Let me *show* you."

I spent a good part of the last few weeks studying every picture I could find of him at events he hosted and inside his home to get an idea of what his taste would lend itself to. And even though the designs are for a wedding and reception, Zen and I were prepared to present an engagement event, too.

"Your next appointment is here, Val. I have him for 3 p.m. He says your meeting was for 2:30," a voice announces over the loudspeaker.

"Oh, I'm sorry, I must have gotten my wires crossed. Ask him to give me a few minutes." He grins to himself, and I get the impression he's not sorry at all.

I glance at my watch. "Our hour is almost up, anyway. We'll just pack up and get out of your way."

"Actually, can you stay? It's my best man who's arrived and we're going to look at a potential venue for the party. If you have time, I'd love to show you."

Zen clears her throat and I look at her. "I've got to relieve my babysitter, I'm so sorry." She looks at me and cringes in apology.

"It's okay. I'll stay. I've got nothing else on my calendar for this evening."

Zen hasn't been gone for two minutes when the door flies open. "Hey, I think there's a mix-up with the time."

The room tilts. I'd know that voice anywhere.

"Dean?" I whisper without turning around.

"The man himself," Val says and walks across the room to where Dean is standing, stock still and looking as shocked as I feel.

His eyes darted from Val to me and back again. "What is she doing here?" he demands.

Val looks completely unbothered. In fact, he smiles. "*She* is my brand-new party planner."

Dean blinks. "Your *what*?"

Val grins. "I know. Isn't it great?"

Dylan Allen

His phone rings and he looks at it and frowns. "So sorry, I've been waiting for this call all day. I'll be right back and then we'll head over together."

Before I can say a word, he's gone and so is all the oxygen in the room.

I'm alone with Dean. I sit in my chair before my legs give out on me.

I glance up at him and wish I hadn't. He looks like he wants to hit something.

"I didn't know you'd be here, Dean." I hate how defensive I sound. I haven't done anything wrong.

"I know," he mutters.

The silence stretches for what feels like an eternity. It's torture standing here like this. So close, but with a wall of time and hurt between us. Our time has passed.

But even in the cold and unreadable depth of his eyes - I can see the boy I loved—the boy I've never stopped loving.

Those eyes were my sanctuary, my safe harbor, and I've missed them so much. Tears well in my eyes and I look down, horrified that he might have seen them.

He looks back at me and there's a flare of *something* in his eyes that makes my heart skip a beat. "I'll be back."

And then, he's gone, too.

I feel a nauseating combination of relief and sadness congealing into a sickening lump in my gut.

I can't believe he was here. I can't tell what he was thinking, but it couldn't have been anything good.

"I'm back." Val stops halfway through the door. "Where's Dean?"

"He said he'd be back."

And I plan to be gone before he makes good on that.

I pull my phone out and message Zen.

Text me back.

Why?

Thanks. Explain later.

"Oh no," I exclaim with exaggerated frowns of regret and hold up my vibrating phone. "I can't stay after all. My mother needs me."

Val's eyebrows snap together in surprise, but he nods. "Okay...We can try another day."

"Absolutely." I hurry to pack up my bag. "Thank you for everything. I'm excited to get started," I say with a vibrant smile even though I want to throw up.

I'm halfway to the door when it opens and Dean walks back in. "Nice to meet you. Excuse me," I mutter and slip past him.

clarity

LOVE IS A HELL OF A DRUG. The rush puts you in a chokehold but the high feels so good you never want to be free of it until you notice you can't take deep breaths anymore.

If it doesn't stop your fucking heart, you'll spend the rest of your life in withdrawal.

I only needed time around that track to see it for the booby-trapped road it is.

I'm a fast learner and it's been twenty years since love beat me in the draw.

That changed today.

I slump into the chair she just got out of. It's still warm from her body and smells like roses. I close my eyes and groan.

"You are such an asshole, Val. What the hell?"

"Listen, I contacted her before I knew she was *your* Milly and before you told me about your run-in with her. She's who Heidi would want. If she'll take the job, I'm going to hire her."

I sigh and drop my head into my hands. "Why didn't you tell me she would be here?"

"Would you have come if I had?"

"No."

"Exactly. You're welcome."

"For what?"

"I'm reuniting two people who should never have split up in the first place."

"She's married, Val."

"So?"

My stomach churns. "No. I don't want to talk about this. That door is sealed shut and locked."

"Is it? You haven't seen her in fifteen years. Don't you want to talk to her? Get some closure?"

"I have closure. She's married."

"Hmmm, she wasn't wearing a ring."

"Yes she was," I insist.

"No, she *wasn't*. I sat across from her for an hour and she didn't have them on."

"She was wearing them last week."

"Maybe...seeing you gave her an epiphany, too?"

I glare at him. Part of me wants to kill Val, the other part of me wants to thank him for knowing me better than I know myself.

I glance at my watch.

"She's gone."

"No, she's at the bar downstairs."

I raise my eyebrows at him. "Really?"

"I own the building, I have access to all the cameras. I saw her walk in and she hasn't walked back out. Go talk to her. What do you have to lose?"

"Nothing I haven't already."

"Right. And what if, by some miracle, she's not wearing that ring for the same reason Nicola's not wearing yours?"

The idea of her being single, that maybe time is finally on our side, makes my next decision for me.

16 /
milly

mercy

IF THE LAST few weeks have taught me anything, it's that happiness is a choice. One I have the power to make every day. Seeing Dean was like reliving the night I lost everything. But, I know how to survive this feeling and I'm determined to not let it drown out everything else like it did before.

And no matter how bad I feel about the state of my heart, I'm relieved that I got that gig. With the potential for more.

It's not quite three o'clock, but it's five o'clock somewhere and I wanted to toast this win.

I stroll into the gorgeous restaurant on the bottom floor of the building and catch a glimpse of myself in the mirror. I bought this suit for today and had my hair blown out again this morning. At least no one can tell I'm a walking mass of chaos.

"Welcome to Claudia's." The hostess smiles at me as I approach her stand.

"Thank you. Is your dining room open?"

"How many are in your party?" she asks.

"It's just me."

"Oh, we don't seat single tops for dinner because we get so busy."

She gives me an apologetic smile. "But the bar is open and you can order from the menu there."

"That sounds perfect." Far from feeling self-conscious for being alone, I'm actually a little giddy. I can't remember the last time I sat at a bar and ordered a drink. I'd forgotten how much I used to enjoy it.

I follow her through the restaurant and admire the space and decor. It's all chrome and glass and red upholstered furniture. It's so sleek and sexy and gorgeous. It would be perfect for an intimate event.

I walk around to the side of the bar that lets me watch people as they come in from the street entrance.

I pick up one of the haphazardly placed menus and immediately know what I want. The drink *Mercy, Mercy*, a citrus and vodka cocktail, is calling my name. I order one from the very young, very cute bartender who appears almost out of nowhere as soon as I look up.

"What's your pleasure today, beautiful?" he says, grinning at me. And I want to ask him if he's even old enough to work here.

"I think I'll have this Mercy drink." I smile back, because why not?

"I'll be right back." He grins, winks, and disappears around the side of the bar.

I glance around, everyone is with someone and I'm caught up in the interactions of people. Kevin and I hadn't been out in years. I don't even know what it feels like to have a drink at a bar.

He drops my drink off with a warning to not drink it too quickly. I immediately pour the entire thing down my throat.

As the vodka works itself into my system, I let myself get lost in the thrill of being here alone and start to think about the benefits of being single.

It's great Dean and I didn't have the reunion I used to dream of… Being single is what I need to do for a while.

It doesn't matter that being near him felt like being home. It doesn't matter that despite the time and distance and how he treated me, the feelings I had for him when I was seventeen were only amplified by the time and distance that should have freed me from them.

I'm about to order another drink when the air fills with fraught energy. I feel a thrill run up my spine; I *know* Dean's standing behind me. Before I can turn around, he slips onto the stool next to me, the sleeves of his jacket brushing mine as he sits.

A tingle moves down my spine, all the way to the tips of my toes and they curl.

I sneak a glance at him and find myself staring into a pair of stunningly clear green eyes. Dean is looking right back at me. This time his expression isn't enigmatic at all. He looks angry and eager to let me know.

His eyes are roaming my face, just as mine roam his and neither one of us says a word. I feel absolutely no discomfort as we look at each other. We used to do this for hours - lay there and stare at each other. Back then, our eyes were full of love and wonder. Now they are full of wariness.

"Hi," he says in a deep, rich voice which instantly sets my pulse to a wild cantor.

"Dean . . ." is all I can manage in response. My eyes involuntarily fill with tears as I watch him. I see his struggle.

He doesn't want to be here, but he can't help it. My struggle is the same.

I want him to go and I hope he never ever leaves.

He drops his head, almost in defeat, breaking our stare. A lock of his hair falls onto his forehead and my hand reaches up out of instinct to brush it back into place.

I stop myself, but before I can retract my hand, he grabs my wrist in a grip just shy of being punishing.

This is the first time I have felt his touch in so long. I want to savor it, but I also want it to stop because I don't trust the feelings it elicits.

He doesn't speak, his hand tightens like a manacle around my wrist.

His head is still down, his posture completely rigid.

"Dean, what are you doing?" I ask him, my voice cracking, overwhelmed with the weight of everything that has happened today.

His head snaps up and he looks at me, the anguish and rage in his eyes steal my breath.

"You got married. Two years after you left me, you fucking *married* someone else." His lips are barely moving as he continues. "You pledged your *life* to someone else. You had another man's *child*." He practically spits the last sentence, and I flinch and look away from the accusation in his eyes.

"What?" I sputter.

He drops my hand and grabs my chin and tilts up until my eyes are back on his.

My skin burns where he's touching me, but I don't want him to stop. "I haven't had a truly good night's sleep since that last night in your house. I never understood how you just disappeared from my life. So when I had this chance to see you, to ask you, I took it. And I'm not sorry."

Confused by the tenderness in his eyes and full of liquid courage, I ask a question I'm not sure I want the answer to. "Why—"

He jerks my hand up to eye level and looks between it and my face. "What are you doing?" I ask and try to pull my hand away.

He tightens his grasp. "Where are your rings?"

My brain feels like it's got whiplash. "What?" I say even though I know exactly what he's asking.

"Your rings. Where are they?" he demands, grabbing my left hand and pointing to my ring finger.

I snatch my hand back. "I took them off," I say curtly.

"Why?" he demands, grabbing my hand back.

This question is a fuse to the Molotov cocktail of fatigue, hurt, and alcohol.

"You don't get to ask me why anymore. Go ask your fiancée and leave me the fuck alone," I shout and stand up from my stool. I open my purse, grab a twenty-dollar bill from my wallet, and throw it down on the bar. I snatch my jacket and walk away.

I need to get away from him. I don't know what's going on or what any of this means, but I need to get home, to feel safe again.

I am almost to the door when I feel his hand close around my bicep and stop me in my tracks.

I turn around to tell him to take his hands off me. But before I can, he says, "No way. You're coming with me."

the truth

WITH MILLY'S arm firmly in my grip, we wind our way through the restaurant. Nothing is as I expected and I can't keep up with the speed of my emotions. And all I can think is *don't let her leave.*

She doesn't fight me until we reach the front of the restaurant and step outside.

"Where are we going?"

"Somewhere private," I say and lead us around the corner to the alley where my driver is waiting.

"Hey, Mr. O." My driver, Greg, steps around from the side of the car and opens the back passenger door as we approach. Without missing a single stride, I step up into the car and reach out and pull her inside with me, placing her on the seat beside me. The door locks engage with a loud click and she pulls the handle, futilely trying to open the door.

"Dean, what are you doing?" She looks at me and if looks could kill, I'd be stone cold dead. "Are you completely crazy? Let me out of this car."

"I didn't exactly drag you kicking and screaming in here," I shoot back at her, trying to remain calm.

"That's because I was too shocked to do anything. What else do you want from me?"

"I want to talk to you."

"Talk?" She spits the word like it's dirt in her mouth. "It's too late."

My anger spikes. "More like overdue. You disappeared without a word. I was reeling and you just...what? Didn't remember to tell me that you were leaving? That I'd likely never see you again?"

"Why in the world would you think I would ever reach out to you again after everything?" she says incredulously.

My anger spikes. "Maybe because you fucking loved me? Maybe because we made promises to each other. My father *died*, Milly and I never heard from you. I went through that alone. I know you had no choice about the move, but...you could have found a way to let me know something. You could have said I want something different."

I reach up and slap the overhead lights on.

She looks like I slapped *her*, instead. Her eyes are wide and glassy with unshed tears. She lets out a shuddering breath. "I did call you, Dean. Repeatedly after your father died. You texted me, asked for space. Remember?" she says, her voice husky with pain.

When I force my eyes back to hers, the hurt in them almost slices me in half. "No, I didn't. And you never called."

"I *called* you. You answered the phone," she repeats. Her voice is softer now, her expression sorrowful. She stops talking and chokes on the sob she tries to hold in.

I feel like my entire world has tipped on its axis. I have so many questions screaming in my head. "No, I didn't."

"You did. And then you gave it to your mother so she could tell me that you didn't want to talk to me. That you hated me and blamed me for your father's death. That your entire family did."

I search her eyes, but I don't need to.

I know Milly.

I don't need to wonder if she's telling the truth, I can *see* that she is.

Thoughts of my mother, our fathers, what all of this means are fleeting and yield to my overwhelming need to touch her. Holding her hand used to ground me and I'm desperate for something to hold onto as gears that have been stuck for years finally click into place and start turning.

She didn't abandon me.

I put my hand out and she flinches as it moves toward her face, but she doesn't pull away. "I've never hated you. I never blamed you. And *you* were my entire family."

She swallows audibly and her tongue darts out to wet her upper lip. Her eyes fill with tears right before they flutter closed. I put my hand up again and this time, I don't stop. I cup her cheek and she leans into my palm.

My hand works into her hair and I tug the piece of elastic holding it back. Her hair goes from this slicked back controlled ponytail, to riotous and wild. I lean toward her at the same time she leans toward me.

Our lips meet in a mutual middle and the years we've spent apart disappear.

Her mouth tastes like it did the last time I kissed her, clean and sweet. Her lips feel like heaven, tender and welcoming.

At the first touch of our lips, it's like we are eighteen-years-old again and our lips are acting on memory. It starts out as tender as all of our kisses ever were, both of us so young and innocent and trying to control ourselves. A gentle touch before we come back together, and her mouth opens almost immediately. It may feel like yesterday, but I *know* it's been years and I have been deprived of this woman, this kiss, this feeling for far too long. I don't hesitate in accepting her invitation, and like a wave held out from shore for too long, my tongue invades her mouth.

We drink each other in.

Her hands in my hair, pulling me closer, her nails scratching my scalp. I don't hold any of myself back. I can't hold back when I'm with her because she is and always will be, the *one*. Every kiss before and since her was just getting me ready for this moment. This moment that I've waited my whole life for. With this woman who has always meant everything to me.

I pull her flush against me and push my erection into the soft bed of her abdomen. She gasps into my mouth and I pull her lower lip in between my lips and suck on it. My lips travel down her chin and along her jaw. It takes my need for her from burning to blazing.

My hands travel up and under her jacket and cup her breasts. She's fuller than she was, but still fits perfectly in my hands. My thumbs rub her nipples through her blouse and she moans, a sound that starts out sharp and ends on a husky exhalation.

"Red," I groan her nickname, that was all I ever called her when we were together.

She breaks our kiss and backs out of my embrace almost immediately.

"No," she whispers and scrambles away from me, pressing her body to the door.

"Milly, I'm sorry."

She laughs without any humor. "Oh, I'm sure you are. God knows I am, too. If I had even the tiniest clue that your mother wasn't speaking for you that night, wild horses wouldn't have kept me away. My father disappearing was terrible, my mother retreating into a shell was painful. But knowing that I didn't have you anymore, *that* debilitated me. I lost *everything* when I lost you. So, yes, I got on with my life and tried to carve out an existence that brought me as close to happiness as I could be without you."

"Red." I move closer.

She puts both arms out, hands up. "No. Don't call me that and don't touch me!" She looks wild-eyed around the car and it is only then that I notice her bag is on the ground, contents scattered. She bends down and starts gathering her things. I bend down to help her.

"I want to get out of this car. Now. I mean it. I want out." She slaps my hands away when they accidentally brush hers as we both pick up the spilled contents of her bag.

"If I had known you called me," I return, feeling like a fool and knowing that I've screwed up royally.

"Don't finish that sentence. It doesn't matter what you would have done then. This is now, and now you're engaged and I'm sick of men who think I'm supposed to dance to their tune. Why don't you go ask the woman you're marrying to do that and leave me alone."

"Milly, it's not that simple . . ." I start, feeling a prick of guilt rising as I realize how, when laid out the way she has, what I've done and said sounds terrible.

"Really? Seems pretty simple to me," she says, her voice losing all of its ice and instead sounding like an erupting volcano. She shouts at me, "You're not God, Dean. You don't get to manipulate people's lives because you've been hurt by something. You didn't have the right to do this to me." She sounds equal parts irate and wounded.

"Do what? Kiss you? I'll never be near you and not want to. And every chance I get, I'll try."

"You're crazy. You're engaged," she snaps.

"No, I'm not."

She blinks and shakes her head like she's trying to clear it. "What?"

"It's been over, but I made it official the day I saw you."

She closes her eyes and her chest heaves. "I can't do this."

"Milly. Come here."

"No, Dean. You need to listen because this is the last thing I'm going to say to you."

My scalp prickles with apprehension and my mind rejects that. But I let her finish. She's waited a long time to get this off her chest and I owe her the chance to without interfering. "I'm listening."

She takes a deep breath and closes her eyes the way she used to right before she did things she was afraid of and brace myself.

"I meant it when I said I was happy to see you. But, I'm done letting people take their pound of flesh and leaving me bloody. Anything we had to say to each other is meaningless now." She straightens her spine and wipes her face.

She waggles the door handle and I tap the glass divider. The door unlocks and she doesn't waste a second leaping out of it.

And then she turns to look at me. "Focus on the future. Forget me."

I meet her eye and hold her gaze steady with mine. "I am. And I can't," I confess.

She gasps and her eyes glisten with tears. "I have to go."

She slams the door shut and I let her go.

For now.

fifteen years earlier

friends

"IS DEAN HOME?" I ask as I stand on the doorstep of the O——' home. It's raining hard and the wind is whipping the water against my back even though I'm standing under their covered porch.

The woman who answers the door, a tiny woman who looks like most of the other women who answer doors in this neighborhood, peers out at me. Her eyes hold suspicion and annoyance. She says in an unfriendly voice, her accent heavy with her native Spanish, "Can I help you? No soliciting here."

Clearly, I don't look like most of the people who ring the bell on the Orleans wrought iron and stained glass front door.

They live in the tony River Oaks neighborhood of Houston. It's anchored by an even more exclusive country club. It once, famously, denied membership to the city's mayor because his wife was Jewish.

My father probably out earns Dean's father exponentially, but we live in the less exclusive neighborhood of Tanglewood.

This is my first time visiting Dean and I was self-conscious the moment I stepped out of my car and started up the grand steps to the front door, but her greeting makes me want to disappear.

Regardless, I try to keep a polite smile on my face. "I'm not selling anything. Dean is expecting me."

"Mister Dean? He knows you?" she asks, and I start to feel annoyed. I'm getting soaked by the rain and it is galling to be treated like this by someone who I'm sure knows exactly what it feels like to be treated as less than in this neighborhood.

"Yes. Look, can I step inside, it's raining really hard." I try to speak calmly, even though I want to push her out of the way.

She pulls at the door as if to shut it when I hear Dean's voice from behind her. "Hortensia, who's at the door?"

I feel relief well up inside me as she steps aside and Dean appears. His eyes widen and he grabs my arm to pull me inside.

"Red, why are you standing outside getting soaked?" he asks as he takes my bag and pulls me into a hug.

I pull away because I'm wet, but also because his question annoys me. I pull my jacket off and hang it on the coatrack that stands in the foyer.

"I wasn't standing outside. Hortensia here thought I was a burglar disguised as a door-to-door salesman and wasn't exactly rolling out the red carpet for me," I snap, annoyance and embarrassment dripping from every word I utter.

"What?" he says annoyance clear in his expression as he looks between Hortensia and me. Hortensia's eyes widen in fear, and I'm immediately contrite. She's only doing the job she was hired to do. I'm sure part of her is conditioned to see other brown people as suspicious. I shouldn't let my anger jeopardize her job here. I'm sure she has people who rely on her and her paycheck.

I walk up to Dean, wrap my arms around his waist, and hug him.

"Dean, it's nothing. I didn't say right away I was here to see you, so she was asking me questions and was about to let me in when you walked up. I'm starving, what've you got to snack on?"

That distracts him, he looks away from Hortensia and turns back to me. He winks at me and says with a grin, "Cheese, of course. Come on."

We get our snacks, Dean's favorite sesame sticks and a cheese stick for me, and head upstairs.

We work together, sometimes talking about what we're reading, but mostly in silence. Soon, we're wrapping up our homework. We've been doing this . . . thing . . . for the last month or so. Dean usually comes to my house, but we study together, hang out, listen to music, or watch television and then he goes home.

I know Dean likes me. I like him, too, but he's the popular guy on campus, and I'm the girl whose only friend is my younger sister.

I already know the guy everyone else sees on campus isn't who Dean really is. He hates the attention. He won the genetic lottery and his parents live a flashy lifestyle. So, kids look at him and see those things. But I can sense his anxiety because I have it, too.

He wishes no one cared how good he was at lacrosse. He cringed the first time he gave me a ride home in his brand-new convertible BMW. He was embarrassed by it and the impression it created.

I think that's why we get along so well. We are both misunderstood. People only see our exteriors and no one bothers to look any deeper. I was so lonely until I met him, and he's already my closest friend. I don't want to ruin this by turning it into something more. We're in high school. He's dated a lot of the popular girls, the ones who won't even sit at the same table as I do at lunch.

"So, what do you want to do now?" Dean asks, breaking my meandering thoughts.

"Actually, I should probably go home." I prepare myself for

him to argue. He always wants to stay at my house late, even when it's past his curfew. He always wants to stay on the phone, even when we're both struggling to keep our eyes open.

He looks at me from his end of the couch and smiles. That smile, it's devastating and makes my heart do a somersault.

"Okay, maybe you should go," he responds. My somersaults stop and disappointment, fresh and hot blooms.

I try to smile as I gather my things. "Yeah, okay, sure. It really is late." I look up at him. He's still smiling that warm smile; his eyes are looking at me the way he always does. But, he's watching me pack up and not asking me to stay.

"Well, my mom will be home any minute. And she hates you," he says, still smiling the same warm smile.

I rear back like he slapped me. I knew his mom didn't love me and only tolerated me because my dad is an executive her husband reported to, but Dean saying she hates me causes tears to spring to my eyes.

"Why would you say that?" I ask him, not able to disguise the hurt in my voice.

His smile disappears and a dark sneer mars his handsome face. He leans toward me on the couch.

"Because it's true, Milly. We all hate you. You killed my father."

present day

priority

I WAKE up with a start and moan softly. I haven't had one of the nightmares in a long, long time.

But after my run-in with Dean, I've had nothing but spotty, troubled sleep. The last words he said: "I am, I can't."

What does that mean?

I don't know what to do.

I slip out of bed and head up to the attic and pull out my old journal from a trunk of keepsakes. I open to a page that's still marked by a paperclip.

"The Milly Life Plan"

Making the list used to be an annual ritual.

I'd ask myself questions - What do I want?

I haven't asked myself those questions in a long time. Or allowed myself to remember the answers.

I flip to the page that's more worn than the other, my heart in my throat as I read them.

1. I want to start a business using my skills and talents

2.Be someone's best friend (besides my sisters)
3.I want to be a good mom
4.I want to travel
5.Dean

How simple life was back then. When I think about who I was before my father left, it hurts. But the truth is, the only thing I didn't do that's on this list was the last one. And now, it's too late.

When I met Dean, I looked at him and knew, despite his outward façade of Mr. Popular, good-looking and rich, he needed a friend. I knew it because I needed one, too.

Besides my sisters, I'd had a hard time making friends because people looked at me and saw a reserved, cold snob. But Dean, he knew differently right away; we just . . . clicked. So much more than that.

I reach up to stroke the ring around my neck as if it will soothe the ache this trip down memory lane has created.

I think about the relationship I had with Dean and my heart aches because I'll never have that again. I want *something* like that again.

I make my list again, and this time, I tear it out and put it in my purse so I can pull it out when I need reminding.

I call this list "Remembering Milly".

1. Forgive my dad
2. Grow my business
3. Feel my fear and do it anyway
4. Have great sex and fall in love again

Immediately I thought about what my sisters would say. Addie, that I'm not reaching high enough. Lilly, that I'm still not taking real risks. But, they have their own journeys to travel.

This is *my* life and I know the things on this list all make my heart race. I'm terrified, thrilled, and proud.

I don't want to start living in the past. Remembering a kind, generous boy who obviously didn't exist anymore. I don't know what to do about Valentine's campaign but I can't walk away from the opportunity. I need it.

Until I know if we'll even have any contact, I'll leave that off my list of things to worry about.

I touch my lips and still feel his on mine.

"Milly, I need your help," my mother calls from downstairs.

"Coming." I trudge down the hall and compose myself before I get to her room. I haven't told her what happened with Dean. I hardly understand it myself; I can't even begin to explain it to someone else.

She and Rabea are leaving for a week in New Orleans later tonight. Her suitcase is open on her bed, spilling over with enough clothes for a world tour. "I'll be right out," she calls from the bathroom.

I walk in and sit down on the edge of her bed. The comforter is a simple white eyelet and the bed's accent pillows are made of the Kente fabric she got from her last trip to Ghana.

When she came to live with us in November after the press conference, I had this room done up for her exactly as it had been in the small house she moved to after Addie left home. Her coming to stay with us was supposed to be temporary, but we've both settled into her being here. She likes her space and independence and I know that she eventually wants to get back to her own house, which is just sitting empty, but for now, it's a perfect arrangement.

I walk over to the side of her bed where she still has my father's picture framed. I pick it up and gaze down into those eyes that are so like mine, sometimes, I see him before I see myself in the mirror.

My eyes sting with tears.

I miss him.

I wonder if he misses us, too.

She comes out of the bathroom, humming to herself and smiles when she sees me sitting there holding the picture. "I love that picture of him." She smiles wistfully and takes it from me to gaze at it with so much longing that I feel like I'm intruding on a private moment.

"I want your opinion on this dress." She puts the picture back and reaches over to dig in her suitcase, still humming to herself. For someone whose life was irrevocably changed when my dad left, you wouldn't know she walks around shouldering feelings of loss, guilt, and pain. She's the strongest person I know. She holds us all together, even at the expense of her own well-being at times. And I don't understand how.

"How can you still have faith in him?"

"How can I not? I made a pledge to him. For better or worse."

"What about the pledge he made to you?"

She shakes her head sadly. "I can't speak for him. I can only do what my heart tells me. And I don't expect anyone to understand."

She holds up a bright yellow dress covered in sequins with a flourish. "What do you think? Too much bling?"

I laugh despite myself. "I don't think that counts as bling, Mom. But I love the color."

She beams. "Me, too. I can't wait to wear it."

"I'm glad you're excited."

"Oh, I'm more than excited. It feels very decadent to do something like this, but I can't wait," she says, her eyes dancing as she stops packing and sits down next to me. She grasps my hands; the joy in her expression dims.

"I also hate leaving you when I know something is bothering you. I didn't want to ask because you seemed so . . ." Her eyes scan the ceiling as she searches for her words. "You seemed so rubbed raw."

Her eyes come back to mine and they are full of understanding. The knot of tension at the base of my throat loosens as I look at her and know I can unburden myself with her—she will help make it better.

So, I tell her about Dean and what happened last week.

"I felt so many horrible things at once, Mom." I finish on a hiccuped sob.

"Oh, Milly. I'm sorry. This must have been a lot for you to process. His mother did that? You never told me."

"How could I? I wasn't supposed to use the phone to call anyone we knew. And I didn't know how to tell you." I implore her to understand.

She drops the blouse she's folding and comes to sit next to me. "I'm sorry I wasn't there for you then."

"It's okay."

"No, it's not. But you're a good daughter for saying so." She pats my hand. "So, Dean wants you back."

I lean away in surprise. "No, he doesn't. He…it was nostalgia."

I can't. Those two words were tortured but true.

"If that is what you need to believe," she says with a knowing smile.

My hackles rise. "It's true."

"Okay dear." She rolls her eyes as she speaks and her words cause a flutter of what feels, suspiciously, like hope. I smother that feeling. Even hope isn't audacious enough to attempt to find purchase in this total quagmire.

I'm incredulous. "Mom, it took me years to get over that conversation with his mother. I married Kevin because I knew the door to a life with Dean was closed—"

"That was your first mistake," she interrupts, with the wry remark. "But, I hope you've learned from it because life is too short to allow your pride to win," she says sadly.

"My pride? This has nothing to do with my pride. He doesn't want me back and I don't want him."

"Milly, I'm not going to try to talk you into anything. But

trust me, love like this, you only get it once in your life. I'm praying you won't squander this miracle of a second chance you've been given."

Her eyes are soft yet full of grave warning. I'm taken aback by this. I haven't thought about Dean's reappearance in my life as a second chance at anything. At least not anything good.

She continues probing. "But let me ask you this; before your life fell apart you had a plan, right?"

"Yes." I always had a plan.

"What was it?"

"I don't know, Mom," I say, but I do know. I just haven't allowed myself to think about any of that for more than a decade now.

But I had a plan. I knew what I wanted. I shake my head. "No, I didn't." And it's true. I knew it was a golden opportunity, but I also felt completely prepared to meet the challenge.

"Then why are you walking away from it? You probably never even have to see Dean."

"Ugh," I groan and my head pounds. "I have to think about it."

"You should call that lady and tell her you've changed your mind and pray it's not too late," she urges, her grip on my hands tightening.

"I don't know . . . And I woke up feeling a little under the weather. I took some cold medicine, but I'm really not feeling up to anything right now. Besides, she never even responded. Maybe she was relieved to get rid of an amateur and hire a real event planner."

"What do you mean under the weather? Do you need me to stay home?" Her hand comes up to touch my forehead. She snatches it back in alarm.

"You're burning up. What in the world?" She looks alarmed as she pulls me up to stand. "I'm going to call Rabea and tell her we need to reschedule. Let me get you to bed."

I sit back down on her bed and shake my head. "No. Go. I

don't feel bad at all. Something has been going around Anthony's school, so I might have picked it up. But you don't need to cancel and stay home. I'll be fine."

She had been planning this trip for so long and was looking forward to it. I couldn't ask her to change her plans now. And I don't want her to either.

She caresses my forehead and her face creases in concern, but she acquiesces. "Okay, but if you get worse, call me and I'll come back."

"Go have fun. You deserve it. I'll be fine."

prodigal mother

I HAVEN'T BEEN BACK to the house where I grew up in a very long time. It's smaller than I remember. It doesn't look like the abandoned husk of an old life that it is. I pay someone to landscape, but the inside hasn't been touched in years.

I slip the key into the lock and meet resistance. I look down at the lock and the key and realize the lock has been changed.

I curse under my breath.

My mother must have done this, but why? And why didn't she tell me?

I pull out my phone and open the app I use to take notes. I make a list of what I'm going to say and exactly what I want out of this call. It's extreme, but I never talk to her without preparing myself, first.

I hit dial. She answers on the first ring.

"Hi, Mom."

"Dean? Is that you?" She's shouting like she thinks I'm at a concert and she has to scream to be heard.

"Yes, it's me. Where are you?"

"In Sedona, we're at a party. What do you need?"

"I'm at the house."

107

"The what?"

"The house," I repeat, shouting this time.

"Hold on."

The call goes silent but stays connected. A minute later, she's back on and the background noise is gone. "What are you doing at the house?"

"I need to get in to see what work it needs before I list it."

"You're listing the house?" she asks in a sharp voice.

"It's mine, right?"

"Yes, but…why now?"

I run a hand over my forehead and pray for patience. "Do you plan to live here ever again?"

"No, but…"

"The taxes on it are ridiculous and it's sitting empty. I'm not asking for your opinion. I called you because the locks appear to have been changed. Where are the new keys?"

"They're with me."

I groan. "In Sedona?"

"Yes. Should I mail them?"

"No, I'll call a locksmith."

"But the alarm."

"What's the code?"

"I don't remember…um, let me see. It's something, Jean-Luc changed it."

"Jean-Luc? Why would he have anything to do with this house?"

"He's my partner, Dean. He cares about me." The unspoken part, "unlike you," comes through loud and clear.

My stomach knots with guilt I can't seem to shake, no matter how unwarranted I know it is. "Just get the code and call me back. I'll be here until the end of the week."

I hang up and try to shake off the tension that seeps into my bones every time we talk.

We're frozen in time; she still sees a disloyal, disobedient, and inconvenient child.

In my eyes, she's still a selfish person who didn't do anything that didn't benefit her.

In the year following my father's death, I let her lean on me because it's what he would have expected from me.

Otherwise, our relationship has remained as it always was - one of tolerance and limited contact.

She doesn't care what I do as long as I don't ask her for anything and the same goes for me.

It's also not lost on me that she didn't tell me why she changed the locks to the house or what business Jean-Luc had setting up anything.

Jean-Luc came into her life a few months after my father died. The details of how they met are vague at best and I preferred them that way. He had "delinquent" written all over his surly face. But, he could have Hannibal Lector and I would have thanked him for taking my mother off my hands.

He was only a few years older than me and a total slob who slept until noon and seemed to live in his Speedos. I couldn't understand what she saw in him the first time I met him. Until I found out that he's the youngest son of a very wealthy French aristocrat and meets the only criteria that's non-negotiable to her - he had what seemed to be an endless supply of money. He's kept her in the designer clothes she loves and bought her the houses in Marseille and Sedona less than a year after they moved in together.

I stalk back to the car annoyed but relieved that I can move on to the next and more important errand on my list.

I give my driver the address we're headed to next.

I have never been afraid of a challenge. In fact, the higher the degree of difficulty, the more motivated I am to conquer it. I've spent more than a week preparing myself to face Milly, and I'm still not sure I'm ready.

I fucked things up with her. Royally. I haven't been able to get her last words to me out of my head. But what is crystal clear to me is that this opportunity at this moment in time isn't something I can walk away from. I've never stopped caring about her. She's never stopped being the one.

Watching my parents' train wreck of a marriage taught me an indelible lesson about love.

If it's not mutual, it's not real.

You can't be in love with someone who isn't in love with you. It's just not possible. Love needs a reciprocal source to sustain itself.

"You never have to force what is yours, son." I'm about to put my father's theory to the test.

I get out of the car in front of Milly's house and walk up the door in long, purposeful strides.

I ring the doorbell twice before the door opens. Milly stands on the other side looking like she has just finished participating in some sort of trial on the television show *Survivor*. One where she has been deprived of sun, food, and sleep for days.

She's pale and sweaty and her eyes are glassy and unfocused.

"What are you doing here, D—" Her sentence is cut off by a hacking cough that forces her to double over. She sways slightly. Alarm sweeps me as I step inside and put my arm around her. She's burning up.

I stand her up and walk her farther into the house. She doesn't resist at all when I pull her into me so she can lean on me for support. I use my foot to kick the door shut behind us. Her head rests on my shoulder and I rub her back as she coughs and I rack my brain for what to do.

Her cough spasm subsides and she pulls back and looks at me. Her eyes are glassy and red. Her lips are dry. She's clearly very sick.

"Milly, I want to take you to the ER, okay? You feel really hot and that cough sounds terrible."

I passed the exit for one on my way here, and I start calculating how long it will take us to get there.

"Let me get your shoes and your purse. They will need identif—" She puts a hand on my shoulder and I stop talking.

"I can't go to the ER," she says. Her voice is hoarse and she swallows hard after she finishes the sentence.

"You need to see a doctor, if you don't have insurance, I can cover it," I say quickly.

"No, it's not that. My son. He's sleeping upstairs. I can't go anywhere. My mom is out of town."

I wish I was a better man than the one I find myself being right now. The mention of her son hurts me. I feel resentment and annoyance, and I know it's wrong. I tamp it down and regroup.

"Okay, I use a service of physicians who make house calls. Let me get you into bed, and then I'll call them."

She doesn't protest, which sends me from concerned to alarmed. I know if Milly had one ounce of strength in her, she would be kicking me out. Instead she sags against me in relief. I stoop to loop an arm under her knees to pick her up and head toward the stairs.

"You need to tell me which bedroom is yours." I prepare myself to be assaulted with remnants of her husband's presence —pictures, clothes.

I push the door open and walk in. I keep my eyes focused on the bed and try not to look around. Milly's eyes are closed, and I feel a sense of urgency to get the doctor in to see her.

I gently put her into bed and cover her with the sheets before I walk back out of the room. Only when I get back down the stairs and pull out my phone do I realize I've been holding my breath.

I dial the number for the physician's service I use. I describe Milly's symptoms and give them her address before I hang up.

It feels strange to be alone in her house. The house where she lived with her husband. Where she's raising her child.

I think about going to my car to wait, but she said her son is sleeping upstairs and with her out of it, I don't want to leave him alone in the house.

I don't want to wander into her living room. I think seeing pictures of her with *him* would make me physically ill. Same for the kitchen. So, unable to do anything else, I sit down on the stairs and wait.

———

"Mr. Picture, wake up."

I open my eyes slowly, blinking against the harsh light coming through the open curtains. Bewildered and groggy, it takes me a few seconds to focus on the little hand shaking my shoulder. I look up and see a pair of huge brown eyes staring down at me. A mop of dark brown curls falls onto his forehead and his grin is missing one top front tooth.

I'm lying on Milly's couch where I fell asleep after the doctor left. He said Milly has the flu. He gave her an antiviral and wrote a prescription for a dose I needed to pick up today so she could start the ten-day course.

She was sleeping. I couldn't leave until I knew she was well enough to look after herself. I'd forgotten about her son and seeing him looking down at me, with a face so much like his mother's, is disconcerting.

"Hello," I say cautiously, not sure whether his smile is a prelude to a meltdown over finding a stranger on his couch.

"I'm a friend of your mother's," I continue as I sit up all the way. I wince inwardly at the lie. I'm hardly her friend, but I can't explain to a kid how I'm in love with his mother and she's not speaking to me, but I plan to win her back.

"Yeah, I know." He frowns and then climbs up to sit next to me on the couch. He looks at me with avid curiosity.

"You look like you do in your picture." My head jerks back a little. I'm well-known in the talent world and appear on trade magazine covers. Hell, *Esquire* did a feature on me when I was named CEO, but he couldn't have seen it. So, I ask him, without any guilt, "What picture?"

As soon as the words leave my lips, his face falls and his shoulders sag.

"I wasn't supposed to say anything. I'm not supposed to look in that drawer." He falls into a full-blown pout, and I decide my curiosity is less important than making sure I don't have to deal with a crying kid.

"I'll pretend you didn't say anything, okay?" I pat his shoulder awkwardly, but my proposal appears to do the trick. He perks up and says, "Okay! Can we watch cartoons now?"

"Do you normally watch cartoons on Saturday morning?" I glance at my watch and find it's just turned 7:00 a.m. Why is this kid even awake?

"Yes. I watch them while Mommy makes breakfast. She's still sleeping, though. Are you going to make me breakfast?"

I blink. I can cook a little, but cooking in Milly's house, in Milly's kitchen with Milly's son, seems like an impossible task.

I'm not quite sure how old this little guy is, but I know he can't cook himself anything. So, I stand up with a smile on my face. "Sure, what do you normally eat?"

He stands up, grabs three of my fingers in his small hand and leads me toward the kitchen.

"Come on, I'll show you," he says as he pulls me behind him.

"If you want to be my friend, you have to make my mommy happy first. You can't make her cry."

I stop dead in my tracks, turn back toward the table.

His face is set in a stern expression that gives me a glimpse of what he'll look like when he's older. He looks a lot like Milly's dad except his hair and eyes are both dark brown.

"Well, little man," I begin slowly, unsure how to answer this. "I would never intentionally make anyone cry. And especially not your mom. She was my best friend." I smile and hope that my answer will cut this conversation short.

He doesn't smile back. He just studies me with an awareness that belies his age.

"If she's your best friend, where have you been all this time?" he asks me, his eyes never leaving mine.

I exhale a big breath, sit back down, and close my eyes for a moment as I try to gather my thoughts.

"Well, friends don't always have to see each other. I lived in a different city, a different state, so I wasn't always able to be here for your mom."

I don't think he understands everything that happened with his grandfather, and that's a can of worms I don't think is my place to open with him. So, I tell him the closest thing to the truth I know.

"I've known your mother a long time. I have always been her friend and she's always been mine. Even when we didn't see each other. And now, I'll be around as long as it makes your mom happy."

He perks up a little at that last sentence and chats to me about his favorite cartoon while we make the waffles and eat.

"All done," he declares with a proud smile.

"How were they?"

His smile spreads into a huge grin. "Really good. When my mom wakes up, I'll tell her so. She loves waffles. She'll probably ask you to stay forever."

He slides out of his chair, picks up his juice cup, and walks it over to the sink then he walks out of the kitchen. He leaves me sitting at the table in awe of the little person Milly is raising. I'm glad he loves her so much. I hope his waffle endorsement will help me plead my case when Milly is finally coherent enough for me to lay everything out for her.

I just hope she'll give me a chance to explain.

reciprocal

"WELCOME to Sweet and Lo's, can I take your order?" the teenage girl behind the counter asks with a warm smile.

"Yeah, a coffee and a sausage and cheese kolache, please," I say with a distracted smile and turn my back to check my text messages: I left Milly at home alone to take Anthony to school. I left a note next to her bedside table in case she woke up while I was gone. Though, given how much she'd slept over the weekend, I didn't expect she'd be awake enough to read it any time soon.

Anthony has turned out to be excellent company. We made it through the weekend with surprising ease. He's very protective of his mother. Funny, smart, curious, and sweet.

I had to figure out his schedule and get him to school but he's a smart kid and knew his routine like the back of his hand.

I pay for my order and hurry out of the bright, inviting cafe. I make a note to come back when I have a chance.

When I walk back in the house, all is quiet. I take some of the bone broth the doctor said she should drink upstairs. She's fast asleep, tangled in her sheets. She looks like she did when she was eighteen and even in the fitful feverish state she's been in, looks so peaceful now. I check the time. She has a few more hours until it's time for her next dose. I smooth some hair off her forehead, wipe it with a cool cloth, and take her temperature. 99.1.

I sag in relief. It's much better than yesterday. I put the thermos down and head back downstairs.

I've just settled down to prepare for a call I have in thirty minutes when Milly's house phone rings for the third time in the last five minutes. The caller ID reads Mary Dennis. I freeze.

If I don't answer, she'll be worried. But… I have no idea how she will react to me being in Milly's house. I can't imagine she'll be thrilled. Milly has always been very close to her mother and given her mother lives here with her, I can't imagine that has changed. She must know what I did last week.

The phone stops ringing and I sigh in relief, but it starts ringing less than thirty seconds later. I'm worried it will wake Milly so I decide to swallow my cowardice and answer.

I clear my throat and pick up. "Hello?"

"Who is this? Where is my daughter?" She sounds pissed and worried.

"Uh. It's Dean. Orleans," I add when she's silent.

"Where's Milly?" she barks at me. "Zenobia called me frantic. Why isn't she answering her phone?"

"She's sleeping." I wince at the way I know that sounds. "I mean-"

"Why is she sleeping at ten thirty in the morning? Why are you in her house? Why hasn't she answered her phone in two whole days?" she demands, her voice becoming louder and deeper as she hurls the questions at me.

"Well, she—" I start.

"You know what? Never mind. I'm coming home. I don't know what is going on over there, but clearly it's nothing good," she says in an angry huff.

"No, no! Everything is fine, I swear," I say quickly, I feel like

I've lost whatever control I had over the conversation and it's spiraling out of control.

"The *hell* it is. Put her on the phone," she almost shouts.

"No, please, listen. I came by on Friday and she had a really high fever. I called a doctor, and it turns out she has the flu. She has medication and is resting," I say this in a rush, afraid she'll hang up and be on the next train before I can stop her. I'm suddenly desperate for her to not return. I haven't had any time with Milly and I need it. I need her to get well enough to talk to me so that I can at least apologize for what I did and figure out how to convince her to give me, us, a chance.

"And where is Anthony? Don't tell me *you've* been watching him," she says, but she sounds less angry and more amused now, and I'm a little offended.

"Yes, actually. I have. He hasn't missed a meal. He brushed his teeth every night and morning. He's at school. We're doing great. He likes me."

I know I sound defensive, but I don't want to leave before I have a chance to talk to Milly. "We're fine," I add when she doesn't say anything.

"Well, well, well," she drawls with a laugh.

I'm so taken aback by her sudden change in tone I don't respond right away.

"Okay, well it sounds like you've got it all under control, Dean. It's nice to hear your voice after all these years, by the way."

"Um. Okay. Thank you," I say, unable to respond to this very cordial statement. It's the last thing I expected from her, and I'm not sure what to make of it.

"Well, I'm sure Milly will call me when she wakes up. But, I'll call to check on her again tonight," she says, sounding almost whimsical.

"Okay," I respond dumbly. She has totally disarmed me, and I don't know what to make of what she's saying.

"Is that all you're going to say? What's the matter with you, son? Are you coming down with something, too?" she asks with a laugh.

"No, I'm sorry. I'm just trying to keep up with this conversation," I say, deciding total honesty is the only way to go right now.

She laughs delightedly, and I shake my head, but her laughter is infectious and I laugh with her.

"Okay, you guys have a good week. I'll let Zen know not to send the National Guard. And, I'll be back on Friday night. I can't wait to see you," she says when she stops laughing and her voice is laced with affection and warmth.

"Okay, Mrs. Hassan," I say reflexively.

"Oh. No one has called me that in years." She sounds wistful and happy at the same time. "It's lovely to hear. Take care of my Milly and Anthony. Bye." And then without waiting for me to respond she hangs up.

I stand there for a minute, replaying the conversation. She did an about face so quickly I'm not sure what to make of it, but I feel a pang of nostalgia after talking to her.

I spent a good portion of my high school years sitting at her kitchen table, swimming in their pool, lounging on her couch. Their home was a happy one, so different from my own.

My mother's indifference and my father's misery created a fog of discomfort I found suffocating. At their house, I could breathe.

She used to hug me, scold me, and treated me like a son. I find myself looking forward to seeing her when she gets back. If I'm still here. Part of me is sure as soon as Milly wakes up and is strong enough she'll send me packing.

Pushing the thought aside, I go back to my makeshift desk in her living room and get ready for my call. I only have four hours before I need to get Anthony from school and I'm desperate to go for a run before that.

I glance up the stairs. Knowing she's upstairs and that I'm

taking care of her gives me a sense of contentment I've never felt before. I get to work with a smile on my face.

awake

I WAKE with a start and find myself in a haze of congestion and with a horrible taste in my mouth. I'm drenched in sweat, my head pounding from the nightmare. It's one I haven't had in years, but, seeing Dean must've revived some of my old fears. I've spent much of my life thinking those things are true, but it's been a while since that nightmare has been so vivid.

My room is dark, but I have blackout curtains so that doesn't tell me anything. I glance at the clock by my bed and see that it's 1:00 p.m.

I groan as I try to stand up. My body is stiff, yet my legs feel like jelly.

What the hell? Memories from yesterday start drifting in, like an uneven cough, it spits out incomplete, unreliable images.

I remember my mother leaving for her weekend away with Rabea. I remember waking up from my nap feeling like I'd been in a car that had been knocked off a bridge, but needing to go and get Anthony. And then, I remember Dean showing up at my door.

But…that can't be.

I pick up my phone and groan at all the missed calls from my mother. My heart stops when I realize three days have passed since the last time I checked the phone. A wild panic grips me.

Oh my God.

"Anthony?" Adrenaline propels me down the hall toward his room.

Has he been alone all this time? I pass the guest room, skid to a stop and take a few steps back and press my ear against the door and gasp, alarmed that the shower's running. I pull the door open and rush in toward the open bathroom door where vanilla scented steam is billowing from and pray I'm not about to walk in on something terrible.

At first glance, I sag with relief. It's not Anthony, but Dean.

Shock straightens my spine and I duck out of the doorway and press my back to the wall. The only way Dean could be in my shower is if I'm dreaming. I pinch myself and groan at the sting of it.

Dean is *definitely* in my shower.

How?

My heart thunders against my chest and I take a deep breath and risk a glance back into the bathroom.

Comfortable with my assumption that he's not going anywhere for a few minutes, I continue to my son's room and sit on his unmade bed. I pull out my phone, dial his school, and hold my breath.

"Hello, this is Milly Bishop, I'm calling to check on Anthony. He's in second grade, Ms. Blair's class."

"Hold on a minute…"

"They're in art, are you picking him up early?"

"No, I just wanted to see if he was feeling okay. He was a little sniffly this morning."

"Well, he's in class and hasn't come down to the nurse."

"Alright, thank you."

I fall back on his bed in relief. By some miracle my baby's safe and at school.

I rush back down the hall to deal with my second crisis. Dean is still in the shower, his back to me. I'm torn on whether or not to get his attention or whether I should let him finish. My eyes make the decision for me, I can't tear them away. I examine him hungrily, searching for familiar parts and pieces.

It's been fifteen years, but the spray of dark freckles across his shoulders is just as prominent now as it was then. Even more so now that the muscles they span are so much broader. Dean always took his fitness seriously, he played on every sports team in high school so he was forced to train hard all year long.

He's got more flesh on his bones than he did at eighteen, but his back is a study of well-honed muscles.

My eyes follow the path of the water as it cuts down valleys and crests of muscular back. His waist is girded with muscle and tapers in from the breadth of his back. My eyes continue their feast, and I drink in his perfect backside. One of his hands is braced on the wall and his head is bowed and then I realize the arm not on the wall is moving up and down in front of him.

My mouth waters.

I forget that I have no idea what he's doing here.

Or that I'm in desperate need of a shower myself.

My body instantaneously remembers how much I want him. The desire that almost overwhelmed me last time I was with him came roaring back to life.

A moan rips from my own throat a second before I can stop it and Dean's head whips around to meet mine. At first they mirror the surprise in my eyes, but as our gazes cling to each other, his lids lower to half-mast and his lips curve into a lazy, sensual smile.

"You're up." He raises his voice so it carries over the running water.

I just stare. He's even more beautiful than he was as a boy standing on the edge of manhood, and I don't have the strength to deal with this right now.

He turns the water off but doesn't turn around. I avert my eyes.

"Have you been here since Friday?"

"Yeah, me and your little guy."

I can hear the affection in his voice but I can't quell my worry. "Is he okay?"

"He's great."

"So, you've been checking on us for three days?" I ask. I feel like I should be asking so much more, but I'm utterly confused. I need to get my thoughts in order.

He smiles at me, gently. "Not checking on you. I've been staying here. You think I'd leave your kid alone while you're basically dead to the world? I've been feeding him, hanging out with him. I took him to school today. He seems okay."

"Oh. Wow. I don't know . . . I don't know what to say," I stammer, completely at a loss.

"Well, how about you let me finish in here, and I'll come out so we can talk?" he says with a smile. And I remember I am standing in the bathroom while *he* is showering. I turn to leave and say over my shoulder, "I'm sorry. Okay, yes. I'm going to shower, too. I'll meet you downstairs."

I call and wave weakly before I turn in a hurry back to the sanctity of the bathroom.

"Milly!" he calls after me, and I stop.

I take a second to gather myself, to try to calm my blush, before I turn around and say casually, "Yes?"

His smile is full-blown and so carnal, I grab the door handle for support at the sight of it. I haven't seen it in so long. His eyes, though, are full of mirth.

"Remember how we used to shower together?"

I nod, my mind melting as the memories come flooding back.

"I was just remembering, too. Come join me. There's plenty of room."

It's only then that I realize the hand not braced against the wall is in between his thighs. I watch his arm move, up and down.

My eyes shoot back to his face, his smile is still there, but his eyes are no longer laughing. They are hooded and serious while he's watching me.

I feel a throb start between my legs and I feel moisture, unbidden and unexpected, as my body responds to his invitation. I bite my lower lip to stop the groan that collects in my throat.

I straighten my back and say with as much indignation as my aroused mind will allow me, "No, that's perfectly fine. I'll go shower in my own bathroom. By myself." I turn and rush out. Dean's laughter taunts me as I make my way down the hall.

I walk into my room and shut the door behind me. I lean against it and try to compose myself. I rip my sweatshirt off, yank my leggings down, and leave a trail of clothes in my wake as I strip and make a beeline for my bathroom.

I turn the water on and hazard a look in the mirror. It's worse than I thought. My hair is a total disaster. My skin looks oily and my lips are chapped.

I hop in the shower and start to wash off days of sleep and sweat. After I've rinsed off, I stand under the spray and I think about Dean.

He's been taking care of Anthony while I've been sick. He doesn't live here.

A part of me isn't surprised. He has always been a caring person. But, another part of me is dismayed. He's a virtual stranger to me now. And our last interaction was far from friendly.

The last time I thought about him properly, all I could muster was hurt and disappointment. Those emotions are still there, but now I also feel a sense of gratitude and comfort that he's here.

My hands skim my torso as I think about him in the shower. My hand caresses the ring that sits on the same long chain as the pendant my parents gave me. My hand brushes my nipple as I play with the necklace and the sensation makes me moan. It's been so long since my body has been this responsive. That kiss with Dean in his car awakened something. I think about Dean stroking himself while he said he was thinking of me and my clit starts to hum. His body is incredible. There was no mistaking the invitation in his eyes and words, and part of me wishes we didn't have so many issues between us because it's been years since I was this aroused.

I pluck my nipples with one hand as the other travels between my legs. I begin to rub my clit as I imagine Dean's hands on my body instead of my own. His fingers, calloused from playing lacrosse, would be rough as they explored me. I imagine his mouth on my nipples. Sucking and licking them and my fingers speed up.

Even though my body still feels weakened from the flu, I also feel empowered in my ability to find pleasure on my own terms again.

One hand is on my breast and the other between my thighs as I think about his hand wrapped around himself. I close my eyes and picture the invitation in his eyes, and I come so unexpectedly I don't have time to think about muffling my cry of pleasure.

I lean against the shower wall as I come down from my orgasm. I haven't done this in so long, but I also can't remember the last time I was inspired to.

As I step out of the shower, I feel clean but tired. I can feel the strain on my lungs as a cough racks my body.

I need to talk to Dean and figure out what's going on. My desire for him may not have waned, but I don't know him anymore and my thoughts about him now are being conflated with memories of who he used to be.

My heart skips a beat when I think about that time in my life. We were so in love. We thought we could conquer the world as long as we had each other.

Suddenly, I'm so tired, I'm not sure I can finish getting dressed.

But, I do.

Dean and I need to talk and don't have much time before I need to leave to get Anthony.

still the one

I'M EITHER a genius or a fool. When Milly walked into the bathroom, I lost my mind.

I *know* I shouldn't have invited her to join me.

I shouldn't have told her I've been thinking of her while my fist was so obviously wrapped around my cock.

But, seeing her standing there, like my fantasy had come true, made it impossible to resist.

I'm glad she had the sense to walk away because if she hadn't, I would have stepped out of the shower and dragged her in with me and fucked her senseless.

I hate waiting for anything, and right now, Milly is standing on the other side of a door that was kicked shut by my idiotic scheme and then, my stupider words. If I want her to open it again, I've got to win her trust. The conversations this will require are riddled with potential land mines that could derail any progress we make. But, high-risk also means high reward. If we can get past the issues in our path, I know I can have her back.

I'm downstairs in front of my laptop, watching the clock so

that I can leave the house on time to get to Anthony's school. I heard her shower running when I stepped out into the hallway upstairs, and I know she's going to come down and talk to me in a few minutes. She probably has a million questions and also wants me to get the hell out of her house.

I hear her footsteps coming down the stairs, and I feel like a man waiting to hear a judgment from a jury. But I'm not going down without a fight.

"Dean?" she calls out as she reaches the foyer. I sit up straight before I respond, "I'm in here."

She walks into the living room, and although her steps are tentative, she's looking directly at me. She looks relieved, which lightens some of the tension floating in my shoulders.

She sits down next to me on the couch, and I take that as a good sign. Without the preamble of niceties, she dives right in.

"So, tell me everything. But start with Friday. I don't understand why you were even here."

Her hands are clasped in front of her and she's playing with her cuticle. It's something she used to do when we were in school. It's her tell. Even when she appeared outwardly calm, I'd know she was nervous when I saw her doing this. I shift slightly so I'm facing her and start talking.

"I came to see you. I felt like a total ass after our last… encounter. I was coming to apologize." I twist my lips in a wry smile. I leave off the part about a second chance.

She doesn't smile back.

"Okay… But, why didn't you just call me?"

Her eyes roam my face. She doesn't sound angry, just genuinely confused. I want to be honest, but I'm trying to pace myself.

"You didn't give me your number."

"I didn't give you my address either."

I wince sheepishly. "Okay, I didn't think you would take a call from me. And I wanted to talk face-to-face. What I did, how I treated you, what I said to you, was wrong. I don't have an excuse. I had been walking around for years with ideas and hopes and then in November they were completely obliterated. It felt like you were disappearing all over again. But this time, I knew where you were. You were someone's wife. You were someone's mother, and you had been for a long time. I was angry and acted like an unmitigated asshole."

That confession sounds pathetic to my own ears, but it is the sincerest truth I can offer right now.

Milly exhales loudly and looks away. Her shoulders hunch and she wraps her arms around her waist. When she looks back at me her eyes are angry; her voice is low and slow when she speaks, as if she's trying to control the incredulity that coats her next question.

"What about Nicola?"

"It's over. Officially now. But, honestly, it's been done for months."

She looks at me, her expression more concerned, but still wary. "Were you together long?"

I shake my head. "Two years." I give a wry smile. "And they *felt* long."

"I know what you mean."

"I forced myself to move on. I was in college, working, then in business school, and then working my way up the ladder at the firm and I've never really slowed down long enough to give myself time to think about relationships. But when I branched out on my own, it felt like time. She was an associate. And—"

"I don't need details. I really don't," she says sharply, her golden eyes sliding over me and shutting me up.

"Yeah. Okay...I just. I'm nervous," I say self-consciously and run my hands through my hair. I've never been able to hide from Milly. I've never wanted to. I don't want to start now. I missed the freedom that comes from being completely honest. Even when I know Milly isn't happy with me, I also know I can trust her with the truth.

"I'm nervous, too," she says quietly and looks down at her

hands. "I don't know what to do with any of this. I don't know what to do with us."

I nod, let out a shuddering breath. "I'm still trying to wrap my head around the fact that I'm here with you. Looking at you. You're close enough I can smell you. I never thought I'd have that again."

"Dean . . ." Her voice is laced with caution and sadness.

"I'm not saying I have you, Milly, but I won't lie and say I don't want you," I persist.

I take her hand gently into my own and put my thumb over hers to still the nervous motion of her fingers. She doesn't pull her hand away, and I take this as my cue to continue.

"Did your friend set that up on purpose?" she asks suddenly.

"Yes and no, he contacted you before he knew who you were to me. But he asked me to come to his office when you'd be there on purpose."

"Why?"

"Because he's a busybody." I smile to myself. "And he loves me. Besides you, he's the best friend I've ever had."

"So... he *really* wants to hire me?" she asks with less skepticism and more hope this time.

"Yes, and if you say no because of me, his fiancée will never let me hear the end of it."

"I don't know," she says, but I can sense she wants to say yes, so I push.

"I'll keep away if you're worried about that, I promise," I say, and I mean it. I'll give her a wide berth if it's what she needs.

She leans back on the couch, exposing her neck and I stifle a groan. That beautiful *café au lait* column of skin is begging for my kiss. She takes a deep breath, and I know she's thinking. So, I don't say another word. I've already pushed too hard. I just need to let her make up her mind.

She sits up after a minute and without looking at me directly, which is so unlike her says, "I don't know. I just need to think. Please don't think I'm not grateful to you for being here when I was sick. I don't know how I would have managed if you hadn't come by. I can never say thank you enough." She's playing with her thumb again.

"I feel a 'but' coming," I prompt, trying to keep the disappointment from creeping into my voice.

"But, after what just happened in the bathroom, I'm not sure it's a good idea for you to stay here." She pulls her hand away and lowers her lashes.

Fuck this.

"Milly, *you* walked in on me in the shower and *you* stayed. I was thinking about you when you walked in. You looked like you wanted to join me, so I extended the offer."

I grab her hand again. This time I turn it palm up and caress the pads of her fingers.

I look at her and see that her face, her beautiful face with its hues of caramel and honey, is flushed, her eyes watching our joined hands. I decide to leave it alone and go back to our original conversation.

"I won't interfere with your party planning. I promise." I tug at her hand to get her to look at me. And when she does, what I see in her eyes causes my hope to surge like a geyser. Her expression says she doesn't want me to go, she doesn't want to say no to me, and she's feeling everything I'm feeling.

It's like the time we lost just disappeared. I know it hasn't. But it fucking *feels* like it. I know we can't just pick up where we left off, but I want to pick up where we are now.

"I'd like the chance to get to know you again. You were my best friend. I've never stopped loving you. And I've never for one second blamed you for anything."

Her eyes search mine and mine search hers. I see everything she feels— she never could hide from me. Her confusion, her fear, her joy . . . and I lay it all out. "I love you. I never stopped feeling that way, and I know that you feel it, too." This makes her head snap up.

"Dean—"

I cut her off. I feel like I'm standing on the edge of a cliff and there is a fifty-fifty chance I'll soar or I'll crash. I decide to jump because I'd rather crash trying to fly than be safe without her. And the upside is so sweet, I can barely think straight.

"A lot of water has passed under this bridge, and I know we have a lot to talk about. But, I also know I've never needed another human being before you. And yes, life will go on, has gone on if we go our separate ways. But I know that my heart is going to stay where it's been since I met you in ninth grade."

"Dean— so much has happened. I don't- " She's more aggressive this time, but I'm determined to get it all out.

"Please, you don't have to say anything right now. Just think about it." I'm close to begging, but I feel like I'm in the fight of my life and nothing has ever felt more important.

She squeezes my hand and releases a long breath before she meets my eyes again. They're shining as bright as freshly polished gold coins. I see a plea for patience in them and I decide to back off.

"I'll leave if you need me to." Right now, I'd do whatever she asked. I know I've pushed her enough for today, and the last thing I want is to make Milly uncomfortable in her own home.

She considers me for a long moment, her eyes always the window to her heart, answering the question before she speaks.

"I don't know what to say. In the last week, you've completely thrown me for a loop. Seeing you again. Finding out we both had the wrong end of the stick. Getting sick and waking up to find you in my house. Finding out you've been here for three days, living here, taking care of my son—of me. That alone is a lot to process. But everything you've just said is a lot to absorb. I need time to think."

"So...should I stay or should I go?"

"You must have so much else to do besides staying here to take care of me."

"Actually, I have been working pretty well from here. My assistant rescheduled all of my meetings this week, and I've been able to do most of them by phone. I had my suitcase in the car, so I've got everything I need." I put my heart in my hand and hold it out to her. "I don't want to leave you. Or little dude. I do need to get back to New York on Friday, but until then, I'm at your disposal." I look at her hopefully while she considers me for a long moment.

"Okay, well, I won't turn down the offer for an extra pair of hands and for the chance to spend some time with you. And thank you for taking care of Anthony," she says with a shy smile.

She glances at her watch.

"Speaking of, it's almost time to go and get him."

I grab my phone from the table. "I have an alarm set. I've been using it to make sure I leave the house on time every day."

She smiles. "Really? Wow, Dean. I don't even know how you figured it all out."

"Well, you've got a smart kid who knows his schedule. And I looked up the school's address online. He's easy and fun. You've done a great job with him."

She beams at me, her pride obvious. "Yeah, he's pretty great. I'm glad he wasn't any trouble."

I grin. "I didn't say that. He hates doing his spelling homework and probably conned me into giving him way too many snacks."

She laughs out loud at this. "He's very persuasive when he wants something." Her laugh turns into a cough and it reminds me she's still sick and hasn't eaten anything since I got here.

"Hey, you must be starving. The doctor said to start you off with bland food. Can I get you some toast?"

"I'm actually really tired again, but I'm so hungry I could eat my own foot," she says with another smile that is so *her* it totally disarms me.

"Okay, let me get you something. Sit here, and while you're eating I'll run and get Anthony. He'll probably tackle you the minute he sees you're out of your room."

I stand up and head toward the kitchen. But there's so much left unspoken between us, and I know we have a lot more to talk about before I can start to relax. But fuck me, look how far we've just come.

snack

I CALL my mother and both of my sisters and Zenobia while Dean is out getting Anthony. My mom apparently knows Dean is here and is thrilled. In a singsong voice, she says, "I told you this wasn't about revenge." I just roll my eyes and don't say anything because I'm not ready for that conversation. We talk for a few more minutes before she and Rabea are off to play the slots.

I can't reach Lilly. She's so hard to get in touch with these days, but I know she will call me back when she gets my message. Addie and I talk for a few minutes, but she's busy preparing for a hearing the next day, so it's a short conversation.

"Mommy!" Anthony's scream cuts through the silence I've been sitting in while I waited for Dean to get back with him.

I stand up and brace myself to catch him as he throws himself into my arms. He climbs up my body and wraps his legs around my waist and his arms around my neck. I wrap my arms around him and caress his head.

"Oh, baby. I've missed you." I breathe into his neck.

"Me, too, Mommy," he whispers back.

And everything is right in my world. This child is the reason

I'll never regret a single decision I've made. Because I couldn't imagine my life without him.

I put him down and look down at his beautiful little face. "How was your day, honey?"

"It was okay. I'm hungry though. Can I get a snack?" And he takes off before I can respond. I watch him run down the hall and disappear into the kitchen.

I look up to find Dean watching us from the door. He's smiling at me, but his eyes look a little sad.

"Hey, thanks for getting him." I walk over toward him.

"No problem. But that carpool lane is ridiculous. Anyone could drive away with him." He looks at the hallway Anthony just ran down and smiles.

"Not really. He wouldn't get in the car with just anyone," I tell him. "You guys spent a couple of days together over the weekend before school started, you dropped him off this morning. He knows who you are."

He tips his head and looks at me like he just remembered something and then looks away to hide the expression. My curiosity peaks.

"What?" I touch his arm and he looks down at my hand. He's wearing a thin gray Henley and I can feel the strength in his arms, the heat of his skin. I love the way it feels to have my hands on him. When he just keeps staring at my hand on his sleeve, I prompt him again, "Dean, what?"

He looks up at me and the expression on his face is so serious I wonder if I even want to know.

"It's maybe nothing. I don't know." He sounds so unsure, so unlike Dean, I move my hand from his arm to his shoulder and step closer to him. His eyes follow the movement of my hand and then come back to rest on my face.

"Don't ever stop touching me," he says, his voice hoarse, his eyes intent.

"I don't want to stop," I respond honestly.

"Mommy, your phone is ringing. It says Jasper's mom."

We jump away from each other just as Anthony comes darting back into the living room, my phone in hand and skids to stop in front of me.

"Thank you, honey. Dean, I've got to take this," I say before I walk to the kitchen.

"Hey, Laila." Laila is the only mother in his grade I've befriended but she's everyone's friend. Because she's nosy and helpful all at once.

"Milly! I've heard some hunk picked Anthony up from school today," she says before I can say hello.

I burst into laughter. I can only imagine the gossip mill at school. "Well, hello to you too, Laila. I'm fine, thanks. It was a terrible bug," I say back dryly.

"Sorry you're sick. But, I'm sure you'll live. Tell me who that man is!" she says, her voice full of excitement.

"Oh, my God. He's a friend. He's been helping me while my mother is gone," I respond, trying to sound exasperated, but unable to hold back my mirth.

"From what I hear he's gorgeous. The teachers who work the carpool lane have been talking about him nonstop. Does he take clients? I'm about to be sick. I need someone to come and take care of me."

I laugh, but it turns into a cough. I also hear the back door open and I get up to see who opened it. I look out the window to see Dean and Anthony in the backyard. It's surreal to see him in my backyard with my son. Two weeks ago, I didn't think I'd ever see him again.

I walk back to the couch and listen as Laila starts talking again. "Oh, I'm sorry. I didn't mean to act like I don't care that you're sick. How are you feeling?" she asks warmly once I've stopped coughing.

"I'm not great, but better than I was a few days ago. Dean, my friend, has been staying here and helping."

"Your friend? What kind of *friend*?" she asks coyly.

"None of your business!" I shoot back, but I'm laughing.

"Oooh, he's *that* kind of friend. I'm so happy to hear this, Milly." I can hear the excitement in her voice.

"Don't get too excited." But really, I'm the pot calling the kettle black. I'm brimming with excitement.

"Okay, well, I'm going to let you get back to your *friend*. Feel better. I'll bring some food around this weekend, okay?"

"You're the best. Thank you for calling."

We disconnect and I walk to the back door and stick my head out. They both look up when they hear the door open and their smiles are two beams of sunshine.

Dean walks over and leaves Anthony climbing the jungle gym he has nearly outgrown.

"I'm glad you're up and about, but maybe you shouldn't overdo it. The doctor said you'd be tired for about a week. Let's get you back to bed."

He puts his hand on my elbow, and I want to collapse into him. It feels so good to be touched by these hands again.

"Okay, sure. I'm a little tired." As if sensing my need, his hand slides up my arm and wraps around my waist. He lets me lean on him as we walk inside and up the stairs. We stop outside the door to my room.

"Thank you for bringing me up. I'm okay, though. Anthony's alone out there." He looks like he wants to argue but nods and drops his arm from my waist.

He leans forward to brush his lips against my cheek. My eyes involuntarily close at the contact. He smells so good.

His kiss is reverent, and I know his eyes are closed, too. I reach up to grip his arm, and he sighs and leans his forehead against mine. Our breaths mingle, my heart races, my nipples peak, and I can feel the moisture building between my legs. We stand there—closer, physically, than we have been in a long time. But my emotions are all over the place.

And I need to think. I need to get my feelings straight. I'm too vulnerable after the whirlwind of today, and I don't think I can fight the feelings stirring to life between us.

Dean and I have agreed to get to know each other again. Who we are now is sullied by everything that has happened since the last time we saw each other. I know we need to talk about all of that before we can really attempt a friendship or anything beyond it.

I pull my forehead back and see his eyes are closed and for a split-second I study his face. His lashes, always a dark brown and totally at odds with his blond hair, rest on his cheeks. His skin is golden and is almost as smooth as it was when he was eighteen.

My hand comes up to caress his cheek and his eyes open. The expression in them stills my hand. He looks like I feel. Scared, excited. He knows we have much to overcome and he's dreading and looking forward to it as much as I am. I break the contact and take a step back.

"Okay, shout if you need me or send Anthony upstairs if he gets to be a handful."

"Okay, but we've been managing on our own since Saturday morning, Red."

Hearing him call me this, so easily, sends a thrill through me.

I head into my room and sit on my bed, thinking about how I got here.

Finding Dean had not been on my list of things to do on my Remember Milly project. I touch the heart shaped pendant on my chest, the one that is demanding I remember everything. Which includes letting myself recall how I felt about him all those years ago.

After seeing him in his office, after the way we parted, I never imagined he would show up at my doorstep. I didn't think I'd want to see him there. But, now, I'm so glad he came.

So, his mother wasn't speaking for him. He didn't blame me. He wasn't lost to me. I gave up on us and him because I thought reaching out to him would hurt him. We have lost so much time.

A sob escapes me before I even realize it's coming. That phone call, that deceit by his mother cost me so much. I would have gone to find him as soon as I could have if I had known. Or would I have? I hate second-guessing my actions because no matter what else went down, the path I took led me to Anthony.

I shake off the chill threatening to come over me. My mother is right, Dean is right, this is a miraculous second chance. I want to give us a try. I want to let go of all of the ugliness between us, but first we need to talk. About his family, his father. About my family, my father, and about Kevin.

It's not a conversation I'm looking forward to, but it is one I know I can't avoid. The one certainty I have, which is propelling me forward, is that there's still something there.

We are not who we used to be. But, I've always worn my heart on my sleeve when it comes to him. When we were young, I felt empowered by how much I loved him. I felt fortunate I had met someone I could love without reservation or doubt. But now, my love feels like a self-inflicted wound. I'm exposed and vulnerable, and I pray I can survive whatever is coming next for us.

A wave of fatigue overwhelms me, and I lie down. I'm assailed by memories, but the one that always stands out, the one I replay often is our first kiss and our first "I love you." They happened on the same day, in the same moment, and I remember it like it was yesterday. I close my eyes and let my mind drift.

Right before I drift off to sleep, I bring my fingers to my lips. I've never stopped feeling that kiss. I've never stopped loving him. I hope we can find a way to get past this because I want to have "great" again.

step one

DINNER WAS WONDERFUL . . . and terrible.

We avoided each other's eyes, focused on Anthony as he talked without pause about his day, his friends, his latest drawing.

He was obviously thrilled his mother was back in the land of the living because he talked more over the course of this meal than he had said during the three days we had spent alone together.

I loved watching them interact, but I couldn't help but wonder about his father. In all of the time I'd been at Milly's house, he hadn't called once. The kid had only mentioned him a couple of times. I couldn't understand how someone could have a wife like Milly and a son as fantastic as Anthony and just leave it all behind. She was all I had wanted my whole life. For her to be the mother of my children had been a fucking *goal* of mine.

I have seen the difference between a household led by parents who loved each other as opposed to what I grew up in. I knew from the first time I ate dinner at Hassan's table that *this* was the kind of family I wanted. I can't imagine having it and walking away from it.

I wonder if her husband will come to his senses and try to reconcile.

My gut twists at the thought. I push it away. There's no point worrying about things I can't control. *"You never have to fight for what is yours."*

She comes down wearing a pair of light gray sweatpants, an LSU sweatshirt, and thick gold and purple socks. Her hair is braided and hanging over her shoulder. Her face is completely devoid of makeup. She doesn't look eighteen anymore, but time has been very kind to her.

She was a knockout in high school.

Now, she exudes sensuality without even trying. Her eyes are twin pools of burnished gold. Her face is a study of angles and curves. All of them come together to give her the look of a Nubian goddess.

Besides her bronzed skin, she's her father's carbon copy, right down to the shades of red in her hair.

She coughs and I realize I have been staring at her. She's standing in the doorway staring at me, too. I extend my hand to beckon her.

"Come sit, you must be tired."

She purses her lips as if contemplating my offer and then walks over to me. Her gait is loose and her hips swing with each step.

I remember holding those hips in my hands when I kissed her in the car. Fuck, but I'd give every penny I owned to do that night all over again.

She reaches the couch and sits down. But she takes a seat in the corner across from me and brings her legs up into a lotus position.

"I'm here. Let's talk. I'll go first," she says her eyes on mine. Not so much a challenge in them, but determination. "I need to talk to you about our parents. I know you said you didn't hold me responsible for what happened," she begins slowly, as if she is weighing every word before she speaks.

I answer this one quickly because I want to get it out of the way. "I didn't then, and I don't now. And whatever financial crimes went on, I still can't believe your father would leave you for anything."

She wrinkles her forehead and her lips pucker slightly. "I don't know. My parents fought in the days leading up to the collapse. And then after, everyone was so convinced of my dad's guilt. And the FBI said we needed protection."

I frown at her characterization. "Said?"

"Honestly, after a few months, things died down. It felt like overkill, but my mother wanted us to cooperate so they would let us live our lives in peace. They were looking for my dad, and they figured we were the best bait they could find. Everything happened so quickly. When I called you…I wasn't even allowed to. They said no one could know where we were."

"Why?" I ask her, giving voice to a question I've wanted to ask her since I found her again.

She looks startled. "Why could no one know where we were?" She says it like it can't possibly be what I'm asking.

I nod. "Yes. Why? I understood why they moved you, things were crazy in the days after your dad disappeared. I understand the name changes—a little. But, did they think some crazy ex-employee was going to hunt you down and kill you? Most of them could barely afford to pay their mortgages. Much less launch a manhunt for four women who hadn't done anything wrong."

She shakes her head and looks at me, and I realize that this is the first time she has considered this. "Didn't you ever want to be yourself again?"

She sighs, considers it and shakes her head. "No. I'd lost everything, I wanted to look forward."

"I know what you mean." She gets to her feet.

"Yes, okay. Listen, do you want some wine or something? I can't drink, but one of us should." She stands up without waiting for my response.

"Yeah, I'll take a glass of whatever you're having."

I sit back and watch her walk out of the room. I know we have a long way to go, but it feels like we could actually build a relationship.

She comes back a second later with a bottle of white wine, two glasses, and a wine opener.

I take the bottle and opener from her, open the bottle and pour a drinks.

"Okay, you were saying?" she says as she plops back down on the couch, this time right next to me. Her expression was completely unguarded and relaxed. It gives me the impetus I need to keep talking.

"Just that...I never blamed you. And honestly, besides the fact that the money went missing at the same time your father did, I've never seen any proof that he's the one who took it."

"Yes! Exactly! Honestly, until they told us about that sighting last year, I didn't even know if he was alive or dead."

"What do your mom and sister think?"

She pops up so she's on her knees on the couch. Her expression excited and relieved at my words. "My mother doesn't really talk about it, but she's never believed my dad would have left us voluntarily. Lilly and I both thought none of it added up, but we didn't have any answers and were just trying to put one foot in front of the other. Addie was so young, and so angry. When I left for college, I tried to put it behind me...carve a life out for myself."

She sits back, seeming to deflate as her story ends.

I bite the bullet and bring up a subject I would rather pretend doesn't exist.

"Is that where you met your husband? At LSU?" I try to keep my voice steady and calm, but talking about this still makes my stomach hurt and my blood simmer.

"You have to understand; I was reeling. I felt so lost." Her eyes drift toward the ceiling and she runs her fingers through her hair at the memory she just recalled. "And then I saw a picture of you with a girl at homecoming at Stanford and I couldn't bear it. I just wanted to feel better...and never be as exposed with anyone as I had been with you. I wanted something certain. And Kevin was there."

Something in my chest constricts to think of her in pain because of me. "I don't even remember homecoming, or much of anything that first year. I just wish...we'd still had each other."

"I see the disservice I did to both Kevin and myself. I shouldn't have married him just to create certainty, but at the time it seemed like the most important thing in the world."

She sighs and leans back. "But, I can't ever say I regret it. Never. Because of Anthony." She runs her hand over her mouth and down her neck and looks away from me.

"He's incredible, Red. And it's clear how much he loves you. If you and your husband didn't have a lot of love between you, I'm happy to know you had him. That you found something good despite all the hurt."

She smiles at me, so sweetly and so beautifully I know she's thinking of her son. "He's everything. I'm so lucky to have him."

"Tell me what happened. Why did your marriage end?"

She tips her head back and stares at the ceiling. She's gathering her thoughts, and I give her a minute. Instead, I study the long column of her throat, and I see the thin gold chain that disappears under her sweatshirt and I remember that pendant she wore every single day.

"He cheated on me. For years."

"And you just found out?"

She leans her head on the back of the couch and closes her eyes. "No. I'd always known. But, it wasn't until Lilly called me out one night that I gave any thought to what a sham of a life I was living."

I wince at the hurt in her voice. "I'm sorry."

"Me, too. We were two people living in the same house because we share a child. It was over long before I ended it."

"Any regrets?" I ask.

She shakes her head and one corner of her mouth tugs up into a smile. "Saying no to that life has opened as many doors as it closed. I'm ready for a phase of my life that's honest, true, real." She smiles sadly at me and I want nothing more than to make sure she has everything she wants.

"Well, anyway, that's it. He gets Anthony every other weekend and my mom handles the switch over, so I never see him."

"He hasn't called once this week. Does he know you're sick?" I ask angry on Anthony's behalf.

"He wouldn't care."

"But what about just to check on his son?"

Her sigh is steeped with resignation. "He loves Anthony, but he…doesn't want to do the hard work. He's down for the fun parts though." She ends the sentence with a huge yawn.

"You should get back to bed." I stand up and grab her hand to pull her up to her feet.

She stops me and I look down to meet her worried eyes. "Are we okay? I know we've got years of catching up to do. But is the air clear?"

I'm very eager to ease her fears. "Yes. The air is clear. I love you." The words slip out before I realize I'm going to say them, but I'm not sorry I did. Even if she can't say them back.

She takes a deep breath and moves to stand so we are face-to-face.

"I love you, too, Dean. I always have." Her eyes dart away. "Saying this makes me feel ashamed because I *did* get married. I *did* plan on spending my life with Kevin."

"I didn't know how badly I needed to hear that," I admit and rock back on my heels.

She flushes and looks up at me with caution in her eyes. "That doesn't mean we can just pick up where we left off. We've changed. You were just engaged. I was *just* married, I have a son.

I'm just starting to rebuild my life. I have so many questions to answer on my own, too."

She's earnest and clear-eyed as she draws her lines in the sand. "There's no rush. I'm not going anywhere."

She grabs my hands as she speaks and her fingers intertwine with mine.

She steps forward and without missing a beat, steps into my chest and wraps her arms around my waist. My arms go around her, and we stand there.

I inhale her, trying to get my fill because I know what this is . . . and what it's not. She's being my friend, and I need to remember this is where she needs me to be right now. But as I feel her breasts pressed against my chest, her pelvis cradling my hips, I renew my resolve to do whatever it takes to win her back.

I'm hers.

There is no one else for me.

We turn simultaneously, and I walk her to her bedroom door. We hold hands, but don't speak as we make our way up the stairs. I press a kiss to the side of her jaw and feel her inhale. I can't help myself as my tongue comes out to taste the skin my lips have just caressed. She moans and leans into me again. I'm hard and don't try to hide it.

She tips her head back and it hits the door. Her hands come up and grab the sides of my waist and I can feel her fingers flexing, and I know she's trying to decide what to do.

But she pulls back, opens her door, steps inside, and closes the door behind her, her face a mask of indecision.

I stare at the door. I'm not feeling indecision about what needs to happen next. I can taste her on my tongue, I want more.

crazy in love

I CLOSE the door behind me and press my forehead against it.

What am I doing? I feel so many contradictions in this moment.

I'm the first to admit I've got a toxic relationship with my memories.

I try to ignore them - and they, in turn, won't let me forget that I'm one bad decision away from ruin.

I sometimes wish I could erase them, and there are moments - like this - where they make it clear I'll never be able to.

My whole body is a live wire. Every single nerve ending is aroused.

It's is nothing new. I'd just forgotten.

All Dean ever had to do was smile at me and anything else that wanted my attention would disappear.

I was so in love with him and would show him that in as many ways as I could. And almost nothing felt better than using my body to send the message.

Why did I send him away?

I reach for the door handle and jump back with a yelp of surprise when it flies open before I've even touched it.

"Have you been there the whole time?"

"I can't leave you anymore than you can let me go."

His hands flex open and shut at his sides and blazing eyes pin me in place.

He looks so beautiful.

"Are you just going to stand there?" I give him a coy smile.

He doesn't return it. "Invite me in."

My pulse is beating a flagrant staccato and my body practically humming with want that grows more intense with every take a step toward him.

He steps toward me, too. His stride is long and aggressive like he's attached to the same thread that's reeling me in, pulling my body closer to his.

Our hands touch, palms pressed together, and a thrill of anticipation dances up my spine.

"I'm not going to walk down the hall. I'm not going to sleep in the room next to yours and wait. Fuck waiting. I don't know if when I go to sleep tonight, I'm going to open my eyes tomorrow. Nothing is promised. And I'm not spending one more day apart from you." His voice is raspy, his eyes burn into me, and my mouth positively waters.

He closes the gap between us and spans my waist with one hand and links our fingers together with the other.

He bends slightly so that we're nose to nose. His eyes capture mine and refuse to let go. In them, I see my own heart's song. One of need, impatience, and love. Right now, life and love are deciding for us. "I know you want to take things slowly, but we have wasted fifteen years. We have let enough come between us, and I'm done."

He looks more earnest than I have ever seen him.

His heart is being held out to me, he's offering himself to me. I'm going to reach out and grab him.

His lips come so close to mine that as he speaks, they touch.

"I know one thing, and *only* one thing, for certain, that

your heart is made of exactly the thing mine needs to feel at home."

My heart is ready to combust but I can't speak.

"I'm not leaving this room unless you tell me you want me to go. We don't have to do more than just be. Like we used to. But, I don't want to spend one more night without you if I don't have to," he murmurs.

My hands slide up his chest and loop around his neck. I'm breathing hard through my nostrils, trying to catch my breath and keep up with my emotions. My convictions, though, are crystal clear. "I don't want you to go."

"Thank God." His mouth brushes back and forth across mine in slow, coaxing, soft strokes that are a strike of flint on the tinder of my desire.

I press my body into his. "I forgot how good you feel."

"Do you feel well enough for me to make love to you?" Dean asks me, his voice tender, his breath hot as it washes over me.

A few minutes ago, I was sure keeping him at arm's length was the right thing to do. But now, I don't think anything has ever felt as right as he does in my arms.

We were inevitable. We've just needed the chance. It's been hurled into our laps. I *have* wasted enough time; I'm ready to start living. Without reservation, without fear, and with *him*.

I only nod in response. His thumb comes up to my mouth and he presses it against my lips. I open my mouth and the tip of it slips inside. I suck it, savoring the saltiness and rough texture of his skin. He groans and in a flash, his finger is gone and his lips are on mine.

This kiss is an ode to our new beginning. I savor it, wanting to remember every moment about it because I know this is a kiss that marks the start of a grand adventure. I pour all of my passion, my love, and hope into it. My mouth feasts on his and his devours mine. We are a tangle of lips, tongue, teeth; a dizzy spiral of lust and need.

His hands grasp the bottom of my sweatshirt and in one swift pull, it's over my head.

The motion breaks our kiss and Dean stands back to look at me. I wasn't wearing a bra under my sweatshirt. My breasts are exposed to his gaze. I take care of my body, but I have also carried, given birth to, and nursed a child. These are not the breasts Dean would remember from our youth.

I bring my arm across my chest self-consciously, but he reaches forward to pull it back down to my side.

His eyes are full of adoration and heat. It's a heady combination. He reaches up to rub the ring that sits on the chain around my neck. He stares at it as he turns it over in his hands.

Then he looks up at me. "You still have this. You're wearing it?" He sounds shocked.

"Yes, for good luck."

"Fuck me. I don't deserve you."

I start to interrupt him, but he cuts me off. "I know I don't, but I'm going to work every single day I draw breath to be worthy."

I duck my head and my arm comes back up to my breasts. He pulls it back down.

"Don't ever, ever hide from me, Red. Your body is beautiful. It's even more beautiful than I remember. I want to see it all. I want to taste it all. I want to *fuck* it all."

He reaches behind him and uses one hand to grip the collar of his shirt and pull it over his head. He exposes his body—all muscle, sinew, and strong bones—to me. My eyes drink him in. He's more beautiful than I remember.

I reach out to touch his beautifully sculpted chest. My hands run all over his golden skin, my hands following the ridges and hollows, the swell of muscle. My fingertips skim his nipples and he hisses out a breath.

He removes his jeans and his boxers and then he's standing in front of me completely bare.

I drop to my knees in front of him, drawn to him like a moth to a flame. His cock is so beautiful, erect and proud. I lean forward and lick the pre-cum that is already on the tip of his cock.

In a voice that suddenly is all gravel he says, "Milly . . . fuck."

My hand circles the base of his cock, and I take him as far into my mouth as I can. The taste of him is unbelievable, the feel of him, hot, smooth skin over rigid steel is intoxicating, and my own arousal takes flight.

I feel his hands grasp my shoulders, and I grip his ass. I'm not very practiced at this, it's not something I did more than a handful of times while I was married, and I certainly never enjoyed it. But the pleasure I'm getting from this is like I'm the one experiencing it.

One of my hands leaves his body and goes between my legs. I feel Dean's cock grow harder, and I increase the already tight seal my mouth makes. My tongue traces a path up and down the center of his cock, and I can feel the surge of cum. I know he's close.

He starts to pull me back and says with a warning in his voice, "I'm going to come, Milly."

I only hold on tighter and move my head faster. The hand that is between my legs also speeds up, and I feel myself getting close to orgasm. I want to taste him, swallow him, and have a piece of him inside my body. He comes with hard, fast thrusts of his hips and a long cry that sounds like a sob.

I swallow everything he gives me and lean back on my knees as I start to come, too. My lips are sore from taking his wide girth into my mouth, but nothing has ever felt so good.

He looks back down at me, dazed and happy. He hooks his hands under my arms and hauls me to my feet.

"My turn," he says with a wicked grin.

He bends his head to take one of my already hard nipples into his mouth and the sensation leaves me scrambling for purchase. A shot of pleasure runs down the core of my body, and

I feel my clit throbbing from my recent orgasm. He yanks my sweatpants down and lays me back on my bed.

He hovers over me and his eyes roam my face like he's committing my expressions to memory. My eyes do the same. He has a slightly wild look about him. His eyes have turned a dark green and his pupils are dilated. His hair is sweat dampened and thick locks of it are clinging to his forehead.

He bends down and takes my nipple back into his mouth. And watching him, his lips attached to my breast, while I feel his tongue licking, is the most erotic thing I've ever seen.

My hands thread in his hair to try and hold him there. But he's on the move, kissing his way down my torso. He gets to the line of my underwear where a swirl of stretch marks from carrying Anthony sit. He licks them, reverently and slowly.

My hand comes back to his head, but this time to caress it. My heart feels so full, joy leaks from my eyes.

His head moves and nuzzles my pussy through my underwear. He opens his entire mouth and sucks me through the lace and silk and then he pushes them aside and takes my already hard and throbbing clit into his mouth and starts a gentle sucking motion.

My mouth falls open in a silent cry and he puts three big, blunt fingers inside of me. He rubs gently, turning his fingers until he hits a spot that makes my hips buck off the bed. And he stays there, stroking, coaxing all while his mouth gives me the sweetest pleasure.

In only a matter of minutes, I'm coming apart. For those seconds, I'm lost in a wave of bliss, pain, pleasure . . . life. I feel it surge through me as Dean holds me to his mouth, his sucks gentling. I sag into the mattress and he pulls my panties all the way down and settles in the cradle of my hips.

"Are you on birth control?" he asks suddenly, and I nod quickly, yes.

"I want to be inside you without anything between us. Can

I?" I nod, an emphatic yes, I want that so much, too. My heart is so full it wants to burst. I can't wait to feel him inside of me.

Dean slides up my body and pulls my legs up to his waist and then I feel him, blunt, wide and delicious, as he slides into me. It is a laborious and long thrust that pulls a keening moan from deep inside me. I lift my hips to bring him all the way inside me.

He turns us, so we are side by side, pulling my knees up to either side of his hips and then he begins to move. My arms wrap around his shoulders and I bury my face in his neck. He feels incredible, skin against skin.

His hands fist in my hair and he pulls my head back to look at him.

"This is us," he says.

"Always," I return, smiling at him.

He drops hot kisses on my face, he licks my neck, he bites my lips, and he moves inside of me, taking his time, making love to me.

"This body, this soul, this love, all of it, only for us. The only other children that will grow inside you are the ones that I put there. The only tongue that will make you come again is mine." His thrusts move in a cadence with his words.

His pace picks up. "Tell me I'm not alone here. Tell me you love me, baby." He's not asking; he's demanding because he knows I have no choice.

My hands claw at his back as he starts to move faster and faster.

My hands thread in his hair and I hold on for dear life. "I love you so much. So much. It's always been you," I moan.

He flips me over, so that he's on top of me again. He puts my feet over his shoulder and starts to drive into me. "Don't ever leave me again," I beg.

He grunts and talks to me while he fucks me. "Leave you? I would have to be dead to ever let you go. I'm serious about you and us." I wince and flex my hips as he hits the top of my womb. "Am I too deep?" he asks.

"You could never be deep enough." I want him to crawl inside my body and live there. I'm desperate in my need for him.

His hands run my torso to capture my nipples. He starts to squeeze them to the rhythm of his thrusts and then I'm coming. Coming so fast and so hard that I turn my head to bite the pillow and my hands scramble to find a hold in the comforter we're sprawled on top of.

"Tell me you like that," he demands.

"I like it."

"Tell me you know it's mine." His fingers coil in my hair and he pulls.

"What are you doing to me?" I beg. I'm so lost in the concerto of sensations overwhelming me.

He pulls out of me, turns me over onto my stomach, and re-enters me. He starts to thrust hard, leans down and bites my shoulder, and then licks it to soothe the sting. He moves his hand underneath my hips, finds my clit and starts to rub it. My orgasm rolls into another one, and I cry out his name.

"Milly. Fuck. Milly. I'm going to come." He's saying this over and over again. And then he grabs my hips and starts to pound into me as he comes. His motions are furious and jerky, and I feel him empty himself into me.

We collapse in a heap of limbs, still connected, and he wraps his arms around me. His chest is sweat dampened and hot as I press up against him.

"Dean, this was . . ." I trail off, unable to find the words.

"I know." He slips out of me and peels away. I feel cold without the heat of his chest.

He comes back from my bathroom with a washcloth he has wet with hot water. He wipes me off before throwing the cloth into the hamper and then crawls back into bed with me. He pulls me to his chest and wraps one arm around me.

I cover his hand with mine and bring it to my lips.

"This is us," I whisper and feel all of the emotion he has just poured into me well up in my throat.

I feel Dean's breathing even out before I let myself relax and start to drift off. I can't stop the tears as they roll down my cheeks. I remember the last time I lay in this bed and cried myself to sleep. This time, the tears flow from a wellspring of joy.

puzzle pieces fit

IT'S incredible how I've lived without her for fifteen years, but the prospect of a week away feels like torture.

I'm afraid to step out of the cocoon we've created at her house. But work calls for both of us and her mother is going to be back tonight.

I'm drinking coffee and checking my schedule for this afternoon's meetings, while Milly is dropping Anthony off at school. It's her first day taking him since she got sick, and I'm glad she's feeling well enough to do it. Yesterday, she slept a lot during the day and I worried that I had pushed her too hard when we'd had sex.

But, when I was showering last night, she slipped into the shower with me and we put that built-in bench to work.

I'm smiling to myself when I hear the door that leads from the garage to the kitchen open.

I look up to see Milly, looking not a day over eighteen, walking through the door. It's still cold in March, and she's pulling off her jacket and kicking off her boots before she walks back in.

I just take her in. She has worn her hair in that single, fat braid since she was fifteen. Her hair is longer now than it was then and the braid's tail wraps around the tip of her breast. And I feel envious of the braid. I get up and walk toward her.

She looks up as I approach and her beautiful mouth tips up into a smile that lets me know she's happy to see me.

"Hey, D." I smile back at her. She hasn't called me that since we were in high school and it feels so good and familiar to hear it on her lips.

"Hey, Red." I wink at her and then lean forward a little to kiss her. I taste the minty sweetness of her toothpaste as her arms come around my neck.

Our kiss goes from a greeting to a prelude and before I know it, she's on the counter, her top up around her neck and her hard pebble sized nipple in my mouth. She is starting to unbutton my jeans when her landline starts to ring.

Her hands still, and I release her nipple with a pop to look up at her. She is staring at the phone with trepidation.

"You okay? You need to get that?" I ask her. She just nods and hops down, pulling her shirt down as she walks to the other side of the kitchen island where the phone is cradled.

"Only my mother, sisters, and the FBI call this phone," she says without turning around.

She looks at the caller ID before she picks up the phone and a frown settles between her eyes. She clears her throat before answering it.

"Hi, Agent Walker." Her voice is civil, but devoid of all warmth. She listens for a second and then reaches into the drawer below the counter, pulls out a pen and notepad, and begins to write. She bites her lip as she writes, her brows drawn together in concentration.

After a few minutes, she finally speaks. "Yes. I understand. I'll contact my sisters and talk to them."

She listens for a few more minutes. "I understand." And then she hangs up. She returns the phone to its cradle slowly and then turns around to face me. She jumps slightly when she sees me, as if she forgot I was here. The look on her face is haunted.

She turns back around hiding her expression.

I walk over to her and put my hands on her shoulders, she relaxes and leans back into me, her head lolling on my chest.

"Red, come on. What's going on?" I speak gently, knowing that whatever conversation she just had unsettled her.

She lets out a long exhalation of air and turns around in my arms.

"That was the FBI. We have been in constant contact since my dad's disappearance. They check in on us, we have to report to them every time we leave the country. They monitor our contact with each other. They are so overbearing. But recently, they got a credible break in their efforts to locate my dad." She sighs and pulls out of my arms.

She looks annoyed and sad. She told me last night about her list, the one she made after her husband left, and that exonerating her father is one of the things on it. And while I don't think he had anything to do with my dad's death, he did disappear with a lot of money. I have no clue how he can come back and be redeemed.

"Okay, so what do they want from you guys?" I ask, prompting gently but impatient to hear where this is going.

"They want us to try another appeal, but honestly, I don't think it will work. If all he needed was us as a reason, he would have come home on his own years ago."

I look at her and think carefully how to phrase my next question. It's been a question I've had since they disappeared.

I walk us over to the center island and have her take a seat on one of the dark brown leather barstools that line it. I sit in the one next to her and swivel so we are facing each other. I look her dead in the eye, making sure my sincerity shows, but that I am also conveying my concern.

"What do you think happened?" Her question startles me.

"I don't know."

"Well, do you have a theory? Do you think your dad had anything to do with the money disappearing?"

"No. He wouldn't have drained the company. It was his baby."

She doesn't stop pacing, but she turns to look at me. "I don't understand something. Your mom, when I called, said a lot of things. I know now that as far as you were concerned they weren't true. But there was real venom in her voice. Her anger at my father, at me, it was real. So why was *she* so convinced he had done something wrong if you weren't?"

I sigh and glance at my watch. It's a few minutes shy of nine a.m. and my flight is at noon. I have time. And I'm going to tell her now.

"She needed an outlet for her venom. But I don't think she was ever really sorry he was dead. She moved on really fast and said she wanted to forget that other life. We never talk about him."

She stops pacing. "Really?" She looks horrified.

"He was going to leave her." I say it aloud for the first time. I've never even told Val.

She comes to sit next to me. "Did she know?"

"I don't think so. I think that the worst part of him dying was that he finally had plans for the future that were all about him. And when he was gone, I lost my one loving parent. I miss him so much every day," I admit.

Milly rushes over to the island and climbs into my lap. She puts her arms around me and rubs my shoulders. She doesn't say anything, just gives me the contact I need. I'm so fucking lucky.

It's only when Milly's lips touch my cheek that I feel the moisture there. I didn't even realize I had started to cry. I've never told anyone the entire story before.

"After he died, I was in a very dark place. When I realized you were gone, I flipped a switch on that part of my life and focused on honoring my dad's memory and make something out of my life."

Milly wraps her arms around me and buries her face into my neck. "Oh, God. I'm sorry you went through this alone. So sorry, D. That you lost your dad and thought you'd lost me, too."

She leans back and kisses me. "You're not alone anymore. We found each other again."

"I know, Red, and I'm okay. Really. It's good to get this out."

I kiss her temple and we sit there holding each other. I feel the energy, the one that has always existed between us flowing. The *connection* which tied me to this woman from the first time we talked. I know her heart and if I don't let pride and fear get in the way, I can always see it very clearly. And I know she doesn't want to go back to the conversation about her father. But we must.

"We need to dig into this thing with your dad a bit more because I have a theory," I say, breaking the comfortable silence we've found ourselves in.

"Of course, you do. Go ahead, tell me," she says with a bit of her dry humor coloring her voice.

"I don't think your dad disappearing had anything to do with the company's collapse."

She stiffens. "What do you mean? What else could it have been?"

"His leaving doesn't make sense and when things don't make sense it's usually because there is another explanation. I don't know what it is yet. But I think we should try to find out."

"We should?" she asks in a voice as skeptical as I've ever heard it.

"Yes, but we have to talk about it more later. I suggest we start with your mom." My phone alerts me to an incoming text and I stand up, sliding her off my lap, I reach into my pocket and pull it out.

"It's my driver. He's outside." I look back at her, hating that I'm leaving in the middle of this conversation. Hating that I have to leave at all. "I'm sorry to leave you right now, but I'll call you tonight when I get to my hotel."

"No, it's okay. My mom should be back in a couple of hours, and I've got a lot to do. And I need to let Val know we're full steam ahead." She smiles and pecks me on the lips. She winks and saunters out of the room. I watch her go. Her ass looks so sweet in that skirt. I hope this week sails by so I can get back to her.

proud of me, too

ONE OF THE casualties of my hyper focus on my marriage has been relationships with people who are not members of my family. But Zenobia changed all of that.

She started out as an employee, but quickly turned into a friend. Her husband was a cardiologist who worked all the time, and her son was a year younger than Anthony. A few months after she started working for me, we bumped into each other at the trampoline park near my house.

Our boys enjoyed playing together and we started having playdates. Our friendship has grown to be a deep and meaningful one that I cherish. And our Sundays at the trampoline park have morphed into full-day visits that include dinner, a movie, and if the boys behave themselves, sometimes we work on our events.

"They've only got eyes for Moana. That gives *us*…" she glances at her watch. " Ninety minutes to talk like adults." She climbs on the couch next to me and tucks her legs underneath her body and props a pillow up behind her and makes a show of getting comfortable.

"Okay, I'm ready. Tell me everything."

"Zen…I don't even know where to start," I admit, my smile so wide my cheeks hurt. I hug my knees to my chest and sigh.

She leans back, grinning wide. "Wow. You're fucking blushing and glowing. Is this, Dean?"

I nod. "I'm in love again. Or…more like, my love has a home again, or something…"

Her eyes widen in surprise. "Already? His dick must be amazing."

I roll my eyes. "I'm not talking about that…It's between us. But, I can tell you *he* is amazing. I can't believe I get a second chance at this and I've never been happier."

She squeals when I'm done. "Oh, my God. That is amazing. Maybe I need to leave my husband and find an ex." She giggles as she looks at me, her warm brown eyes sparkling with delight.

"Except you're obsessed with your husband and hate all of your exes."

She bites her lip, but she can't contain the smile that spreads on her face. "Yeah, I mean, we could make more of an effort, but I know he loves me."

She grabs my hand. "I'm so happy for you. I mean, I know it's happening fast, and you're cautious, but I think if you have a chance to be with someone who makes you look like that, you should go for it."

I let the giddiness I've been tamping down rise for the first time. I was afraid she'd say I was crazy to be talking like this. That she's encouraging makes me feel like this could actually be real. "We have a lot to work through, but he is *it*, Zen."

"Life is short. And if nothing else, this is your chance to make up for over a decade of orgasm deficient sex."

I look around to make sure the boys are out of earshot.

"I *know!*" I squeal back. And then I sober up a bit.

"Oh! I meant to tell you, I heard back from The Blue Lassos and they're free on the night of the party."

I clap my hands together and beam at her. "Thank the *Lord.*

Oh, this is going to be amazing. Thank you for not letting up on that."

She nods with a proud smile lighting up her face. "Like a dog with a bone. We're going to knock their socks off and make everyone who dumped us jealous AF."

I laugh, tickled by the pettiness and the truth of her words.

"I'm proud of you, Milly."

"Why? I haven't done anything." I try to wave her words away, but she takes my hand and squeezes it tight. Her eyes grow solemn and glisten with unshed tears.

"It's not easy to fall on your face in front of the whole world and get back up and keep moving. You've gone through a lot, been down. You could have stayed there, but you didn't. Being a single mom isn't easy. Dealing with life changes isn't easy. But you're doing it."

I'm too choked up with tears to respond. I squeeze her hand back and mouth, "Thank you."

She gives me an encouraging smile and I return it. We turn to watch our kids and I let my mind stay in the moment we just shared. I'm proud of myself, too. I had to claw my way here, but I'm stronger for it. I feel like anything was possible. I know I'm capable of more.

I *like* the feeling. And now that I have it back, I won't ever let it stray so far from me again.

sixteen years earlier

price of a kiss.

"HEY, MILLY." I look up and smile at the burly lacrosse player walking out of the locker room.

"Hey, can you tell Dean I'm here? He's not answering his phone."

He smiles, but his eyes narrow in confusion. "Uh..." He glances over his shoulder. "Dean's not in there...He wasn't at practice either."

"Hmmm, okay..." I look up at the clock over the door. We were supposed to meet before his game. It's our tradition to do a two person huddle. He said it helped him find his calm and focus. I loved the chance to be with him before he got on the field and I had to share him with everyone else.

He was a crowd-favorite on the lacrosse field. Fast, tireless, and graceful with quads that understood the assignment.

I walked away from our usual meeting place, dejected and confused. I call Dean twice more, but stop when it keeps going to voicemail. I see Dean's car as soon as I reach the student parking lot. It's where it was this morning, right next to mine.

I approached the flashy three series and shrug my backpack off one shoulder so I can unzip it. I pull out a pen and my notebook and start scribbling a note to leave on his windshield. As I get closer, I can see his silhouette inside the dark car. His forehead rests on the steering wheel, his shoulders hunched and my stomach tightens with worry.

I rap on his window and his head whips up. A second later, the doors unlock and I open the door and climb into the passenger seat. "Hey. What gives? I've been waiting for you for almost twenty minutes. And you're about to miss your own . . ."

He hits the overhead lights and my words trail as soon as I see his face. He's not crying, but he looks like he wants to. My annoyance disappears and is replaced by alarm. I lean across the center console right away and put my arms around him.

"D, what's wrong? What happened?" I ask him urgently, trying to keep the level of unease I'm feeling out of my voice.

He looks at me, his eyes full of hurt that tugs at my heart. I stroke his face and push the hair back from his forehead.

"Red. I knew you'd find me," he says, his voice breaking. He puts his head in my neck and hugs me to him tightly. He doesn't make a sound but his tears wet my neck and his shoulders shake.

I feel so helpless. I want to ask him what's wrong, but I wait and let him get out whatever he needs to.

After a few minutes, he pulls away and drags his arms across his face.

My arms feel empty without him in them but I let him have his space as he takes deep breaths to compose himself.

"Oh, shit. Red, I'm sorry. I... didn't mean to dump on you like that." His voice is strained with the effort keeping it steady.

"D, why are you sorry? I'm not. I'm just glad I found you. What happened?"

He leans back in his seat, exhales a long breath, and closes his eyes.

I stroke the side of his neck. "It's okay if you can't talk yet."

"No, I can talk. I need to." He expels a short, mirthless chuckle. "I mean...I've always known my mother doesn't give a shit about me as long as I stay out of her way. She's never made that a secret. I've gotten used to it." His voice is remarkably devoid of emotion.

My blood steams at his words. I hate that she has the power to make him feel this way. "Did something happen tonight?"

"She got rid of Spider," he says, and I can't catch my gasp of horror before it's out.

"No." I clamp a hand over my mouth.

Spider is the English Cocker Spaniel his father surprised him with on his birthday last week. And in that week, Dean had fallen head over heels for that dog. And she knew it.

"How? Why?" I ask, unable to form a coherent sentence.

He opens his eyes and looks at me, his expression mournful and defeated.

"She said he barked at her this morning and scared her. But it could have been anything. She doesn't want me to have anything that makes me happy." He sounds so glum and broken my own heart breaks for him. He leans forward and puts his head on the steering wheel.

"Am I unlovable? I mean, if my own mother doesn't love me, how could anyone else?" I can tell even though this is the first time he's asked me this aloud, it's a question he has pondered seriously.

I'm shocked this boy who is so giving, talented, and funny could even think this.

"Of course, you're not unlovable," I say to him, the vehemence in my voice causes him to glance up at me. His eyes, normally so white and clear, are bloodshot with his tears. He shakes his head in disagreement.

"How do you know? I mean, you can't know that . . ." He puts his head back on the steering wheel and closes his eyes.

Watching him, knowing how badly he needs someone to be strong for him, I decide to put my fear aside and be that someone for him. If there has ever been a moment for me to have the courage of my convictions, it's now.

I lean over the console and put my lips to his ear and whisper, "I do know, Dean. I know because I love you. I love you so much. You're the best friend I've ever had, and you're an incredible person."

He goes still, his eyes, full of agony a second ago, are now full of hope when he turns his head to look at me.

"You love me?" He says each word slowly, like he has to think about each one before he can utter it.

I nod. My heart in my throat. I thought when I told him how I felt, I would feel vulnerable and scared. Instead, I feel free. The way he's looking at me, with so much hope and the beginnings of happiness in his eyes, makes me feel like right now anything is possible.

His hand comes up and strokes my cheek with the back of it. His fingers sweep across my forehead and then dive into my hair.

He places a kiss on my forehead and my eyes fall closed at the contact.

"Dean . . ." It's a plea. I'm asking him to kiss me, and he doesn't make me wait.

He tilts my head slightly, rubs his nose down the side of mine and then his lips touch mine, soft, and sure. Right then, in this moment, I know for certain, this is my person. That we have something special and are meant to be. I've been kissed before. But nothing has ever felt like this. The touch of his lips does just what I thought it would. It sends my heart into a complete free fall.

"Dean?" I say his name when he pulls back a little. I want to get this thought out before I'm too far gone to think straight.

"Yes?" he responds as he drops kisses on my cheeks.

"That kiss—it wasn't free. It will cost you," I whisper, eyes open and locked on his.

"What's the price?" he asks, drawing back slightly. His eyes are like a force field, they hold me in my place, forcing me to be totally honest.

I put my palm on his chest, over his heart. "I want your heart . . . and I want it forever."

He doesn't miss a beat. "It's yours, Red. It has been for a long time. I love you, too."

He leans forward and my eyes close as his lips take mine again. This time it's not just a quick press. His lips lock with mine in a dance that seems to be timed to the beating of my heart.

When his tongue sweeps my bottom lip and my mouth opens for him, our breaths mingle and I could live on that air for the rest of the night. With one kiss, his capture of my very soul is complete and final.

This is us. And always will be.

present day

loud and clear

I STARE at the screen of my phone, where my mother flashes over and over again.

I was having a good day, too.

"Dean, it's your mother," she says as soon as I answer.

"Yeah, I know. What can I do for you?"

"I swear, you treat me like a stranger. I'm *fine*, Dean. Thank you for asking."

I'm not a good son.

I'm not proud of it, but it doesn't keep me awake at night, either.

She's been using me as her personal pin cushion for so long, I've stopped feeling the pricks. But over time, they've shredded that nearly innate boyish affection I used to feel for her and left gaping holes held together by an obligation borne of our biological connection.

"Glad you're fine. But," I glance at my watch. It's only 9:30 a.m. here so that means it's 8:30 a.m. where she is.

I can't remember a single day when she was awake before 10 a.m. when I was growing up. It was my father who got me ready for school until I could do it by myself. "Isn't it a little early for you?"

"Yes. But your fiancée called me this morning in quite a state. She says you've broken off the engagement."

I laugh more with disbelief than humor. "You've never even met her before. Why do you care?"

"What do you mean?" Her voice rises an octave with her indignation. "I'm your mother, of course I care."

"You've got an odd way of showing it."

"Don't we all?" she retorts. "Why did you end your engagement?"

"What did she tell you?"

"She said you told her that you don't love her."

I sigh, not hiding my impatience. "I don't. She shouldn't have called you."

"I'm glad she did. I've decided to come and see you." She's the only person I know that can make something like that sound threatening.

"See me where?"

"In Houston."

"I'm on my way back to New York." My heart gives a thud at the thought of being back in that city with her.

"When will you get back?"

"It's not a good time. And I don't know how much longer I'll be there. All depends on the house. Do you have the code?"

"I'd like to come now. Help you and Nicola patch things up," she goes on as if she didn't hear me.

I swallow a growl of impatience. She's the very last person on this planet I'd go to for relationship advice. *If* I needed it. "There's nothing to patch up. My mind is made up and I've already moved on."

"You're being impulsive. She's good for you."

"You don't know what's good for me. You barely know me at all."

"I'm your mother. I know you better than anyone. I created

you with my body. I know you down to the molecule. No one could know you better. I know I haven't been a loving mother, but it doesn't mean I don't love you."

I wasn't prepared for those words. She hasn't said them to me in so long and it's like a drop of water on a dry patch of grass - just enough to remind me how parched parts of my heart are, but not enough to make a bit of difference.

"Mom, I'm sure you mean well." I'm not sure at all. "But this is a dead-end conversation."

She sighs dramatically. "Fine. I don't really want to come to Houston anyway. Why don't you take a couple of weeks to cool off and then the two of you can come down to Sedona for a nice long weekend before Jean-Luc leaves for Marseille."

"I don't need to cool off and the only place Nicola and I are going is in opposite directions."

There's a beat of silence. Long enough that I think she's run out of steam. "If that's all. I've got a fli-"

"She told me about the wedding planner." Her quiet declaration has the desired effect - my heart leaps into a wild gallop and blood rushes in my ears so loud I can't think.

Fuck.

The mere *mention* of Milly used to be a hairpin trigger for my mother. It had been a long time since she'd come up in conversation. I thought the years had mellowed the irrational and disproportionate anger she felt toward her. But I can hear from the steely cold of her voice that her feelings haven't changed and are very close to the surface.

"Is *she* why you ended things?" Her voice is grave with warning.

This is a minefield conversation that I need to navigate carefully. My mother's got a vindictive streak and she used to speak of making the Hassans pay with anticipation that made me glad we didn't know where they were.

"No, she's not. I was going to do it before we came to Houston. I don't love or trust Nicola."

"She's married and has a *child*, Dean," she says, disregarding my answer completely. "And her father is the reason *yours* is dead."

I bristle and dread makes my stomach feel like I've swallowed lead. She's lucky I'm a patient man. "That's not true. And you know it. Milly's not her father. She was a kid, just like I was."

"She disappeared and never looked back, and you're still defending her?"

I haven't told her I know the truth because I couldn't without also telling her that Milly and I were back in touch. "Thank you for your concern about Nicola and me. It's misplaced."

She chuckles softly. "Oh Dean," she drawls. "You're so much like your father." Her taunt hits its mark but I won't ever give her the satisfaction of knowing it.

"And you're so much like yourself. I've got to run." I hang up.

God, I hate how easy it is for her to get under my skin. I put my phone away and close my eyes for the rest of the ride to the airport.

My phone rings again and I answer it with a terse, "What do you need?"

"Dean, it's me."

My head starts to pound. This day is going from bad to worse. "What do you need, Nic?"

"I wish you wouldn't be this way. I don't know how else to say. I'm sorry," she whines. I can't believe I used to like the sound of her voice.

"You've said it, I've heard you, and I forgive you. But it doesn't change the fact that I don't want to spend the rest of my life with you."

"Dean, please, I know you're still angry. You have more money than you know what to do with. Why do you care so much about how I spend it?" She continues whining in my ear.

My good mood has completely evaporated. Conversations with Nicola drag me back to a place I don't ever want to be again.

I sigh, long and loud. "This is the *same* conversation we've had for months."

I have to go back to New York this week for a couple of meetings, but I don't intend to see Nicola. I've found it remarkable how quickly I got over her once I saw her for who she really is.

"I don't care how much you spent. I don't care about anything other than you getting ready to move out when the lease is up in three months," I grind out.

We're pulling up at the departure terminal and I'm eager to end this call.

"Well, that's actually what I'm calling about. I need a little more time. Work hasn't been steady—"

"You have three months. I'm not responsible for your living situation. Figure it out. I've been fair and let you stay there without having to pay a dime of rent. I paid off all the credit cards and lines of credit you opened. If you can't get a job acting, then think of something else. That's what regular people do."

"How can you do this to me?" she wails so loudly I have to pull the phone away from my ear.

"Do what, exactly? Give you a free place to stay? Not call the police when you essentially stole from me and pay for all the shit you bought with that stolen money? Is that what you mean?" I return.

Greg opens my door, my carry-on in his hand. I'm done with this conversation.

"I'm at the airport. I have to go. Don't call me unless it's to let me know you've turned over the keys and are moving out. You have until June." I don't wait for her response and hang up.

I step out of the car and take a big gulp of the cool, spring evening air. It feels cleansing after my conversation with Nicola.

I walk toward the terminal, eager to get to New York. I want to get through this round of meetings and then get back to Houston and Milly and her little guy.

I can't believe my luck. Milly's given me another chance. She still loves me. She's wearing my ring around her neck. It's crazy early, but I want to put another one on her hand. I don't want to take any chances that I'll lose her again. It is crazy and she's not an object to be won or lost.

We've lost so many years. But I know that I've got to find a way to reconcile her and my mother because there's no escaping the fact that she's part of my life. But I can't have them in an endless war.

My gut twists at the thought. My mother and I barely speak and I know she'd make Milly walk over glass to atone for her perceived sins before she'd ever let us live in peace.

Finding out what really happened to my father and Milly's would go a long way to mending the rift between them. But the only thing that would do that would require us to go back in time and rewrite history.

unbothered

"WHEN IS this going to be over?"

The loud whisper came from Rachael. She's sitting in the row behind me, next to Kevin, at Anthony's school Easter program.

I roll my eyes and only my mother's warning squeeze on my thigh stops me from turning around to tell her to shut up.

This is my first real event at Anthony's school since Kevin and I split. I was hoping an evening free of any drama would show them I was still the same old boring Milly. This is Anthony's second year at this school and this is only the second time Kevin has bothered to attend any of his performances. It makes my stomach sour that what should be an evening of pride and happiness is something he'd use in his bid to gain custody of Kevin.

Anthony's class is up next and I keep my attention on the stage and ignore her griping.

When his class comes out, Anthony scans the crowd for me and when we make eye contact he gives me a huge grin and a thumbs-up. He's the spitting image of my father when he smiles and it tugs at my heart to think of him missing all of this.

The music cues and I want to cry with pride as he takes his place on stage and starts to sing.

The performance is a perfect disaster as only school programs can be. I stood up when he started so that I could get a better view to videotape the performance.

When he's done, he jumps off the stage and comes running toward me. I barely have time to open my arms before he's hurling himself into them.

"Mommy, I was awesome!" He grins up at me, his eyes sparkling.

"Yes, little man, you were." I kiss his head and see my mother coming to join us.

"Nana, did you see me?" he shouts as he wriggles out of my hold to go to my mother. They hug and she teases, "No, I didn't see you! Were you on the stage?"

"Nana! I was! I was right there!" He points to where he was standing and looking like he can't believe what he's hearing.

Just then, Kevin and Rachael walk over.

"Anthony. Good job, son," Kevin says, his voice full of genuine warmth and happiness.

"Daddy!" Anthony sprints to his father, and I feel a pang of sadness in my chest for him. He loves his father more than he loves almost anyone and seeing him is something he relishes, especially now that it's so infrequent.

I'm surprised Kevin is here. But I'm glad. I hate for him to miss these moments because we're raising Anthony in two separate households. I can't believe this is my life. I can't believe I'm watching the man I used to think would be mine forever hug my son with one arm while holding another woman's hand with the other.

"Kevin. Hello," my mother says with a tone as cold as ice.

Kevin has always loved my mother. She treated him like her own son and since his parents are both deceased, he loved the attention she lavished on him.

"Good evening, Mary." He lets go of Rachael's hand and can't quite meet my mother's eye.

"I would ask how you are, but I can see you're doing just fine," she says, again her tone clipped. She turns her gaze to Rachael but doesn't address her.

"We're going home, Kevin. It's a school night and it's late," I say, trying to end this encounter.

"Well, I was hoping I . . ." Rachael jabs him in the ribs. "I mean we could take Anthony out to dinner to congratulate him," Kevin stammers, not looking at me.

I want to slap him. I feel people watching us as they congregate in their own little family clusters. I want to get out of there.

How dare he even propose such an idiotic thing? "It's Thursday. It's seven p.m. and he is seven years old. He's already had dinner, and now, he is going home to take a bath and go to bed," I respond as calmly as I can.

"I told you she'd say no," Rachael whines loudly.

I kneel down in front of Anthony who is watching our exchange with big, anxious eyes.

"Honey, say good night to Daddy, okay?" He nods at me and walks over to give his dad a hug. I lock eyes with Kevin, but speak to my mother.

"Mom, can you please take Anthony home with you? I just want to say good night to his teacher."

Without a word, my mother takes Anthony's hand and walks him out, saying something to him just as they reach the door that makes him laugh.

I watch them walk out and as soon as I see that they have left the room, I turn back to Kevin.

"That was really low. I'm not sure whose idea this was, but don't use our son as a pawn in your games."

He gives me a pained look. "I just want to spend some time with him."

"Then take him to the park on the weekend, come read to

him before he goes to bed, but you don't take a seven year old out to dinner on a weeknight," I hiss.

"You can't tell him what to do," Rachael interjects, loud enough that the remaining people in the gym all turn to look at us.

"Lower your voice. This is where Anthony goes to school every day. Do not come here and embarrass him *and* me because you didn't get your way." My voice is low but angry.

I look at Kevin not bothering to disguise the hurt in my eyes. "I don't even know who you are anymore."

I turn and walk out of the school's assembly hall feeling a dozen pairs of eyes on me as I try to walk out with as much dignity as I can.

Just as I get outside my phone rings and a number I don't recognize comes up. I let it go to voicemail and get into my car.

I'm beyond humiliated. I don't want Kevin back and after my night with Dean, I know that at the very least, our sex life was completely lacking. Yet, to see he has moved on, that he's with someone else hurts. To think this vile person will have access to my son makes me feel like burning something down.

I push the button to start my car to begin the short drive home. Almost as soon as I get ready to put the car in drive my phone rings again. I look at the clock on the dash and it's almost seven p.m., the time Dean calls, my mood lifts as I answer.

"Dean?"

"Hello?" And just like that my buzz is gone. It's Kevin. "Yes, Kevin?"

"Who's Dean?" he snaps.

"None of your business. What could you *possibly* want?" I snap back.

He's silent for a beat, as if deciding whether to pursue this line of argument, but then he says in a tone that is rushed and quiet, "Look, I just wanted to apologize. Rachael said she wanted to try and get to know Anthony, I wasn't thinking about it being a school night."

"Fine," I say with a calm I'm not really feeling. "Fine? That's it?"

"You've called, you told me why you did what you did. What else should I say?"

"Shit. You're such a bitch," he snarls. And then he hangs up.

"Takes one to know one," I mutter to myself.

I'm turning into our driveway now. As I pull into the garage, I just sit there contemplating the evening and the state of my life in general.

I sigh and my forehead hits the steering wheel. I start thinking about Kevin and decide that I'd rather not. Stunts like the one he pulled tonight make me worry that our relationship is only going to get more acrimonious.

I pull my phone out and open my voicemails. That missed call was Dean, and it is the most pleasant of surprises when his voice floods my car's speakers.

"Hey, Red. It's me. I miss you." I can hear the longing in his voice and my heart and thighs clench in unison. "It's been such a busy week, but I'll be back tomorrow. Can I take you to dinner? I was thinking Claudia's again, since that seems to be our place. Wear your hair up, so I can take it down. I miss you. Call me."

I listen to it, on a repeat loop for five minutes before I get out of my car and go put my son to sleep.

try me

MY CAR PULLS UP outside my Greenwich Street office. I'm in a rush to get done with my day and hop out before Greg can open the door for me.

I stride into the lobby and swear under my breath, but keep moving when I see Nicola is sitting in the reception area waiting for me.

This is the last thing I need.

She hops out of the seat and speed walks over to stand right in front of me and stops me short.

She's smiling like we are best friends rather than exes who parted under very acrimonious circumstances.

"What's going on? I have a busy morning," I say before she has a chance to speak. I want her to hear the impatience in my voice and know I'm not in the mood.

Her eyes flash with hurt, but she's a terrible actress and I know she's faking it.

I roll my eyes and sigh. "Cut the shit and say whatever you've got to say."

"Wow, Dean. A few months ago you were prepared to spend the rest of your life with me, and now you're acting like I'm a

185

fucking door-to-door salesman trying to sell you new windows," she says angrily, dropping the pretense of hurt.

"As far as I'm concerned, you might as well be a door-to-door salesman," I drawl back.

She gasps and this time her anger isn't feigned. "Fuck you."

"Ah, there you are. You've got about forty-five seconds to tell me what you want before I get on the elevator."

"Fine, I need money. I know you don't want to give me any, but you owe me. I talked to a lawyer; I could sue you for emotional distress. So, if you don't want a big mess, just give me what I need, and I'll go away."

This woman is incredible. I actually thought she couldn't be any worse than she already showed me. But she has proven me wrong.

"Sue me. Go ahead. I'm late for a meeting."

Her eyes widen, and her mouth opens and shuts, making her look like a fish. I shake my head at her in disgust and start to turn away.

She grabs my arm to stop me, her nails digging through the fabric of my suit jacket.

I look at her closely. She's a beautiful woman, probably what a lot of people would consider stunning. Blonde, blue eyes, flawless skin, incredible figure, ridiculously talented in bed. But that's where her beauty stops.

I snatch my arm away. I don't want her contaminating the good Milly's touch has left on me. Her touch feels like a taint, and I don't want it anywhere near me.

"How can you do this to me?" she wails.

"You came here to blackmail me. I called your bluff. Let's see what happens." I don't have to feign my boredom at this point.

"I know you're seeing someone. If you don't stop this, I'll move on and never take you back."

I'm too shocked to hold back my laughter. Fucking tabloids. "You think I'll come back to you? Nicola, move on. I'm in love with someone. I'm moving to Houston and I'm selling the condo."

She steps back, aghast, her tan skin suddenly pale. "What?"

"You have until June to find a place. If you want to try suing me for whatever fantasy some lawyer put into your head, go ahead. I'm late."

I turn and walk toward the elevator. When I step in one and turn to push the button for my floor, I see her walking hurriedly toward the entrance of the building. I hope it's the last I see of her.

milly

date night

I SPENT the morning working on a presentation and then spent the afternoon at Anthony's school volunteering in the library. I tried to be more engaging than I normally am, but all this led to was me fielding about half a dozen "sympathetic" questions about Kevin and the woman he brought with him last night.

"She looked *so* young."

"I don't know how you managed to sit through that entire performance with your husband and his *girlfriend* right behind you."

"They must be serious if he brought her *here*."

They all look at me with sympathetic smiles. I return it with one of my own. "Honestly, I'm too busy getting my back blown out to care."

My mother always says that misery loves company. I declined the invitation to their party and I left there feeling pleased with myself, but also hoping I wasn't counting my chickens before they hatched. I'm terrified of how much I feel and how quickly. But… I'm not afraid of heartbreak anymore. If it happens, I'll either going to crumble or stand up straight. Right now, I'd take odds on the latter.

For the first time in ten years, I'm thinking about a future that is based on what *I* want and not feeling guilty for it.

My business is thriving. My son is watching his mother prove that she can do anything she puts her mind to and therefore, he can, too.

And…I've got a date tonight. With a gorgeous, blond Adonis who I had *sex* with last week.

Who loves me.

Who waited for me.

Who never gave up on us.

I shiver in anticipation of tonight.

I can't wait to see him. I'm not sure if it's him or if it's my newfound freedom, but I feel like breaking more rules. I want to shock myself tonight.

When my mom got back from New Orleans, she peppered me with questions about his stay. I tried to be as vague as possible because even though I'm certain of his feelings for me—everything feels so new.

She dropped it, but I know she only gave me a temporary reprieve. She's with Anthony, and I can hear them roaring with laughter in his bedroom as I start to take off my clothes to get ready to shower.

My phone rings just as I turn the water on, and I see it's my sister, Addie. She's in London, basking in the glow of young and happy love. She doesn't know about Kevin and me. I haven't told my sisters yet. I don't know why, but I just can't. It might be a matter of pride, but I know deep down they always thought it was silly of me to get married so young. I also think that Lilly, in particular, never liked him very much. I've sworn my mother to secrecy for now. I'll tell them when I'm ready.

"Hey, Ad!" I answer brightly.

"Hi, sis," she responds in a flat monotone voice.

"Oh, babe. You sound so glum." I wish I could wrap my arms around her.

"I am. I'm miserable. It's cold. I'm hungry," she whines.

Addie isn't a whiner. Unless she's talking to me. Then she reverts to the little sister who whines and wants me to pick her up and put her in bed with me.

"Addie, the only two things you can do anything about are hunger and misery. Go and get something to eat and call Simon."

"I can't call Simon. He's busy. You're always free. So, I'm calling you instead. And yeah, I'll go and get something to eat. I didn't call to talk about me. I just wanted to say hi. How are you guys?"

"Fine." It comes out in a high-pitched squeak that sounds ridiculous.

"Okay . . . well, can I talk to Anthony or is he already in bed? I miss him. I should come visit soon. During his summer break?"

That sends a course of panic through my body. I'm not ready for her or anyone to come visit, yet.

"We'll come see you. Anthony loves flying," I say hurriedly, trying to dissuade her from making plans to come here.

"Okay, whatever. I just need some Anthony time. Soon." She doesn't sound convinced and I know I need to end the call.

"Hey, I'm getting in the shower. Go eat."

"Why are you showering? It's like six thirty. Did you and Kevin just fuck?" She snickers.

"You are so crass, Adelaide. I have to go. Go eat," I snap.

And without giving her a chance to say anything else, I hang up. I can't help but laugh as I get in the shower.

If only she knew.

finger licking good

MILLY WALKS into Claudia's ten minutes past seven. And the minute I see her, I forget about the time. Milly knows how to make an entrance.

She is wearing a red dress, its only closure a zipper that runs from top to bottom in the front. It fits her like a second skin. It is long sleeved and hits her right below her knee.

She turns around to say something to the hostess, and I get a view of her back. There is a wide, exposed zipper that is open from the middle of her shoulders up. It is so tight she couldn't possibly be wearing any underwear beneath it.

My mouth waters as I think about her immaculately groomed pussy. The deep V in the front of the dress lets me see she's wearing the chain with that pendant and my ring hanging from it.

She strides toward the table where I'm sitting, her eyes never leaving mine. Her hair, rather than being up as I requested, has been blown into pin straight strands which shimmer with every step she takes.

She looks like Hera descending Mount Olympus. She's more beautiful than Helen of Troy, and I would be willing to battle an entire nation for her. And unlike that poor schmuck Paris, I would fucking *win*.

I stand as she approaches our table and walk toward her. The restaurant is crowded. The bar is standing room only and between the background music and the conversation, it's loud.

Yet, as I cut through the crowd and tables that are separating us, our eyes never leave each other, she's the only person I notice.

"Red, you're beautiful," is all I say before I lay my lips on her and kiss her. It's not a deep kiss, but it's demanding and hungry. She leans into me, her scent—roses—is intoxicating.

She moans when I pull my lips away. Her eyes are hooded. And I remember the Milly who had always thought public displays of affection to be tacky. But tonight, right now, it's obvious she doesn't care.

Our eyes hold and I smile down at her. "Come. Let's sit down and eat."

I take her hand and lead her back to our table. It is away from the crowded bar area, and more of a booth than a table. I let her slide in first and then sit down next to her.

Our waitress appears and she orders a glass of white wine, while I order a whiskey.

"So, how was your week?" She turns so she's facing me. I put my arm around her shoulder, pulling her close to me.

"It was rather ordinary. How was yours?"

"Busy. I had a lot of meetings this week, but my Friday is turning out to be a real winner." She grins.

Her grin is infectious, and I find myself grinning back.

Our drinks arrive at the table and she immediately takes a long sip. And then she looks at me and says, "Tell me about your fiancée."

It's not what I am expecting her to say. I know my expression changes and she must see it, too. Right away I feel the mood at the table shift from lighthearted to tense.

"Never mind. I'm sorry. It was a stupid thing to ask. I didn't mean to ruin the mood," she says quickly before I can respond.

"No, you haven't."

"I'm sorry."

"Why? I want to tell you. I was an asshole. I didn't love her. I should never have asked her to marry me. In the end, it turned out she was just like my mother. With me for my money and status. She was stealing from me. I called it off, but we were trying again. But, I knew before we came to Houston that it was over. I only came because it was you." I glance at her to gauge her level of disgust at how I handled that.

My muscles relax when all I see in her eyes is concern. She squeezes my hand. " I want to kick her ass because she hurt you and kiss her because she also left you free to be with me. How'd she take it? Do you have loose ends to tie up?"

I sigh in relief and shake my head. "She's still living in the place we shared. I've given her a few months to find something else, but that's it."

She smiles and it reaches all the way to her eyes, which are the color of beaten gold in the waning light.

She takes my breath away.

Every single time.

I hold her gaze and return that smile."I was always free to be with you, Red. I've always been yours," I whisper.

She grins at me and winks. And I want dinner to be over so I can get her home and out of that dress.

I try to remember why I asked her to dinner. I want to date her, like we never got the chance to. I wasn't even planning on taking her home tonight. So, I steer my mind back to our date and keep the mood light.

"How long have you been planning events?"

Her face lights up. "Since I had Anthony. I started small, but it's grown in leaps and bounds."

"You love it?"

"Yes. Even though...brides and sometimes their parents can make me forget that."

"You seem really good at handling upset clients."

She rolls her eyes and shakes her head. "I'm the mother of a seven-year-old boy who is very honest in all of his observations. So, believe me when I say, I have a pretty thick skin and I've yet to have a client as ungovernable as a three-year-old child."

I shake my head in wonder. "You're a mom."

"Yes, I am." She smiles at the thought of her son. "Do you want children?" she asks me.

"Yes, of course," I answer quickly. It's something I've always wanted. "Do you want more children?" I ask her in return.

"Yes, so much. Anthony would be a great big brother, and I always wanted a large family."

"Why didn't you have more after Ant Man?" I ask.

"Kevin didn't want more, and honestly, now I'm glad. It would make our custody battle so much more stressful if we had more than one child."

I touch my forehead and wince in apology. "Shit, Red, I haven't even asked how that's going. You've got a good lawyer, right?"

"Yes, I have the best lawyer. And it's going okay, we have a hearing set, but we can't even file for divorce until next year, so we might have to do this again once that is final."

She takes a large gulp of wine, and I can sense her stress.

"You're not worried, right? I mean, you're his mom. You seem like a model citizen—despite your proclivity for wearing dresses that make men want to rip them off your body." I wink at her. "You should be okay."

She laughs at this but says, "I hope so. But, let's talk about something else."

"Fine by me." I pull her closer to me. She seems to welcome the closeness and burrows herself into my side.

"Let's talk about how much I thought about you and your pussy this week."

At that unexpected, but welcome subject change, I feel her relax. She puts a hand on my thigh and says, "Did you?"

"Yes. I've thought about you with your legs spread apart while I eat you 'til you cry and beg me to stop."

I put my hand on her thigh under her dress. I run it slowly up her leg until I get to the middle of her inner thigh, and then I start to knead the flesh there.

She sighs, I can feel the heat coming from her pussy. I know she wants my hands to give her relief.

"Tell me, Red. Tell me what you need," I whisper in her ear.

I look around the restaurant, but no one is paying any attention to our little corner.

She closes her eyes and breathes. "I need you to touch me, Dean."

"No. Don't be a lady with me. I want you to tell me what you want."

Milly doesn't curse. She doesn't even *think* the words I want her to say. But I can tell she wants to . . . I can see the pulse thudding in her throat. that she wants to find that part of herself and explore it.

Her hips are moving in small circular motions in time with my hand on her thigh. She needs release.

"Tell me right now, or I will stop." My voice is rough with need.

"Touch my pussy, Dean. Please, fuck my pussy with your fingers," she whispers, and my hand flies up her leg and does just as she asks. As I suspected, she's not wearing any underwear.

I slip two fingers inside of her and her eyes fly open as they stretch her swollen, sensitive flesh. My thumb presses down on her clitoris and I apply a firm pressure while I start to move my fingers in and out of her.

"Your wish is my command," I whisper in her ear.

She looks at me, her golden gaze locked onto my green one.

Dylan Allen

And it feels like our hearts are the only two still beating in the entire universe. We are completely alone in this crowd.

"This feels so good," she chokes out, and I can tell she wants to say more, but the words won't come. They are trapped in her throat.

"I want you to sit here, baby, with my fingers inside of you. Our waitress is coming to take our order. Can you do that?"

She shakes her head to say no. She's so close, and I know that the idea of her being here while my fingers are inside of her threatens to send her over the edge. This public act is a turn on for her; I can feel her grow even wetter on my fingers.

"If you can't, I'll have to stop," I whisper.

"Don't stop," she whimpers and then bites down on her lip. She plasters a smile on her face as our waitress comes back. She rattles off the specials for the evening, and I know neither of us barely hear a word she says. I tell her I'll have the fish and Milly orders a steak.

Just as she walks away, I start to move my thumb over her clit, watching her face intently. It is a portrait of all of the different shades of pleasure. When I touch a spot that makes her clench around my fingers, I start to rub and in less than fifteen seconds she's coming.

I put my mouth over hers, swallowing her moans as she comes. This time, I kiss her with my tongue, and I can taste the tartness of her wine mingling with the tang of my whiskey.

I pull my fingers out of her as she comes down from her orgasm. I put them under my nose and inhale. She smells so good.

"Divine," I whisper. I pull out my napkin and wipe my fingers clean. "That's just to tide me over until later."

She's clearly stunned at what we've just done in public. She sits back and watches me as I take a sip of my drink, while I watch her in return.

"Red, drink your wine. The night is young."

falling

I'M LEARNING SO MUCH about myself. Apparently, being fondled in public turns me on. I also really like feeling free to be wanton while having a sexual experience. Sex with Kevin was... sex. We did it in bed. At night. He got on top of me, I came and then he got off.

We never made out or flirted beyond this. At least not after our first year or so of dating. And even while we were in a place where we had sex more regularly, we always did it in bed with the lights off.

My experiences with Dean are completely foreign, yet it feels so natural.

We're done eating dinner and sharing a *tres leches* dessert that feels as decadent and sinful as our entire evening.

I realize we never really got to date like this before. We were in high school, dates were movies and doing homework together. And even though we've already made love, and are in love, tonight feels special.

We've talked about everything from politics to religion. We had such different upbringings. He was raised in an agnostic household and called himself spiritual rather than religious. I was raised a devout Methodist. Yet, we had very similar views on issues of morality and ethics.

Dean talks a lot about his passion for seeking out and cultivating talent. Helping people find the right audience and making sure they don't get taken advantage of. He joined the Creative Artists Agency straight out of business school and left after only two years to join Definitive Artists.

"So, Dean. What is your talent?" I ask him, letting him turn my hand over in his. His other hand comes up and starts to draw circles on my open palm.

He looks relaxed and happy.

"Seeing talent," he says simply. "I'm good at knowing what other people are good at. I just need to spend some time with them in their natural habitat, and I can figure it out," he says with such confidence and excitement. I'm so happy he's doing something he loves.

"When you're not working, what do you do?"

"I work out, I read, and I listen to music. I learn the newest dance craze from Kidz Bop," he deadpans.

I laugh out loud. I can't help it. "You can't be serious."

"Oh, I'm dead serious. It's how I know what's going to be hot next. The kids are always ahead of what adults are buying. One day, I'll show you."

And so, our conversation continues. We talk about Dean's love for music, dance, and reading historical biographies. He's reading Alexander Hamilton's right now and tells me a great screenplay is floating around, looking for money to produce for Broadway.

I stifle a yawn and glance at my watch.

"Oh, my goodness, it's almost ten thirty," I exclaim as I glance around the restaurant for the first time in a while. The din is gone. The place is basically deserted, most of the tables have the chairs turned upside down on top of them.

I hadn't noticed anything as Dean and I talked. I was totally absorbed in him and listening to him talk about college in California, business school in Chicago, and then life in New York. The only thing he hasn't talked about is his mother. It's not a subject I want to broach.

"Is it?" Dean says without looking away from me. "Time flies," he says with a slow, sexy smile I feel in between my legs. I swallow hard and take a sip of my water.

"It does. But, I've got to get home. I have to be up early for soccer, and then I've got a ton of errands to run."

I'm trying to sound casual. I wonder whether or not a man like Dean, one who seems to live in a world full of glamor, late nights, and even later mornings, really wants to get involved with someone like me. I live by schedules and my son's schedule always comes first.

"I understand, tonight was nice. It feels like we are getting to date. I like it. What are you doing on Sunday?"

I scan my internal calendar quickly. Kevin's picking up Anthony tomorrow afternoon and he's supposed to spend the night and come back Sunday morning.

"I could see you tomorrow night if you're free," I say, trying not to sound as unsure as I feel. I've never asked a man out; I've never been so forward. But this is Dean, he's already mine in so many ways.

"Yes, I am. I can pick you up. Say around six?" he asks. "Sure. What do you want to do?"

"I want to fuck you, Red," he says immediately and my jaw drops.

"But, I think the question you're asking is 'what are we going to do?'" he murmurs as he leans across the table so that his mouth is close to mine.

"Yes, what are we going to do?" I whisper. I bring my head closer to his, too.

"I want to show you something, I think you'll like it. Dress casually." I feel a shiver of anticipation at the promise in his voice.

He leans forward a fraction and his lips brush mine. My eyes close from the absolute pleasure the touch brings. I lean in and flick my tongue out to lick his lips. His hand comes up to wrap around the nape of my neck and he takes control of our kiss. His tongue enters my mouth, probing, seeking, and then taking.

My hands come up on either side of his face and then dive into his hair and he groans into my mouth as my hands rub his scalp.

Our kiss goes from passionate to wild. Dean's other hand reaches out and he snakes his arm around my waist, pulling me flush against him.

Our teeth are clashing, our lips dueling, and I've never ever even known a kiss could be like this. I feel like I'm being allowed to reach for something spectacular for the first time in my life. I forget everything as we kiss, as we taste, explore, and make promises for later.

And then the crash of plates as they hit the floor brings *me* crashing back down to earth. We are in a restaurant, in public, and if Dean had taken me right here and now I wouldn't have stopped him.

"I can't get enough of you. I can't . . ." Dean says as he pulls back, the sounds of the restaurant pulling him back as well. He looks as dazed as I feel as he glances around.

"How did you get here tonight? Did you drive?" he asks me, still looking around. He seems nervous and it's making me nervous, so I pull myself back from him and start to gather my things.

"No, I took an Uber. I was going to order another to get home," I say as I pull my purse up from the seat.

He looks back at me and grabs my hand that is reaching into my purse. "No, Red. I'll take you home." He smiles, focused on me again, whatever distracted him, clearly forgotten. At least by him, but I'm not exactly comfortable.

"What's wrong, you seem nervous," I say, trying not to sound like I'm annoyed, but wanting him to know I've noticed.

He sighs and leans back in his chair with his eyes closed.

He's very tan. I'm fascinated by him, and as I wait for him to speak, I just look at him. He's pinching the bridge of his nose with his fingers, and I'm struck by how gorgeous his hands are. So long, his fingernails, cut short, but not blunt, almost tapered, and he looks like he should play the piano.

He opens his eyes and those beautiful green pools stare at me for a minute before he starts to speak.

"I'm pretty well-known in entertainment circles. Houston isn't exactly New York or Hollywood, but a lot of TV shows film here now. Celebrities use their platforms for causes they care about which means testifying before Congress. And where celebrities go, so do photographers. I represent some very, very famous people, and I do my best to make sure that I stay out of the spotlight."

Understanding dawns as does some unease. The last thing I want is to be in the spotlight.

"So, making out like a horny teenager in public is probably not the best way to do this. I understand, I got carried away. It's all of the delicious wine you plied me with tonight." I try to lighten the mood with a joke, but I'm suddenly very concerned about getting involved with someone who lives any part of his life in the public eye.

"It's not the wine. It's just the way we make each other feel." He drops a kiss on the tip of my nose and stands up suddenly.

He puts his hand out for me to grab. "Honestly, most of the time no one cares about me. I'd just like to keep it that way. Are you ready?"

"Definitely, yes," I say, and I'm ready. I need to think, and I can't do that when I'm anywhere near this man.

"I think I'll call that Uber. There is really no need for you to make that kind of drive tonight." I start to dig in my purse for my phone.

He stills my movements with a hand laid across my forearm. I look up at him.

"I'm not letting you go home in an Uber." He pulls me to

Dylan Allen

standing and leads me out of the restaurant. "I'm not driving, Greg is."

"Dean, I don't need you to take me home; I don't want you to think you can direct my life. I'm fine," I insist, as I pull my hand out of his grasp.

He stops and blows out a breath.

"I'm not trying to direct your life," he says slowly, like he's trying to be patient. I feel my ire rise. "I just want to make sure you get home safely. Forgive me if I'm not thrilled at the prospect of sticking you in the back of an Elantra driven by a total stranger. I know you're capable of getting yourself home. Would you humor me and my paranoia and let me drive you home?"

I feel slightly ashamed. He was just being nice, and I'm being difficult, but I won't go quietly into the night.

"Thank you. I'd love a ride, but please next time just ask me instead of ordering me."

I turn and walk toward the door. I can feel the weight and the heat of Dean's gaze on my back, and I add an extra twist to my hip with each step, just as I reach the door, I hear him groan.

It makes me smile.

red flags

"IT'S HOT AS HELL. Isn't it still winter?" Val and I step out of the cool air conditioning of Le Peep in Rice Village. It's not even in the morning and the sun is blazing.

"You forgot where you are. It could be forty degrees in the morning and 90 degrees by afternoon. That's why we wear layers."

"Duly noted. Nothing changes." And I'm glad. Le Peep was a favorite of my dad's. He used to meet clients and mentees for breakfast here almost every Saturday and started taking me with him when I was thirteen. Walking in there was like stepping back in time. It felt good to be back.

"Where are you off to?"

"I'm meeting your lady at Venue in the Heights to sign the contract for the event."

I nod in approval. "How's that going?"

"Great. We'll have the invites ordered before the ink is dry and then it's full speed ahead. Milly's a magician."

I smile, proud as hell of her. "Tell her hi." We have a date tonight and I'm stupidly excited to see her reaction to where we're going.

"I will. Where are you going now?"

"Back to my office. I've got calls with Universal's team at Peacock and I've got to prep."

We slap hands and say goodbye. "Thanks for breakfast. It's nice having you close enough to do things like this."

"It is."

"Maybe we'll make a Houstonian out of you, yet."

"Don't get ahead of yourself." But the thought doesn't make me itch like it used to.

"Dean?" I turn in the direction of a voice I recognize and smile when I see it is who I thought.

"Hey, Mr. Holly," I greet him with a warm smile as he approaches my car, smiling wide.

Ed Holly had been my dad's insurance agent and one of his best friends. I hadn't seen him since my dad's funeral.

"Good to see you look so well," I tell him as we shake hands.

He's almost seventy, and other than having a lot less hair than he used to, looks as fit and vital as he'd always been. He'd been a runner like my dad. "Dean, I told you to call me, Ed, son. You are a sight for sore eyes. Even though I do get to see your face in magazines now there's nothing like seeing you in person." He pats my shoulder. "You look so much like your father."

My heart aches but not in a bad way. "I know. I get glimpses of him in the mirror sometimes. How's Mrs. Holly?" She was so kind. She always sent my dad home with something delicious, sweet, and homemade. My mother couldn't stand her.

"Oh, everyone's great. I've got two grandchildren now. I'm going to retire in a couple of years. And I've found an agent I'm grooming to take over my business. Can't leave my clients in a lurch now, can I?" he returned jovially, his accent showing his East Texas roots.

"I think no one could ever take your place so it'll feel like a lurch even if it's not."

He laughs and waves away my compliment. "How's your

mama? She doing okay? I heard she moved to Arizona. I've been keeping up with you online. And I'm glad you're doing so well. It must be a relief to be able to take care of her now," he says while patting my shoulder.

I can't hide my confusion while I say, "She doesn't need me to take care of her. She's got dad's life insurance policy and her rich boy toy. So she didn't have to wait for me to make it big to settle right into her life of retired luxury."

His brow furrows and I can tell that, now, he's confused too. "What life insurance policy? Did he buy one from someone else?"

The hairs on the back of my neck stand up. "No. She said he bought it from you. She showed me the money deposited in her account. It was almost ten million dollars. She said she paid off his debt and paid off the house with it."

He frowns. "I mean, I know she paid off the house, but the only debt they had was hers. You know how your mother liked to shop. But I thought that money came from...I don't know. They didn't buy a policy from me though."

"Ed, do you still have a PI who works for you?"

"Yes, now...if you want me to look into your mama, you might have to hire someone else, I do her estate planning, too."

"Not my mom, her boyfriend, Jean-Luc."

His eyes narrow in understanding. "I'll have him call you."

paint

"YOU'RE WEARING THAT?" Rabea says from her perch on my couch. She's visiting my mother tonight.

Kevin came to pick Anthony up earlier and it was uneventful. Anthony was excited to spend the night with his dad. I'm a nervous wreck, but I hope it will work out. As much as I'm starting to dislike Kevin, I recognize the need for Anthony to have a good relationship with his father. So, I've sent him off with a smile and encouragement that he should have a great time.

"What's wrong with what I'm wearing?" I look down at my black skinny jeans, gray knit top, and some cute but comfortable ankle boots. "He said to dress casually."

"Well, I guess you're not trying to get any tonight then," she says and turns back to whatever she's watching in the living room.

I continue down the stairs, through the living room and into the kitchen where my mother is busy getting something ready for them.

"Oh, Milly, I'm so excited, *The Sound of Music* is on tonight!" She starts talking as I walk in even though her back is to me.

"We're going to eat schnitzel and sauerkraut in honor of the movie. It's almost ready."

She turns around, takes me in, and her smile falls slightly. "Oh. You look . . . nice," she says with a forced cheeriness.

"Oh, my goodness. He said to dress casually!" I throw my hands up and run out of the room. Clearly, my outfit lacks any sort of sex appeal.

I go back up to my bedroom and rip my top off and step into my closet. My mother and Rabea had been so excited when I told them about Dean and even though I've asked them to keep it to themselves for the time being, they are both acting like I'm going to the prom tonight. Rabea's sudden appearance tonight couldn't have been less obvious.

I decide on a camel-colored blouse that ties at the waist with a thin gold belt. I don't want to look like I spent hours working on my outfit.

I'm just fixing my ponytail, which is high and tight, when I hear the doorbell ring.

"Shit!" I grumble. I race downstairs to open the door for him before my mother or Rabea can.

He's early.

I sprint down the stairs. But hear my mother's voice before I'm reach the bottom step. I close my eyes and steel myself for what I will find when I walk into the room.

"It's one of my favorite movies. I usually watch it every Christmas," Dean is saying to my beaming mother as I walk into the room.

They all turn to face me.

"Milly!" my mother exclaims as if she didn't expect to see me.

"Yes, Mother?" I say as I stand here, feeling for a moment like I was intruding. Dean starts toward me then, and once his back is turned to my mother and Rabea, they both smile beamingly at me like Prince Harry just swooped in and asked me to marry him. He places a kiss on my cheek, inhales and says so only I could hear, "Red . . . you smell divine."

I squeezed my thighs together as I remember him using that same word last night at the restaurant. "Hi, Dean." I smile in return.

"Hi, Milly," he says, this time audibly for everyone.

"You remember my mom, Mrs. Dennis," I say dumbly.

He gives me a look that says he thinks I'm crazy and smiles. "Uh, yes, Milly, I do."

"I told him to call me Auntie Mary again," she chimes in, smiling like I just brought her a bottle of her favorite marmalade.

"Okay. And this is . . ."

"Oh, he knows. I'm Rabea," Rabea interjects. She *winks* at Dean and then smiles at me innocently.

"Well, since you've met everyone, I'll just grab my jacket and we can be off." I grab his hand and ignore his grin as I pull him toward the front door.

He stops to look at the pictures that line the wall between the front door and the living room, all of them of Anthony at various stages of his life. Some of them include me. Some include his father. Some include us together. He stops to look at one of the three of us.

"You were a beautiful family," he says, reaching out to stroke the picture. "That man is an idiot." And then he continues with me toward the door. Rabea and my mother are hot on our heels.

He turns around to face them.

"Very nice to see you both. I'll have to take you up on your offer to watch *The Sound of Music* next time it's on."

I open the door and call out, "Night, Mom. Night, Rabea. See you!" And walk quickly down the stairs to Dean's waiting car. This time, instead of his hulking Escalade, it's a gorgeous white Tesla.

"Wow, you don't do anything halfway." I laugh and slink down into the gorgeous, tan leather interior.

He closes the door for me and walks around to the driver's

side. I've always loved the way this car looks. But right now, all I can look at is the gorgeous man who is striding past the front of the car.

He's wearing a long, wool coat, but each step causes it to blow back. It reveals the white sweater he's wearing and the dark blue jeans that mold to every single inch of his long legs. He looks like he could be a model. His blond hair, long on top, moves with him, and I can't believe this beautiful, interesting man is my date.

He gets in, touches a screen, and the car comes to life. It's like being in a spaceship, a very quiet spaceship, as we head out of my subdivision and down San Felipe toward the Galleria.

"How was your day?" he asks as he turns his radio down. I watch his fingers caress the center console and imagine them caressing my side and feel my nipples start to pucker.

I have no idea what song is playing, but I like it and start to relax.

"Oh, boring. Soccer, grocery shopping, cooking, cleaning." I pause as my throat tightens. "Then Anthony's dad came for him."

He glances at me as he continues working his way through the normal traffic on this main thoroughfare of Rivers Wilde.

"How was that?"

I let out a deep exhale. "It was fine. It's not easy. I hate that he's sleeping under a roof that's not my own. But he's with his dad, so . . ."

"Your mom lives with you, right?"

"Yeah, she does. She moved in when all the craziness with my dad started and she just never left."

"How is that? Having her live with you?" he asks after several minutes.

"It's great, especially now that Kevin is gone, I think Anthony's adjustment has been easier because she has been around."

"She's always mothered everyone. Your son is lucky to have her."

"Yeah, he is. So am I. It's funny now that I have some distance from my marriage, I realize she never really mothered Kevin. I don't think she disliked him, but I don't know if she likes him either."

"Do you think she can really forgive me? That she'd trust me with you again?"

I brush his words away with the flick of my hand. "There's nothing to forgive."

"I want you back. Completely."

I stop breathing. "What?"

"I'm not a young, romantic fool. So, I'm not going to do or say anything crazy, but I feel something when I'm with you I've never felt before, Red. So, I'm making the most of this second chance. I want to spend as much time with you as possible."

My heart goes crazy with happiness, I smile and nod my agreement. "Of course. I'm just saying I can come and see you, too."

He shakes his head. "No. I don't want that."

"Okay...." I'm confused.

"Listen… I only came down to see you, get the resolution I thought I needed and planned to go back. My life is in New York. Or, it was."

"Was?" I ask, breathless with emotion I haven't felt in more than a decade.

"Sorry. I just… I want us to be really clear about what we are doing. I've waited a long time for you, spent a lifetime regretting what I didn't say. I'm not leaving anything to chance. I don't want to be your long distance lover, I don't want any space between us at all. I'm going to take that ring off your neck and put it on your finger, and make you promises I'll die to keep. And ask you to make me promises, too."

I look around the car, reeling slightly from what he has just told me. I am a combination of excited and scared and all I can say is, "Right now? In the car? Aren't we going somewhere?"

He laughs at me then and says, "When the time is right. For now, let's go have dinner." He claps his hands together excitedly.

He pulls back into traffic. "I know I got a little intense there, but I just needed to let you know how I'm feeling, Red."

I want to say so many things and yet I have no clue what to say.

So, I just say the first, honest thing that comes to mind. "I feel the same way."

He reaches across the center console and grabs my hand. His hand is big and warm. And even though his job involves him sitting behind a desk, his palms are very calloused.

"He's the only man I'd ever been with besides you." I feel the start in his body through his hand, and I look at him. "He was my college boyfriend and we got married as soon as I graduated."

I swallow before I continue. "Besides Anthony, I don't really have any accomplishments to show. I'm not sure what you think is so special about me."

I look down at our joined hands. I hate that I sound so negative about myself, but I feel like I'm just being honest.

"Lucky for you, you've found a man whose talent is spotting what's special. You've already found something special, but I'm going to let you come to the realization yourself. Just know, I don't have the time or the inclination to blow smoke up anyone's ass."

He grins at me as he pulls into a parking spot on a side street. As he cuts the ignition, I hop out of my side. He walks around, takes my hand in his and we walk down the street together.

all fired up

"STAY WITH ME TONIGHT," Dean says as we stand next to his car, his breath hot in my ear. He has me caged in with both of his arms and his eyes are pools of endless temptation and fire as they pin me in place.

We went to eat at Los Tios. It's been here since we were in high school and the drinks are just as strong as they were back when we had fake IDs and zero tolerance. The two margaritas I had with my meal have caused me to lose all my inhibitions.

"Yes," I rasp out. I am lost in a whirlpool of Dean—lust, alcohol; and my own desire to experience things I've only ever dreamed of.

We get into the car and drive to his hotel. Our hands are linked during the entire drive over and stay that way until we enter his suite.

As soon as the door is shut, he backs me against the door.

One of his hands coasts down my body gently and then with a rough grab of my hip, pulls me against him. I feel his erection, hard and large, against my stomach and I can't . . . I can't get close enough.

"Dean," I whisper, my chest heaves like I've been running. I feel wild in my desire for him.

"I can smell what you need, baby. Let me give it to you."

He makes a trail of kisses down my neck, hot, open-mouthed kisses that make me so wet I can feel it on my thighs. He stops at my breast and through the silk of my blouse and the lace of my bra, he sucks my nipple into his mouth.

There is no inhibition, and my groan is deep and long as the sensations shoot from my breast to my core and leave me almost too weak to stand.

He doesn't move to my other breast, rather continues his descent down until he's kneeling in front of me. He presses his nose to my center and pulls in a deep breath.

He stoops over and yanks my boots off my feet, throwing them over his shoulder without even glancing to see where they might fall. Then he reaches up, unbuttons my jeans and in one swift and hard pull, they and my underwear are down my legs and flying over his shoulders after my shoes.

"I've been dreaming about tasting you. I've been fucking my fist thinking about you sitting on my face."

He looks up at me with a devilish grin on his face. He sits, puts his hands on my hips, and pulls me to his mouth.

I whimper at the first touch of his tongue to my clit.

My hand goes into his hair, wanting to hold him in place as his tongue plays a concerto on me.

Suddenly, he lays back, pulling me with him, until I'm sitting on his face.

"Perfect," he breathes against my sensitive skin. He spread my legs wide and then his tongue inside of me, probing me while his thumb presses on the bundle of nerves. He rubs, and licks and then his mouth replaces his thumb and he sucks my clit into his mouth. It is exquisite, causing my body to move on its own. I have no control over my thrusting, begging hips, and all I know is the orgasm I'm chasing.

It feels like I'm dying and being born again. My orgasm

explodes out of a spiral of tension at the center of my body, and I'm screaming as I come and grind myself into his mouth as he holds me to him, as if he can't bear to let me go.

I don't have a chance to recover before Dean picks me up and moves me down his body. He whips his shirt off his head and wipes his face. I blush.

"Sorry. I got carried away," I say to him as I attempt to shift off his lap.

"No, you didn't. But you're about to." That mischievous grin is back and I smile back, confused but amused.

His grip on me tightens and then in a display of strength that leaves my mind boggled, he wraps my legs around his waist and stands up like he doesn't have my one hundred sixty-pound frame wrapped around him.

He turns me around and lays me down on the bed. His eyes roam my face as he reaches down and pulls my blouse over my head.

He reaches behind me and unsnaps my bra and then pulls it off.

And when I see the way his eyes light up as he looks me up and down, I feel like a goddess.

"Milly," he breathes and I gasp again.

His big, right hand comes up to cover my left breast and it's a small handful and disappears under his tender grip. I feel my nipple bead against his palm. Our gazes are locked and he licks his lips as he looks at me.

"You are fucking perfect."

He bends, head dipped, and moves his hand to take my nipple into his mouth. My back bows and my hands surge into his hair, holding him in place as he suckles me. He wraps both his arms around my waist and strokes his tongue against my nipple, and then my entire breast. He licks and nips and bites and sucks, and by the time he turns his attention to my other breast, I'm a writhing bundle of nerves.

My body is seeking release and relief. Again.

My hands run up and down his massive, muscled shoulders, and I marvel at how smooth, almost velvety his skin feels.

He moves over me, every muscle in his arms and shoulders rippling as he practically prowls his way up my body.

His lips touch mine, briefly and softly, and his hand comes up to caress the side of my face.

"You are more beautiful than I deserve."

He kisses me again, this time it isn't brief or soft but hard, passionate, and deep. He puts his hand between our bodies and his fingers glide against me, and past the lips of my pussy that are so sensitive his touch causes me to shudder.

He reaches for my hand and puts it between us. "Put me inside of you, Red."

I take a hold of his cock, marveling at how hard he is. He feels like a steel pole, wrapped in velvet in my hands. I guide him to me. I'm slick and he slides inside without any resistance. We both hiss at the initial contact, the sensation making my heart race and my breathing shallow. Our eyes meet and we grin at each other. We're both giddy over how *good* it feels.

He braces himself above me on his forearms and with one hard thrust slides all the way inside of me. I feel the walls of my pussy contract and cling to him. It feels so right to have him inside of me and yet, my body, unused to the size, registers some discomfort.

"Are you okay, baby?" he gasps as he moves his hips, settling even deeper into the cradle of my thighs. He brings one of my legs up, holding it under the knee and watches my face.

I reach up and brush a lock of blond hair out of his eyes and smile. "Yes, so good. I'm great."

Then he starts to move, his hips make slow thrusts, each one a statement. Each one saying he feels me, he wants me, and he never wants this to end.

I raise my pelvis to meet each thrust, and I feel like we are partners in a race, each of us doing our part to get us across the finish line.

I feel my orgasm building as he puts his face in my neck and bites the tendon that connects my neck to my shoulder. He growls and starts to pepper my shoulder and chest with kisses.

The pace of his hips slows and forces mine to do the same. He bends again and licks my nipple. The sound that leaves my mouth is close to a wail. He looks up.

"Red, I could stay here, attached to this juicy nipple all day. I want to suck it until you can't fucking speak. I want to fuck you until all you know is the feel of my dick inside of you."

I can only pant in response, my eyes are having a difficult time focusing, so I close them.

"Your body is making me feel like this is my first time at the world's best amusement park. I want to ride everything, over and over."

I whimper, I can't speak under the pressure of the pleasure pulsing through me. He cups my calves and drapes my legs over his shoulders, putting me at an almost ninety-degree angle while he moves deeper and deeper inside of me. Each thrust, painful and turning into a sharp pleasure that has my orgasm stacking up inside of me.

"Feels so good, Dean," is all I can say as he starts to slam into me. And without touching any other part of my body, Dean fucks me into an orgasm that is so powerful, I feel completely wrecked by it. We kiss as we catch our breath. Dean gets up to use the bathroom and I fall asleep before he even gets back.

When I wake up, I'm alone in bed. I can hear Dean in the other room typing on his computer.

I glance at the clock and see it's three in the morning and I remember I need to get back home no later than eight o'clock. Kevin's bringing Anthony home at nine this morning because he has his piano lesson. I want to get there with plenty of time to be ready to face him.

I sigh, feeling the delicious aches of our lovemaking as I turn over and go back to sleep.

labels

"CAN'T YOU GO ANY FASTER?" I hiss at Dean, one hand covering the speaker on my phone. We are in his car, speeding down Sixteenth Street toward Silver Spring. When I don't get a response, I glance up at Dean and find him staring straight ahead. I can see his jaw flex in annoyance. I'm about to reiterate my question when my mother's unusually panicked voice pulls me back to our conversation.

"Milly, he won't leave. Anthony's gone up to his room, but he's just sitting here, saying he needs to speak with you."

She's whispering, obviously trying to keep Kevin from hearing our conversation. I feel a wave of guilt at the idea that she's alone and uncomfortable with him.

I planned on being home two hours ago, but I overslept. I woke up to my phone ringing. My mother's anxious voice had me out of bed and pulling on my clothes before I even checked to see if Dean was awake or still sleeping beside me.

He's been awake, for hours apparently, and he had no idea I needed to be home so early.

He's been quiet since we got into the car. He insisted taking me home would be faster than me trying to call a car. I didn't feel like arguing that point because my sole focus was getting home and getting rid of Kevin.

Now though, as I've talked my mother down from her third call in the last twenty minutes, I second-guess the wisdom of taking him home with me for Kevin to see.

It has been three months since our separation. But, I don't think I want him meeting Dean now, or ever.

"Mom, we will be there in less than ten minutes. He can't do anything to you, and I promise he will leave as soon as I get home."

I pray I am not overstating my abilities and hang up before she can say anything else.

I lean back into the seat and close my eyes. I try to gather my thoughts and calm myself with the time I have left.

"Milly, are you going to tell me what's going on? You act like you've been caught cheating on him. He's at your house. So what?" His voice is cold and clipped.

I open my eyes and look at him again. He's sporting stubble and his hair is finger mussed. We only had time to brush our teeth and throw on clothes, but I think he looks like he could have stepped out of the pages of a Ralph Lauren commercial right now.

I avoid looking down at myself. I already know I don't look like anybody's commercial.

"I don't feel like I've been caught doing anything. I would have liked to have been home when Anthony got there, but otherwise, the only thing that's bothering me is that my mother is upset."

I know I sound as clipped as he did. But I don't care. I'm tired, annoyed, and not sure what he's getting at.

"Well, he better not say shit I find disrespectful or we are going to have a problem," Dean clips.

Oh, dear Lord. This is equal parts annoying and hot. But I know I don't want to even know what Dean means by "a problem."

I reach for his hand and he looks up at me. His eyes, so clear and full of anger, leave me momentarily speechless.

"Milly, I'm your man. What do you expect me to do?" he asks when he sees my expression.

My chest constricts, I'm scared and delighted all at once.

"So, I'm going to let you know right now. If that mother-fucker even looks at you the wrong way, we're going to have a problem. He has no say, at all, in how you live your personal life. He has no say, at all, in anything that doesn't have to do with your son."

His hand grabs more firmly onto mine, and he looks back out of the window. The muscles in his jaw flex. I can feel his annoy-ance and wish I wasn't so attuned to him. And immediately take the thought back. This... knowing between us. The draw, the need, the comfort, the heat, I've only ever felt it with him is a life source.

Him beside me makes me feel like I can face anything.

I squeeze Dean's hand and look out the window on my side of the car just as we turn onto my street.

Kevin's Mercedes sedan is parked in front of the house and my stomach tightens.

When we pull into the driveway I don't wait for Dean to come to a complete stop, I jump down and march up to the front door.

My mother opens it as I approach. "Thank goodness you're here. He's pacing, talking to himself," she says as I walk into my house after her.

I don't look back to see if Dean is behind me, I can feel him. "I'm sorry for all of this . . ." I whisper, my throat suddenly tight with unshed tears.

"You have nothing to be sorry for," he returns and then he draws me into his arms.

We stand there and for the first time since I woke up, I feel a sense of peace and calm settle around my shoulders.

I walk into the living room and see Kevin standing there, dressed casually in jeans, a T-shirt, and running shoes.

"Hello, Kevin," I use an unaffected voice, as I slow my pace to stroll into the living room, my mother hot at my heels.

"Mil, where have you been?" he says, looking agitated. His normally handsome face is marred by a sneer.

"Out," I return shortly. I'm not trying to antagonize him, but I also don't want him to think he can walk in and demand to know my whereabouts.

"Yeah. I know . . ." He trails off and his eyes move over my shoulder where Dean is now standing.

"Who is this?" Kevin snaps.

"This is my . . . this is Dean," I stammer, and I want to groan for not having a response to this question ready.

"I'm Dean Orleans. Milly's boyfriend." Dean reaches around me and puts his hand out for Kevin to shake.

Kevin ignores his offered hand and only gawks at him. I want to gawk, too. My *boyfriend?*

I speak instead. "I'm home. What do you need? My mother says you need to speak with me. What is it? Couldn't you have said it over the phone?"

This seems to wake him up. "It's a private, *family* business. I'm not talking about it with him here." He tips his head in Dean's direction.

I roll my eyes and sigh. "Okay, then why don't we set up a time to talk about this over the phone?" I look at Kevin, raise an eyebrow and wait.

"It can't wait. I need to talk to you now," Kevin insists.

"Look, either tell me now or call me later. I'm tired."

And I mean it. I'm tired and I'm anxious for him to leave. Dean walks over to me, puts his arm around my waist and pulls me against him.

"I'm going to get going. I know you're eager to see your son, and I've got to get home for a call and get ready to get back to the office tomorrow."

I want to beg him to stay. "Okay. Yes. Thank you." I hug him again, reveling in the feel of his hard body.

He leans down and presses his lips to mine—it's a soft kiss, yet it's also heavy. I want to wrap all four limbs around him.

"Have a good week. Can I see you soon?" he asks, pulling away from my mouth, but holding me in his bottle green gaze.

I smile at him as he draws away. "Yes, that would be nice. I'll plan something."

"I love you. Go lay down, I'll see Kevin out."

Kevin rears back. "You don't need to walk me out of my own fucking house, man. I need to talk to my wife. You need to leave."

I bristle, stepping away from Dean and toward Kevin.

"Don't you *dare* call me that. You lost that right a long time ago. Even before you left. This may be half your house, but it is *my* home. You need to leave. Now."

"You can't do this." Kevin starts toward me.

"Man. Don't take another step toward her. I'm fucking telling you right now, if you do not leave on your own, I will put you out," Dean rumbles, stepping between Kevin and me. This time, I decide not to stop him.

My mother hasn't said a word since we walked into the room. I look at her to find her staring at Dean, eyes wide and glittering, with a look of utter surprise on her face. I need to get this scene over with. Now.

"Please. Just go," I plead, not caring how I sound right now.

Kevin looks between the three of us and then shakes his head in resignation and anger.

He turns to face me. The expression on his face is soft, his annoyance and arrogance completely gone. For a moment, it reminds me of the old him. The Kevin I married, and I feel wistful and sorry. Sorry this man, the one who looks capable of contrition and honesty, isn't really who Kevin is. Sorry for our younger selves who thought they could build a marriage on insecurity and mediocrity.

I step toward Dean, wanting to make a point.

Kevin's swallow is audible, before he says quietly, "Mil, I'll call you tomorrow. I miss you."

I turn to my mother. "What was that about?"

"Nothing. I just wanted to remind him you are stronger than you may appear."

Not satisfied, but not willing to push it right now, I just say, "Right." I turn to leave the room and she calls after me. "I like him."

For the second time today, my heart catches. I didn't realize how much I needed to hear this until she said it. And I also realize that although she treated him with kindness and respect these are words she has never said to me about Kevin.

I smile to myself as I start up the stairs to my son's room. He passed out on his bed, his sweet mouth parted, and his arms and legs splayed wide.

I run my hand over his curly head of hair and lie down beside him. The rest of the world melts away, as I drift off to sleep again.

40 /
milly

picture

DEAN'S BACK IN TOWN. I feel a flutter of excitement as I see the text pop up on my phone letting me know he's landed.

We've talked every night this week and they have been long, deep conversations about our lives, our families, our ambitions. Our chemistry is crazy. I remember now how no one understood why we were so into each other, so quickly in high school. We couldn't help it. Only people who'd been in love like that would understand. And I'd learned that the love we had was something special.

We may have been apart for all this time, but we've been strong as long as we've been anything.

And the sex...well, let's just say it's been a revelation. Even when he's not here.

Phone sex is our foreplay and after a week of it, and dancing on the edge of my climax, never quite getting there...I'm nearly feral with need by the time he gets back to town.

I've grown bolder, too, and every night when I slip my fingers into my panties and bring myself to orgasm with only the sound of his voice and the images he evokes, I feel like another link in the chains I've bound myself with have fallen off.

223

The party is coming along. Val is a dream client. I can't really tell how he feels about his fiancée, but the attention to detail he's putting into the event tells me more than anything he could say. I hope like hell she loves what I do for the engagement party because their wedding is going to be spectacular.

Work is picking up again. I'm almost fully booked for the rest of the year. I'm afraid to be happy because everything is so perfect. Better than it's ever been. I have everything I want and some I hadn't even dared to dream.

I hum to myself as I stir the simmering pot on the stove while I go over my week. I'm making a very simple but delicious chicken marsala dish for dinner. I've invited Dean over to eat with my mother and Anthony.

I'm nervous about all of us sitting down at the same table again. It's going to feel like old times but with my father gone and my son present.

I haven't heard from Kevin, whatever was so important last week clearly has lost its urgency. I'm glad, I wasn't looking forward to talking to him.

"Mommy! I drew your friend a picture!" Anthony shouts as he runs into the kitchen. He's waving a piece of paper in his fist and is beaming from ear to ear.

I put down my wooden spoon and kneel down so we are eye to eye with each other.

"Look, it's me and you in a spaceship! We're going to discover the galaxy."

He points at the barely recognizable people in the picture he's drawn. His version of me has blue hair and pink teeth. He sees himself as a person with green spiky hair and a big blue grin. I love it.

"It's amazing, baby. He's going to love it." I stand back up and start stirring again.

"Mommy, I'm hungry, can I have a snack?" he asks as he wanders over to the pantry.

"No, sir! We are eating in about thirty minutes and you'll ruin your appetite." I smile as I anticipate his groan of protest.

"Mommy! Please. I'll have one of my Rice Krispies Treats," he begins to negotiate.

"We don't have Rice Krispies Treats, babe." I smile at him over my shoulder. He has a very severe soy allergy and they have it as the main ingredient, so I have banned them from my house.

"Yes, we do. Rachael bought me a bunch last weekend, they're in my–oops."

"You what?" I stop stirring and watch him.

His eyes fill with tears as he looks up at me. "It was supposed to be a secret," he wails as he looks at me.

I feel anger, hot and quick rising in my chest. I keep my face neutral as I stoop down to him again.

"Oh, honey. You know we don't keep secrets from each other. But Rachael is new and so maybe she doesn't know," I say to him, trying to soothe him and keep my own fury at bay.

"But she will be mad at me, Mommy. She told me not to tell anyone," he cries and I see red.

I take a deep breath and then pull him into my arms. "You're not in trouble. She won't be mad at you. She made a mistake, and she probably already knows it." I pat his shaking shoulders as I plan my conversation with Kevin.

"Can you go upstairs and get your backpack for me, sweetie? I need to see what's in it and get rid of the Rice Krispies Treats. You know why you can't eat them, right?"

I have made sure he knows all of the things he can't eat and he also knows the potential side effects if he does eat them.

"Yes, Mommy. They would make my tummy feel really bad," he says woefully before he pulls away and heads up the stairs to his room.

As soon as he's gone, I pull out my phone and text Kevin.

I need to talk to you about Anthony. I'll call you tomorrow.

He responds right away.

What's the matter with Anthony. I can talk now.

I can't. Nothing is wrong with him, no thanks to you. Tell what time tomorrow and I'll call.

And then I turn my phone off. Dean will be here any minute and I've got just enough time to take a shower. Anthony comes back with his backpack and I take the offending snacks out. He pouts as he leaves the kitchen.

My mother is still getting ready, so I turn everything off, check the table setting one last time and run upstairs.

Ten minutes later, I'm dressed in jeans and a T-shirt, coming back downstairs, I know Dean is early and my mother is entertaining him.

I walk into the room and find Dean on the floor, shoes off, sitting with Anthony looking at a pile of his drawings.

"These are great, little man. You drew them all?" Dean is praising Anthony.

"Yes, I did! I've got more upstairs!" he declares, his voice full of delight and then he jumps up and starts to turn and leave the room when he sees me.

"Mommy! You're finally here. Dean really likes my pictures. He wants to see more," he says as he races past me on his way up the stairs.

Dean and I lock eyes and my mother's presence is the only thing stopping me from running to him. He looks delicious and my eyes take in their fill, as he does the same from across the room. I can feel the crackle in the air between us as his smile spreads, and he stands up. We just stare at each other for a moment.

My mother coughs and breaks our reverie. I look at her, and she's smiling at me.

"Hi, Mom. Sorry I wasn't down when he got here."

"Why are you sorry? I'm not. It gave me a chance to talk to him before you came and stole his attention." She winks and then passes me on the way to the kitchen. "I was just going to get some wine. I'll be back."

"Oh, no, I'll do that," I stop her. "Sit and relax."

"I've been relaxing all day, you've been on your feet cooking. Go sit down." She pushes me farther into the room and leaves.

When Dean and I are alone he walks over to me in four ground eating strides and before I can even say anything, his lips are on mine. It feels as good as a breeze after standing in stifling still heat. I immediately melt into the kiss. It is an urgent hello more than a demand, but my mouth opens under his and I groan when I feel his tongue touch mine.

We stand there, kissing each other, my hands around his neck, his at my waist. These lips of his, supple and smooth, know mine. They were made to mate, and they fit together so well. The kiss goes on for what could be minutes, or days, until I hear Anthony's voice, tiny and confused.

"Mommy?"

We jump apart and my focus is immediately on my son. He's standing there with his binder of drawings in his hand. His little face is full of confusion.

"Mommy, why are you kissing him?" He's looking at Dean with a wary eye.

"Anthony, baby. Mommy . . ." I have no clue what to say. I feel like I've been hit between the eyes with a brick. I look over my shoulder at Dean.

"Is he my daddy now, Mommy?" He points at Dean as his lower lip starts to wobble.

Dean bends down in front of Anthony. "Hey, buddy. Mommy is kissing me because we are friends and sometimes when mommy makes a new friend, she kisses him to tell him she likes him. It doesn't mean your daddy isn't your daddy anymore. He will always be your daddy." He reaches out to touch Anthony's head and I gather my thoughts.

"Anthony, you know how Daddy lives with Rachael now?" I ask him. He nods slowly.

"That doesn't mean she's your mommy, okay? She's Daddy's friend who will help take care of you when you're with Daddy."

I feel like I'm floundering and not making sense, but Anthony brightens up and says excitedly, "Is Dean moving in with us? Like Rachael lives with Daddy?"

I have to stifle my gasp of shock and also control my urge to laugh. "No, baby, he's not moving in with us. We are just friends. He's here for dinner."

"Oh, okay . . ." he says as he screws his little face up and looks back and forth between the two of us.

"Well, can I still show you my pictures?" he asks Dean, his expression tentative.

"Absolutely. It's been my favorite part of tonight." He takes the folder from Anthony's hand and walks over to the couch with Anthony following him.

I go check on my mother and the food.

"Kissing looks gross." I hear Anthony return just as I turn the corner into the hallway that leads to my kitchen.

My mother is leaning on the counter drinking wine and staring out of the bay window over the sink.

"Hey, you okay?" I ask as I grab a glass and pour myself some wine.

"Yes, just giving you two some alone time." She sounds distracted and slightly wistful.

"Mom, what's wrong?"

"Nothing. I'm just glad you finally have something like this." She touches my arm and gives me a sidelong glance. "And it makes me miss your father," she finishes, sighing and tucking her chin into her neck.

"Oh, Mom. I know we never talk about it, but I know you miss him. I do, too."

She looks at me sharply. "Do you?"

"Of course, Mom. He was everything…"

Her face searches mine before I see her eyes soften with empathy and understanding. "It's hard to think about, honestly. It's like half of my soul is gone, and I just don't understand how or why," she whispers while looking out of the window again.

Her voice is laced with so much sadness I feel tears threaten my own eyes.

"What are you going to do? I mean, what if he never comes back?" I ask her, because I don't understand her lack of anger when she talks about him.

"Then it means he can't. I know if he left us it wasn't because he wanted to be rich and free more than he wanted to be with us. Something happened. I don't know what, but I know, in my heart, he didn't leave me. He wouldn't. He couldn't. The love we had . . . *have* is something you only get once in your life. I want him home."

"If they find him, he will be arrested. He will be tried, and he will go to jail," I remind her.

Her voice has risen in volume and her eyes have regained their focus. "And they don't have any evidence, Milly. Not really. The money went from the company's account, to his and then to that offshore account that was like a black hole. They have the van rental, they have his trail until it disappeared near the border. There was nothing to indicate he did anything but run."

"But, if he didn't do anything wrong, why did he run?"

She looks at me and shakes her head as if to clear fog from it. "I'm sorry, Dean is here for dinner. Let's not bring all this up."

I look toward the living room where I hear peals of laughter from Anthony and sigh. This is a conversation I've been waiting for so long to have, but now isn't the time.

"Okay, but we can talk more later?"

She pats my hand and starts toward the living room. "Yes, honey, we can."

————

"This is delicious, Red."

Dean smiles up at me halfway through dinner. The chicken came out perfectly and everyone's been busy eating and conversation has been light at the table.

"Thank you. It's actually an old recipe of my mother's." I look at her and smile warmly. She's a wonderful cook, always has been, and even though she cooks a lot of dishes from her native Ghana, she also has a wide repertoire of dishes from all over the world.

"Well, then my compliments to you, Mrs. Dennis." He smiles at her.

"When Milly was first born and I decided to stay home, learning to cook different dishes was one of my biggest projects. This was actually a favorite of their dad's, too."

He starts to cough, and I jump up to beat his back while my mother fills his water glass.

"Are you okay?" I ask him as his coughing subsides. Anthony is staring wide-eyed like he's watching a scene in a movie.

"Yes, sorry," he says between coughs. "Something went down the wrong way." He clears his throat and touches my arm which is now resting on his shoulder. "I'm okay. Really." He looks imploringly at me, so I sit down.

"You were saying? This was a favorite of your husband's?" Dean prompts my mother.

She looks at him wistfully, but then smiles and continues.

"Yes, he loved it. In fact, when he was in the mood for it, he would hint by bringing home a bottle of the marsala wine and leaving it sitting on the countertop where I could see it." She laughs and then blushes. "Oh, excuse me. You probably don't want to hear me reminisce about him."

"No, I don't mind. I was very close to my dad, and since he died, my mother and I have drifted apart. I don't get to hear anyone tell stories about my own father . . ." He sighs a little and then looks at us. "Sorry, I don't mean to be maudlin," he apologizes.

"You're not and telling stories about your dad can be your thing." She smiles at him, and I feel a warmth blossom in my chest. This is my mother. She's such a nurturer and she always knows what to say.

"I'd rather hear stories about Milly, actually. The college years. What I missed," Dean says with a smile that is positively rakish. I note, though, that he's changing the subject. I let it go. I understand how sad and hard it is for him to talk about his father.

"Oh no, you wouldn't. There is nothing to tell," I exclaim. "Anyway, aren't you the slightest bit curious about the party I'm planning for your friend."

"Yes, I am. I just didn't think you'd want to talk about work tonight. But, if you want to tell me, I'm all ears," he says as he takes another sip of his wine.

I fill him in on the venue and the progress I've made in getting the event planned. I start to tell him about the guest list Cristal sent over to me for a head count when Anthony interrupts.

"This is boring. I want Mommy stories instead and Picture Man can tell us his stories, too!"

We all look at him as he clasps his hand over his mouth. "Who's Picture Man, Ant?" my mother asks him.

He looks at all of us wide-eyed, his eyes resting on me for a long moment. And then they fill with tears. I get up and walk over to him, crouch down, and put my arm around him.

"Anthony, who is Picture Man?" I ask him quietly.

He looks at me and shakes his head, but lifts one tremulous finger and points it at Dean.

Dean doesn't look surprised, so I turn on him.

"Care to tell me what that means?" I ask him, knowing I sound as concerned as I look.

"I have no clue, Red. He called me that the first time I met him, but didn't say why." He looks at Anthony, his eyes full of compassion and says, "Sorry, bud."

"What is going on here?" I demand and stand up.

Anthony grabs my hand and looks at me with his big beautiful eyes.

"Mommy, I'm sorry. I was looking for candy. I looked in your drawer and saw that picture you have of him in there. I didn't know who he was, but it's in your secret drawer with all of your secret things I'm not supposed to see." He looks down at his lap.

And my relief washes over me. That is the most benign explanation he could have given at this point. I look up from him and my mother and Dean are now watching me, waiting for *me* to explain.

"It's okay, baby. Don't feel scared about telling me anything, okay?"

He nods, I kiss my son on the head and I walk back to my seat and sit down. And I give my mea culpa.

"I have a picture of Dean and I that I keep in a drawer by my bed. I've always kept it there, and I guess he found it and recognized you. Since he couldn't ask who you were, he assigned you a name. Picture Man," I say and smile at all of them. I look at Dean, but he's standing up.

"Dean?" I start to stand up, too. He doesn't respond but leaves the room and walks straight back to my kitchen.

This is the last thing I expected. I dash after him.

As soon as I walk through the swinging door that divides my kitchen from the dining room, I feel a pair of hands grab my waist and push me against the wall.

Dean has the fiercest look in his eyes, and I'm totally confused.

"I just needed to kiss you in a way that I couldn't kiss you in front of your mother and son," he growls and he lays a kiss on me that curls my toes and makes me wish he was staying the night with me.

We walk back to the table together and sit down. "You okay, Ant Man?" he asks.

Anthony nods and smiles a little weakly.

"So, how about some Mom and Picture Man stories?" Dean says to him and his smile brightens immediately.

My mother shoots me a knowing look while laughing. "Milly, you've been overruled. Just sit back and enjoy it."

I gasp and feign annoyance. "Fine! Gang up on me."

Dean reaches across the table to hold my hand, while he says with a wink and a smile, "Get used to it."

mine

IF YOU'D TOLD me two months ago, I'd be up at seven on a Sunday morning teaching a kid the latest Kidz Bop moves, I would have rolled my eyes. If you had told me I would be doing it because a kid I'm totally crazy about texted me forty-five minutes ago and said he couldn't sleep and asked me to come over, I would have laughed in your face. But, here I am with Anthony, learning the moves to Meghan Trainor's "All About That Bass."

And I'm happy as shit he found his mom's phone and texted me instead of waking his mom or grandmother up. He wanted me, which makes me feel like I won the lottery.

I've always wanted kids, but thought it wouldn't ever happen. And I know he's not technically my kid, but getting to know him as part of my reconciliation with Milly has been one of the best things that has ever happened to me. He's a great kid.

Milly's still asleep and so is her mother, so when I hear the back door to the kitchen open, I get up and rush to the kitchen expecting to find an intruder. Anthony is completely absorbed in the cartoon and doesn't appear to hear the door.

What I find is worse than an intruder. It's the fucking idiot of an ex-husband of hers. Letting himself into her house like he still lives there.

This motherfucker.

He freezes when he sees me. His face moves through different expressions—panic, surprise, recognition, anger—so quickly it's almost funny. Almost.

I stop in the kitchen entrance and plant my feet.

"What are you doing here?" I ask him, keeping my voice neutral. I don't want to wake Milly up or upset Anthony.

"Are you fucking kidding me? I'm the one who should be asking you. This is *my* fucking house!" he shouts, clearly not at all concerned about waking anyone up or shielding his child.

"Yo, man. Milly is asleep; your son is in the next room. Keep it down."

"Get the fuck out of my house, *man.*" The sneer in his voice is as clear as it was the first time he spoke.

I exhale impatiently, trying to hold my temper in check.

"Look, clearly no one is expecting you. Why don't you call and come back later?" I ask in one last attempt to be reasonable.

"No, you fucking asshole. I don't know why you think you can tell me what to do in my own house, but I'm not listening to you. Your opinion doesn't matter to me," he says dismissively and starts moving toward the center of the house.

I step in front of him, forcing him to stop walking.

I have almost five inches of height on him and more than thirty pounds. We are toe-to-toe and his nose is in my neck.

"My opinion may not matter to you. But this isn't your home. Milly isn't your wife. You don't have any right to be here. You need to get the fuck out, now. If you wake her up, upset her mother, or *her* son, you will have a problem with me. Don't let this pretty face fool you, if any of those people even look uncomfortable, I will fuck you up. In every way you can imagine."

He takes a step back. I take a step forward.

"Man, you don't scare me. I've been married to Milly forever.

You just got here. Don't think you're here long-term." He steps back again and sneers at me.

Just then, Milly walks into the kitchen. Her robe is tied tightly around her. Her hair is loose and her face is flushed with sleep. For a second, I lose my train of thought; she's so fucking beautiful.

"Kevin, what are you doing? Dean? When did you get here?" She looks back and forth between us.

Kevin bursts out laughing. "You're not supposed to be here either? You tried to act like you spent the night." He dismisses me by turning to face Milly.

"I came to talk about your text. What's wrong with Anthony?"

"I told you nothing was wrong with him yesterday," she snaps and walks into the kitchen. She walks over to the coffee maker and switches it on. "Tell your girlfriend to stop feeding him food he's allergic to. He had a stash of Rice Krispies Treats in his backpack she gave him. *And* she told him not to tell me. We don't keep secrets. That's not okay." She turns around to face him. He actually looks shamefaced.

"About that, I'm thinking I was hasty about moving Rachael in with me. The whole situation . . ." His voice falters, and I can hear his uncertainty and regret. Idiot.

"*What* whole situation?" she asks slowly, her eyes narrowed on him. I lean back on the counter to watch. I have a feeling this is about to get really good.

"This man you're shacked up with. He's just walking in your house. He's taking advantage of you. Using you and when he's tired of it, he'll drop you. "

And this time, I can't control my laughter. It erupts from me and Milly shoots me a look. So, I try to stop it. It's hard. This guy is unbelievable. Does he know Milly at all?

"No, I used to be a doormat. And you, being an asshole, have always enjoyed that. I'm glad you decided Rachael's amazing pussy was worth more than our marriage. I'm so grateful to be free of it... So maybe it really *is* an amazing pussy. Miraculous even." She snickers and shakes her head.

"Milly, please, let's just talk," he begs, panic infusing his words.

"No. I don't want to talk." She looks at me and beams. "I want to go upstairs and go back to bed . . . with my man. Who by the way has always been my man."

I want to pump my fist in the air, but I just wink at her. Kevin looks like he might throw up.

She starts to walk out of the room but looks back at him once more. "Let's just stick to talking through our lawyers. We have a custody hearing in six weeks and then we can get on with our lives. Don't come back here unless it's to pick up Anthony or drop him off."

She gets to the door and crooks her finger at me. And I'm no fool. I grab the man who *is* a fool and walk him to the door, push him out, lock and engage the alarm.

I pop my head into the living room and see that Anthony has drifted off to sleep on the couch.

Then, I run up the stairs after my woman.

home

IT'S A BEAUTIFUL EVENING.

The sun's slow set is framed by the archway where Val was on his knees asking Heidi to be his wife.

I wasn't convinced about him and Heidi, but he was. I'd never seen him truly nervous until we arrived at the venue. Now that the moment has arrived, he looks and sounds like he doesn't have a doubt in the world.

Heidi had been shocked when she walked in. Whether she was designing the surprise or not, there was no mistaking the genuine joy on her face when he got on one knee in front of her just as the sun moved behind them. The blaze of orange and red made a halo around them. This was it - the moment he had been waiting for.

"My dearest Heidi," he began, his voice shaking with emotion. "From the moment we met, we've been in sync. You understand me in a way very few people can and the years we've spent together have opened my eyes to possibilities I'd never imagined. I can't imagine my life without you in it. Will you do me the honor of becoming my wife?"

Tears streamed down Heidi's face as she nodded her head,

unable to speak. He slipped the ring onto her finger, and they embraced in a warm hug. And then he led her through the archway where we were all waiting and the lights that had been dimmed to hide us came on.

Milly has really outdone herself. There are so many details I would never have considered that she's put into place, which are making the party a stress-free evening for our guests. She even rented out the entire parking lot next door so that guests had a place to park—easy and free. The venue was a huge space made of warm white stone that made the cavernous room feel cozy. There were fairy lights strung up in the trees and tables laden with flowers and candles. It was magical and elegant and everything went off without a hitch. The caterer killed it, the band took it to another level.

Everyone was having a good time.

I'd been surprised to see his stepmother and her daughter, Honoree, there. Rey, as we called her, was Val's first love. I don't think he's ever gotten over her, but he's never let himself explore what's between them.

It's almost time for my best man's toast and I scan the room until I find Milly. She's talking to the woman manning the buffet.

She looks stunning. Her dress, a stunning red thing, sits completely off her shoulders, showing the caramel colored span of silk that is the skin of her neck, her chest, her shoulders, and her upper arms. It fits her like it was made for her. It shows off her incredibly tiny waist and her generous hips and ass. Her hair is straight, parted in the middle and pulled back into a low ponytail. She has a thin gold chain with her heart pendant and my ring around her neck. And she's wearing the sexiest strappy high-heeled sandals I have ever seen in my life. I can't wait to have them up over my shoulders when I fuck her tonight.

I will never get over the fact that this gorgeous woman is mine.

I'm making my way over when I hear a familiar voice call my

name. It halts me dead in my tracks and prickles dread down my spine.

Nicola. What the hell is she doing here?

I turn around slowly. And freeze when I see my mother standing next to her.

I don't say anything as she walks toward me because I am *completely* lost for words.

"Dean, aren't you going to say hello?" Nicola purrs. Her flinty expression contradicts the smile that curves her mouth. I look at my mother who is smiling at me like she's daring me to say what I think.

"Mother. Good evening." She's a true beauty. All blond hair, dark eyes, and perfect features. She was always the subject of my classmates' "MILF" lists. And she loved it. Much to my father's dismay.

"Dean, hello." Her smile slips a little. She walks toward me and I press a light kiss on her offered cheek.

I straighten and look between them, the ice in my veins spreading by the second. "What are you doing here?"

"I was invited. I've known the groom since he was a child and my son is to be the best man. You can hardly be surprised."

"And why did you bring her?" I nod at Nicola.

"Because, she told me that you dumped her for that wedding planner and I thought it was only right that she came and warned her potential clients that she'll not only steal your man, but that she's got a father who the FBI has been trying to find for fifteen years."

"Mother is only here because of me. I called her after I saw that picture. I knew I had to intervene before you made a fool of yourself."

My mind moves, processing what she said. "You're only going to make a fool of yourselves," I warn them between gritted teeth.

"Maybe, but at least everyone will also know what kind of person she is."

My gaze snaps to my mother. "Why do you even care?"

Oblivious or indifferent to my mother's growing unease, Nicola smiles sweetly at her. "She thought maybe seeing me again would make you realize what a mistake you've made. And of course, I couldn't miss the opportunity to save another bride the heartache of having her lure her future husband away."

She says all of this in a nonstop monologue. While she talks I look at my mother, completely incredulous she would dare meddle in my private life again. She's never even wanted to meet Nicola.

"Mother, this is low, even for you."

She shrugs. "I'm just trying to help this young woman. She reminds me so much of myself."

"You need to leave."

Nicola gasps. "Why would I leave? The show is only starting." Her voice is laced with a vindictive glee that makes me shudder.

"You are making a mistake. If you leave now, I won't hold it against you."

I smile unpleasantly at them and turn to walk away, now desperate to find Milly.

She's not where I saw her last. I walk around the room looking for her, but also stopping to talk to employees, competitors, clients, and friends who have shown up tonight. The room is full, and it takes me a while to get through the crowd.

I feel a tap on my shoulder and turn around to see Cristal standing behind me.

"It's time for your speech." She motions to the small podium set up in the front of the room. So, I walk over to say the words I've prepared.

I stand in front of the podium and scan the room. I see my mother and Nicola standing off to the left of me, both of them glaring at me. I dismiss them, my eyes traveling the room until I see Milly, standing to my right, next to a pillar. She's watching

Dylan Allen

me with unabashed love in her eyes. I wink at her, causing her to grin and wink back.

I turn my attention back to the room and tap the microphone to get everyone's attention. My remarks are brief and pointed. I know people didn't come to hear me speak. I toast my best friend and his soon to be bride and turn the festivities back over to the MC.

I walk straight to Milly, put both my hands on her waist, and draw her into me. She braces her hands on my side and keeps me from pulling her too close.

"You look incredible tonight, Red. I can't take my eyes off of you. I can't wait to have my mouth on you," I whisper in her ear.

She sighs and leans her head forward so it rests quickly on the front of my jacket.

"You looked amazing up there," she murmurs as she gazes up at me.

"Let me take you home," I whisper.

She shakes her head. "I can't leave. I have to mingle. Make sure everything goes smoothly. But when I get home, I'll make it up to you."

She smiles seductively yet sweetly and looks at me through her lashes.

My gut clenches and I can't make myself smile back. Her expression flattens. "What's wrong?" she asks.

I can't bring myself to say it.

She takes a sweeping glance around the room. Suddenly, her eyes widen and her smile drops. She pulls away from me and looks at me.

"Dean," she says gravely and swallows.

"I'm sorry," I say because I know she's already seen my mother. "I didn't know she'd be here."

Milly grimaces and looks back at me. "I did. I saw her on the guest list this afternoon. Last minute addition."

I hate the worry on her face. "Ignore them, just focus on

having a good night," I say as I rub my hands up and down her arms.

"Seeing her again was jarring," she admits, her eyes darting back over my shoulder.

"Listen, if you're uncomfortable, I will ask her to leave," I say, and I mean it.

"Oh, no. You can't do that to your mother. That would be terrible. And not for me. Please, I'll be fine."

She steps out of my embrace and smiles at me brightly. I fall even more in love with her at that moment. She has more grace in her little finger than my mother does in her entire body.

I smile back at her, and her smile wavers. I frown. "What?"

"Nicola is here."

I close my eyes and groan inwardly. This is a fucking shit-show in the making. I turn around to face them and lean down to whisper into Milly's ear, "Ignore her, too."

She whips back to stare at me. She looks horrified. "Why is she here?"

"I didn't know she would be here. I'm sorry," I mumble, feeling like the world's biggest ass. I hope the mess this scene is about to create isn't something I can't clean up. I look at Milly, silently begging her to understand.

To my everlasting surprise, Milly's look of trepidation and surprise transforms into a smile. She steps closer to me until she's tucked into my side. My arm automatically goes around her waist. I look at the two women who are now standing about three feet away from us.

"Dean, this is embarrassing. I can't believe you're flaunting this in everyone's face," my mother bites out at me as she stands with one hand on her hip, and the other one locked through Nicola's.

I feel Milly stiff slightly beside me.

"What exactly am I flaunting, Mother?" I ask calmly, even as I feel my anger rising exponentially.

"Everyone knows who she is. Everyone knows she's responsible for our family's biggest tragedy. And you're walking around here like Romeo and Juliet!" The volume of her voice has increased.

A few people glance our way. Milly steps out of my hold but grabs my hand. When she looks up at me her eyes are molten with anger. But when our eyes meet, I smile at her and she smiles back. My anger tamps down a little at the way her smile reassures me. She looks back at my mother and Nicola.

"You need to keep your voice down, Mrs. Orleans. This is a very special night for Mr. Hayford and his fiancée. It wouldn't be fair to ruin it because of our history."

"And who are you to tell us what to do?" Nicola snaps at Milly.

I lean forward slightly. "Nic—"

Milly's hand on my forearm stops me. She looks at them again. "Please, let's all go into the office in the back and talk."

And without waiting for anyone to respond, she turns and walks away. I follow her and know my mother and Nicola will follow as well because they are obviously spoiling for a fight.

I trail her through the double doors that lead to the administrative section of the venue. She steps through the first open door.

I hear the click of heels behind me, and I know the two troublemakers are hot on my heels.

They follow me into the room, and as soon as they walk through the door I shut it.

Milly is leaning against the desk that is in the corner of the room, "Mrs. Orleans, you were saying?" she says politely to my mother.

My mother actually sniffs and turns her nose up at Milly before she turns to face me.

"I understood when you wanted to walk on the wild side in high school. I mean, it was cute. Her father was powerful, but now on top of everything else that's happened, it's crazy for a man like you to have a woman like her," she nods her head at Milly, "on your arm."

I'm stunned speechless. I look at Milly to see if she's okay, and she looks speechless, too.

"I mean, you have Nicola. She's perfect. She comes from a nice family. One we know isn't associated with theft and God knows what else. For all we know he's some sort of terrorist."

She flings her hands in the air for emphasis as she talks, but this manages to shock me out of my stupor.

"What did you say?" I ask carefully. My anger is held in check only by the fact that this woman is my mother.

"Well, who knows what her father was into. He's from Syria. And he ran away with all that money. God only knows. And it doesn't even matter. It's because of people like him and the other scumbags at Enron that your father is dead!" she yells at me.

Before I can even catch my breath to respond, Nicola chimes in. "She was our wedding planner and now you're with her? If you don't want me to tell everyone out there who she is and what she's done, I'll need a nice wire to my bank account tonight."

Like a key made to fit the lock on the door to my anger, her words slide in and unleash it.

"You have lost your fucking mind. To waltz in here after you stole from me and tried to blackmail me."

She gasps and takes a step back.

"And there's only one terrorist in this room." I turn to my mother. You've never pretended to care about what might be best for me. But this is low, even for you. I know what you told Milly when she called me after my father died. I know you decided not to tell me she'd called even when you knew I was distraught without her. You—"

"Dean, please," Milly's voice cuts into my tirade. Her hand slips into mine and she gives it a squeeze.

Her eyes settle on Nicola and her smile is positively lethal.

"Nicole," she says sweetly. And I have to stifle a laugh at her deliberate use of the wrong name. "I completely understand you being crazed because you've lost your chance with Dean. It must be what it feels like to have a winning ticket to the lottery and having the wind blow it out of your hands."

She winks at me and this time a bark of laughter escapes me. She looks back at Nicola.

"But, you don't know anything about me. I'm assuming that his mother didn't bother to tell you that I didn't steal his heart two months ago, it's been mine since he was fourteen years old. And it will never ever be yours." She shakes her head in what looks like genuine pity. "I'm really sorry for you."

She turns to my mother and raises her eyebrows, her smile conspiratorial. "And guess what, I know you have never liked me. And that's okay." She squeezes my hand. "You gave birth to this magnificent human being. And somehow, despite your best efforts, he's a loving, hardworking, and generous person. You don't get to swoop into his life and try to destroy everything he holds dear just because you're bored. You are his mother. I was raised to respect my elders, so I'm not going to say everything I want to. Just this." She steps back to my side and wraps her arm around me. "He's your *son*. And instead of supporting him, you've manipulated him and lied to him. Instead of helping him chase his happiness, you've tried to drive it away. I'm not a young, vulnerable eighteen-year-old anymore who can be run off by some harshly spoken words. You can't separate us. Not with insults. Not with threats. Not with manufactured guilt. I won't let you hurt Dean again."

She smiles up at me, her eyes shining with tears, and one escapes to run down her cheek. My finger brushes it away. She leans forward and puts a soft kiss on my lips.

She looks back at my mother, her eyes glitter with anger and her smile disappears. And even though Milly doesn't move, my mother takes a step back. "You should leave. Now. Don't make a scene, just go. Both of you. Now."

My mother looks at me, her eyes full of apathy. "You've

always been your father's son. I was trying to help you. Marriage isn't about love and devotion. Ask *her* mother where that got her." She tips her chin at Milly. "It's your life. I'm leaving for Marseille in three days. I'll be gone for the rest of the summer. I'll call you when I get back."

She looks at Nicola and shrugs. "I tried. But clearly, you've lost this one. Have some pride and let's go."

She turns and walks out of the room without another word. Nicola looks at me for a second, starts to speak, but then she turns away and follows my mother out of the room.

Milly turns her body into mine and pulls me into a tight hug, her shoulders are shaking. When I pull her face back, I see she's crying.

"Dean, I'm so sorry . . ." she sobs, her eyes mournful. I'm taken aback. "Why are you apologizing?"

"Because you don't deserve any of this. You should have nothing but love. I'm sorry I've always been a source of tension between you and your mother."

I grab her chin and force her to look me in the eyes.

"Listen to me because I want you to understand me." I wait for her to nod before I continue.

"I've been alone most of my life. Until I met you in high school, everyone always looked at me and saw this big athletic guy with blond hair who was good at sports and solid academically. I had a car sophomore year. I lived in a big house. Everyone always thought those things were who I am. Even my parents, they were proud of all of the things I accomplished. That's all they talked to me about. It was really hard to know that the things which made them proud really had nothing to do with who I was. They didn't care that I was someone who defended people from bullies. They had no clue I hated cheese or that my childhood best friend moved away in the middle of our freshman year of high school. Or that I was so lonely, I used to have to force myself to go to school, every single day with anxiety that was nearly paralyzing. And then I met you. And

Dylan Allen

suddenly someone was asking me questions about myself rather than asking me for favors. You treated me like I was a person.

"You were my first true friend. You were the first person who noticed how miserable I was from the attention and made yourself my bodyguard."

She giggles a little. "Well, that's my strength, or my talent, anyway." I glance at her, happy for the moment of levity.

"What's that, Red?" I ask, already knowing what she will say.

"I'm a great judge of character and I have the courage of my convictions," she says with a grin. And that's exactly right.

I drop a quick kiss on her parted lips."Yes you do. You've always been the only person who has tried to look beyond the exterior." I grin at her. "We had to go through hell to find each other, but... if that's what brought us here, I'd live my lonely, miserable childhood all over again."

"Oh Dean. You're the love of my life." She cups my face.

"And you're the love of mine. And one day, you're going to be my wife and have my babies."

Her tears are flowing freely again, and I lean in to kiss her lightly.

I wrap an arm around her shoulder and pull her into my side.

"We can practice when we get home." It's her house, but anywhere Milly and I are together is home.

She looks up and smiles at me before she nods at me. "I love the sound of that."

248

contact

ANTHONY HOPS in the car from his place in the carpool lane
my mood lightens right away.

"Hi, Mom!" he shouts.

"Hey, kiddo. How was your day?" I smile at him in the
rearview mirror as I pull out into traffic and head to the airport.

"It was great. I'm building a robot!" He grins back at me.

I smile fondly as we get onto the Beltway and head south to
Hoby Airport.

"That's awesome, kiddo. Can you get it to clean your room?"

He doubles over with laughter—I love how easy he is to
entertain. "Okay!"

I glance over my shoulder quickly and say, "And guess what?
I have a surprise; we are on the way to pick up Auntie Lilly from
the airport."

"She's coming here? Yay," he squeals and then pauses. He
looks thoughtful for a few seconds before he continues. "Do you
think she will bring me those cookies I love?"

"I think you already know she will."

"I love it when she comes."

"Me, too."

He grins and pulls out the Kindle my mother bought him last Christmas. He's already an avid reader and I love it so much. He sits back and settles in for the car ride to the airport.

When we arrive, Lilly's already at the curb and waves wildly as we approach.

I'm glad she recognized my car because I might not have recognized her. Her hair she's always worn in a shoulder length bob that is always blown into a perfect blunt edge and expertly highlighted with shades of caramel and gold. Today, it's short, like Halle Berry pixie short, and platinum blond. I stare at her, mouth agape as she gets in the car.

"What?" she asks me with a look of amused annoyance on her face. "You look like I showed up with a baby instead of a new hairstyle. Close your mouth before flies land in there," she snaps.

She turns around to grin at Anthony.

"Hey, baby cakes! I missed you. When we get home you better give me lots of hugs and kisses." She beams at him.

If Anthony notices her hair he doesn't say anything, he just grins from ear to ear. This kid loves his aunts and they in turn dote on him.

"Hi, Auntie Lilly! Did you bring me cookies?" he asks.

Lilly jumps excitedly, rummages in her purse, and turns around while holding up a huge paper bag triumphantly. "As if I could ever forget." She hands him the bag, and he opens it immediately.

"Anthony, what do you say?" I admonish.

"Thank you, Auntie Lilly!" he chimes back at her.

"Anything for you, baby," she sings back at him.

She turns around to face the front as we pull out of the airport and gets her bag settled on the floorboard.

"How are things?"

"Good. Mom is excited to see you."

"I'm excited to see her, too. And eat whatever she's cooking."

I smile and glance at her out of the corner of my eye. "I want to tell you something, but I don't want you to freak out."

She leans back and looks at me with feigned shock. "What? Milly's keeping secrets? Don't let me find out you've started dancing for dollars." She laughs out loud at this.

"Shut up. My son is in the car, and I'm trying to tell you something!" I hiss.

"Okay, sorry." She sounds anything but. "Go ahead."

"Kevin and I have split up—"

"Fuck, yes," she whispers and pumps her fist.

"Gee, thanks, Lil."

"Sorry, Milly. You know what I think...and that little guy is the only reason I'm glad you got with him."

I reach over and slap her leg.

"Ouch, you know I'm right, Milly," she says.

"I have more to tell if you'll shut it," I snap at her.

"Holy shit, I'm shutting up. Tell me!" she begs.

I grin at her and say, as neutrally as I can, "Well, I'm seeing someone. And it's serious."

She lunges over the center console of my car and wraps her arms around my neck. "Oh, my God! That's awesome!" she screeches in my ear.

"Let go. You're going to get us killed." I push her off, but her reaction pleases me.

"Who is he? Tell me everything!" she demands.

I glance at her quickly and smile before I say, "It's Dean."

"Dean?" she shouts. "From high school? Holy *crap*. I'm so happy for you. He was so hot. Is he still hot?" She's bouncing in her seat.

I can't contain my giggle and blush. "Yes, he is. And it's amazing. I'm so happy. I've never been so happy. I mean, he's just . . ." I sigh and lean forward on the steering wheel.

She looks at me, her eyes wide, and her mouth open.

"Oh, my God. You're in love." She drags out the "o" in love and puts her hand over her heart.

"I am. And it's amazing. Life in general right now is." I glance in the back seat, Anthony still is absorbed in his Kindle and happily eating his cookies.

"How are you? I'm glad you're here…but surprised, you hate Houston," I say, carefully.

"I do but I love my family. It's been a long time, and I miss you guys," she says as if something important and rare hasn't just happened.

I try to hide my surprise and am about to ask her what she means when my phone rings.

The number displayed on my car's console shows a UK cell number. I hit the Bluetooth button on my steering wheel to answer it.

"Hello?" I say cheerfully.

"Hello, Milly?" Simon's baritone, sexy as hell, British accent comes through the speakers on my phone.

"Hi, Simon," I say cheerfully, genuinely pleased to hear from him. This man has single-handedly pulled Addie out of her self-imposed emotional isolation and has given her back to all of us. I adore him.

"Simon, I'm here, too," Lilly says in a chirpy tone I don't hear very often.

"Uncle Simon, hi," Anthony chimes from the back seat.

Simon's rich laughter fills the car. "Well, this is a treat. I didn't expect to catch all of you, but it's great I did. I had to wait for Ad to go to bed before I could call." He pauses, maybe for dramatic effect, and Lilly and I look at each other with raised eyebrows.

"Well, don't be so cryptic! Spit it out!" Lilly snaps.

"I want to ask Addie to marry me when we're in France two weeks from now. I want you all to be there. If you can make it, I'd love to make all of the arrangements." This all comes out fast and low. And when he's done, the car is completely silent. I'm stunned and happy, and also sad that my baby sister is all grown up.

"Hello?" Simon says tentatively into the silence.

"You're getting...married?" Lilly says surprised and gives me a wide-eyed glance.

"Well, I'd like to ask her. I mean, do you think it's too soon? I just thought it felt right, but if you guys think—"

"Hell no, it's not too soon," she interjects.

"And of course we'll come," I chime in. "You don't have to make all of the arrangements. Just tell us the dates, and we'll be there," I say, my heart is about to burst with happiness.

"Speak for yourself, Milly. Please make my arrangements," Lilly snaps.

"Lilly! Simon ignore her," I say.

"Why? He's rich," Lilly quips back. "Simon, don't ignore me. She's speaking for herself."

Simon's laughter bursts through the speakers. "I insist on it, please. It would be my honor. It's a surprise for Addie, so please keep it mum. I'll have my secretary send you dates and once you're sure they work, we'll buy the tickets. I've booked a block at a very special hotel in Paris."

I remember something suddenly. "You've already talked to my mother?" I ask cautiously.

"Yes, I called her first. To let her know my intentions and to get her blessing. She was very enthusiastic." I can hear the smile in his voice and can only imagine how happy this makes my mother.

He's such a gentleman, Addie did so well with this one.

"Well, this is all wonderful. Let us know what's happening and thank you so much for calling."

"Thank you for being so excited. I think it's going to be very special. I'll call you soon. Bye for now."

The line disconnects and Lilly and I squeal. Our baby is getting married. How amazing. We all already have plans to travel to London in September for Cara and Louis' wedding, so this just adds to the excitement of it all.

We spend the rest of the ride home talking about Addie and Simon. I forget that I didn't get a chance to ask Lilly any of the questions I had for her about her life in Miami.

secrets

MY MOTHER'S soft sobs are audible as soon as I get downstairs. I rush to the sitting room and gape at the sight before me.

I was upstairs for ten minutes putting Anthony to bed and when I left, they were laughing.

Now, my mother's face is pinched and Dean's is full of alarm and they stop talking as soon as I walk into the room.

"What are you talking about?" They both look at me, then at each other and there's silent communication happening that unsettles me.

"Someone tell me right now, or I'm going to start jumping to terrible conclusions." I walk farther into the room and stand in front of them with legs braced, arms crossed and wait.

Dean grasps my hand and my mother looks away.

"It's my fault. I was just talking to your mom about our conversation a few weeks ago. About your dad and how his disappearance didn't make sense."

I look at him in shock that he would broach this subject with my mother without talking to me first.

"We were supposed to do this together." I rush to sit next to my mom.

"I know, it just happened," he hisses back, looking suddenly just as angry as I feel.

"I know thoughts of your dad's disappearance chase you even when you're sleeping. I want answers, too. I want to know what happened to the company our fathers built together. I want to know where your dad is, too. I want to clear both of their names. I just...I can't believe they would do the things it looks like they have."

His tone has turned as gentle and imploring as his touch and I feel tears prick my eyes. I look down at my mother. She's staring at the ground with her shoulders shaking. "Mom? Are you okay? I'm so sorry to upset you."

She looks up at me and her face is streaked with tears. I haven't seen her cry since the day my father left. I am startled by how old she looks right now. It is as if the years of holding in her anger, pain, and worry have suddenly caught up with her.

"Oh, Milly. I'm sorry. I should have told you sooner. I didn't know what to do so I did what seemed best." Her voice is uncharacteristically hesitant, and she doesn't meet my eyes. My internal alarm goes from mild to raging. "Mom, what do you mean?"

I try to keep my voice calm, but my worry is impossible to mask.

I sit next to her on the couch with Dean next to me, his hand resting on my back. I grab both of my mother's hands and shake them gently. She looks up at me but her eyes are unfocused.

"Mom. Please. Whatever it is, you don't have to face it alone."

She looks at me, and with a deep breath squares her shoulders and draws her hands from my grasp.

"I think it's better to show you, instead. Wait here." She stands up and walks out of the room without another word.

Dean and I stare after her and then looked at each other. "I—"

"How—"

We both start to talk at the same time. "You go ahead," I say.

"Listen, I'm sorry. I didn't mean to bring it up without you here. I didn't plan it. She sat down and asked about my mom. I told her we didn't really talk much since my dad died. She said I should try to reach out to her and reconcile. I told her I needed to talk to her about what she had said to you all of those years ago . . . and then I just said it."

"Said what?" I prompt when he doesn't continue.

"That I never blamed you; that I didn't think your father could have done what it looks like and that I wanted to know why he disappeared so it wouldn't be a dark cloud over us anymore."

"What did she say?" I urge, my annoyance forgotten, for now.

"She snapped at me that it was none of my business and said I didn't know what I was playing with. So, I asked her what she knew. She started crying. That's when you walked in."

My shock wars with my worry.

My mother has been keeping something from us. My stomach twists and a strange numbness makes my limbs heavy. I'm not prepared for this.

"Red, say something," Dean's urgent whisper interrupts my thoughts.

"I'm sorry . . . I can't. Not until I know what she's going to say."

Dean opens his mouth to speak, just then my mother walks into the room carrying a small plastic box—slightly smaller than a shoe box and clear. It's full of papers that, from where I am sitting, look like letters.

"The day your father disappeared, I wasn't at the grocery store like everyone thinks. I was following him. He'd been behaving strangely for several weeks. We were always so close, but for about a month before he left, he'd been distant. I thought it was because of work, but my gut told me I was wrong."

"But he and your dad were fighting." She turns to look at Dean.

"They never argued," Dean rebuts.

"Well, a week before they disappeared, they nearly came to blows right outside this door."

Dean and I exchange alarmed glances.

"What did Dad say happened?" I ask her.

"Nothing. He said it was work. But, I could tell it was more than work. About a week before he left, I went into his office and looked through his drawers. I didn't know what I was looking for. I'd never done anything like that before, but I had to see if there was anything abnormal or out of place. I found a statement from his investment advisor informing him of penalties associated with liquidating your retirement fund before you turned sixty-five.

"I knew then something was horribly wrong. I asked him as soon as he got home. He was furious. He spoke to me in a way I'd never imagined possible. Told me to mind my own business. I was shocked, hurt, angry, but also even more suspicious than ever.

"He hadn't slept at home since the night of our argument. But the night before he left, he came home and he begged for my forgiveness. He said there were things he couldn't tell me, but he loved me, loved our family, and would do anything to protect us. It's the very last night we were together.

"The next morning, he got up to take Addie to school; I was supposed to be running errands. He kissed me goodbye like nothing was wrong, but I could sense everything was wrong. So, I followed him.

"After he dropped Addie off he went to the bank, and then he picked up a rental van. He drove to the mall and went inside through the old Macy's entrance. I sat in my car and waited, I waited for hours, Milly, until I got a call from the police. They were looking for him. The company's bankruptcy filing had just been made, and they were looking for him. The FBI wouldn't tell me what he had done, other than he had taken a large amount of money and they wanted to talk to him.

"Then they put it on the news and sent the police and social services to your schools to pick you up.

"I went home, straight to his office, and opened his safe. It was empty except for this box which had my name on it."

She hands me the box with trembling hands.

There is a yellowing piece of paper stuck to it that simply says, Mary.

I open the lid and inside are envelopes with her name on the outside.

"What are these?" I ask as I sift through them. They all look the same.

She shakes her head and exhales, a sad, weary sound that guts me.

"When we were dating, he would write to me every day. I would get to work and there would be a letter on my desk. I kept them all, in order by date, in the box in his safe. I was confused, but I started opening them and each one had a piece of paper with a word on it." She nods at the box.

"Look, Milly."

I do. My heart pounding, I open the box. I pull out the stack of envelopes, there are dozens of them, and I open each one. I pull out the little slips of paper and lay them on the table. I don't allow myself to look at the words as I lay them out.

But I hear Dean say, "Holy shit!" as I lay the last one down and I bring my head up slowly, afraid of what I'll see.

Spelled out on small pieces of paper is this message.

"I'M SORRY. I didn't know what else to do. Had to leave. Don't tell anyone. Don't trust anyone. Keep the girls out of this. When you hear from me again, call this number. You can trust him. I'm coming back to you. I love you always."

Then on a final piece of paper, larger than the rest and crumpled, is a note not in his handwriting.

"The Fauquier Bank. Account No: 672348111, Routing No: 7645100000034"

"What does this mean? He was being blackmailed? Do you know this bank?" These questions are shot off, rapid fire.

It is Dean's hand on my knee which makes me pause.

"What?" I look at him impatiently.

"Give her a minute to answer," he says and raises an eyebrow in her direction.

She has her arms wrapped around her waist and is rocking slightly. I immediately wrap an arm around her.

"Oh, Mom, I'm sorry. This must be so hard for you."

"No, Milly, it's not. I'm so relieved. I wish I'd had the courage to show you sooner. I wanted to do what he said, to not involve you. You and Lilly were gone so soon after we moved and Addie was so angry at me, I just kept quiet."

I turn to Dean. "I've wondered if the FBI knows more than what they are saying. Because I've never thought their actions, moving us, hiding us, searching for him so vigorously, was a proportionate response to someone who was accused of stealing money."

Dean's eyebrows lift. "Maybe."

"Half of me wants him to come home so we can clear his name," my mother continues in a haunted voice. "The other half wants him to do whatever it takes to stay alive so maybe we can find each other again one day and live free with whatever time we have left."

I'm trying to catch my breath and make sense of everything I've learned. I should be upset that she's kept this from me for so long, but I'm not. We all survived the best way we knew how.

"What are we going to do?" I ask no one in particular. My mind is moving from possibility to possibility at a mile a minute. "We have to figure this out. Find out where the money is, at least."

"There is one more thing," my mother says quietly. "And I feel crazy even saying it aloud." She glances up at us furtively. "I think...I *feel* like I saw him."

"What?" Dean and I both shout at the same time. I jump off the couch like it's on fire.

"See, I shouldn't have said anything," she says mournfully.

"No, I'm sorry. Please go on, I mean, it's just shocking, but if you saw him . . . then tell us," I stammer.

"Well, it was right after that whole craziness happened with the media being tipped off to where we were last year. I went out for a walk in Rivers Wilde, it was a week or so after the madness died down. I was just strolling. I went to that cupcake place, you know the one with the stupid lines out the door? What's the name?"

She is snapping her fingers, trying to remember, and I have to bite my tongue. "It's not important. I'll look it up later."

"Okay, fine. Anyway, I was in line, like the lemming I am, waiting and someone bumped into me, knocked my purse off my shoulder. I bent down to pick it up. But before I could reach it, someone got it for me. And Milly, the hand that put it in mine, I swear on my life it was your father's. I thought I was going to faint. But when I looked up, he was gone. I mean, gone. Like a ghost. I didn't see anyone on the street who looked like him. I got out of line and sat down on one of those benches and cried.

"And this young girl, who had been in line in front of me, came out and handed me a cupcake. She thought I was crying because I lost my place in line. Kwasia!"

I burst out laughing. Dean looks at me, confusion marring his lovely face.

"That word, *kwasia*, it means 'idiot,'" I explain. He only nods but doesn't seem amused.

He looks back at my mother. "You saw him." He isn't asking as much as he is affirming.

"I don't know. I think so. I mean, I've been married to him for thirty-four years, I know his hands," my mother says, her tone almost defensive.

"I believe you," Dean says. "Hiding in plain sight, I mean. And then keeping a close eye on you after you guys had been exposed."

"Yes, I think so, too."

"You are all so matter-of-fact about all of this. It's like you're discussing traffic and not the fact that my father, who has been missing and a wanted criminal for more than ten years, is possibly living close by!" I scream at them.

"Baby . . ." Dean starts to say.

"Don't 'baby' me!" I shout.

"This isn't about either of you. Sit down and stop shouting!" my mother admonishes me.

And that was all it took. I felt ashamed for my outburst. She was right. I needed to calm down.

I sat down.

"What do we do?" she asks, her eyes, usually so steady, look to me for calm.

"I don't know," I answer honestly.

Dean slips his hand into mine and squeezes. "Call your sisters tomorrow. Let them know what you have learned and decide how to go from there. But I don't think you should take what the FBI has told you at face value. Also, call from my office. Don't use your phone. Maybe they have you guys under surveillance."

My eyes widen, and I know he was right. They always know when we have and haven't been in communication.

———

It's still dark in the room when I open my eyes again. I feel Dean's absence from my bed before my hand touches the cool pillow where his head should be. I sit up. My body feels like it needs a good long workout, and I have a horrible taste in my mouth. God, after that marathon confession from my mother yesterday, I fell asleep without brushing my teeth.

I'm in the middle of brushing my teeth, with the shower running, when I hear my bedroom door open. Dean walks into the bathroom and leans against the doorframe, arms crossed on his chest. He's a sight for sore eyes. He's dressed in sweatpants and a T-shirt. His feet are bare; even his feet are beautiful. I know what I must look like. So I'm shocked when the first thing out of his mouth is, "You look beautiful this morning, Red."

He's looking at me like I'm holding the secrets to the universe in my hand. I finish brushing my teeth and wipe my mouth before I respond.

"Oh, you must be blind."

I'm drying my hands when he comes up behind me. He wraps his arms around my waist and lays his chin on my shoulder. Meeting my eyes in the mirror, he says, "No, I have perfect vision."

I can't stop the smile that creeps across my face.

"I'm going to make a call. Let me know what time I should have the car ready," he says as he starts toward the door.

"You're going to work from here today?" I ask. We hadn't talked about when or how to tell her about our relationship. So I had decided to keep things to myself.

"Is that okay?"

"Of course. Yes, please, stay as long as you like."

"Don't say that. I might never leave."

My breath escapes in a trembling exhalation. "Dean, we're in love." I can hear how wondrous my tone is. We've exchanged this sentiment so many times, but somehow, hearing him say it so casually feels amazing.

"Yes, babe, we are." And then he wraps his arms around me in the sweetest embrace I've ever experienced. He lays his head on top of mine, and we stand there silent for a full minute.

He releases me, walks me to the shower, and opens the glass

door. "Get in, I'm late for my call." And with another quartet of kisses to my cheeks, forehead, and chin he leaves.

It's only when I'm washing my hair and soap gets into my open mouth that I realize I'm grinning. The bubble of joy that has been bouncing around in my gut turns into a geyser. And I'm so happy I start to sing.

surprise

DEAN CALLS JUST as I'm getting into bed. I answer before the second ring.

"Hey, how's LA?" I ask.

"I miss you," he rasps in return.

I smile and cradle the phone. "I hate that I won't see you before we leave for France."

"Fuck *that*." His voice sends chills down my spine and gooseflesh spreads all over me.

"What do you mean?"

"Are you asleep?" he asks, sounding sleepy himself.

"No, getting into bed. What about you?"

"I'm at your front door," he says, his voice low and sensual.

I'm out of bed and heading to the front door in a flash.

"And I'm hungry."

"I have some leftovers in the fridge." I start walking again.

"No, Red. I'm hungry for you. I want you to ride my face. I want to fuck you until you're spent. Then, I want to fall asleep next to you."

God, I love him. I can't believe how much. "You can have all of that." I rush down the stairs.

"This week without you has been unbearable," he drawls down the line.

"I know exactly what you mean." I reach the front door and fling it open.

Without breaking my stride, I fling myself into his arms and burrow my face in his neck, breathing in the scent of his aftershave. I flick my tongue out and revel in the salt of his skin.

His arms go around me and he lifts me off my feet. My legs wrap around his waist and he walks us into the house, kicking the door shut behind him.

"I'm so glad this back and forth is over," he murmurs into my ear. He presses kisses on the side of my face and down my neck. And I do the same to him. Our lips meet and our kiss burns hot and fast, a beautiful melody of lips and tongues and co-mingled breaths that transports me every single time.

He carries me up the stairs, taking two at a time, and walks into my bedroom, shutting the door quietly.

He puts me down on the bed, and I get a good look at him. He's wearing a beautifully cut navy blue suit with a white shirt, his cuff links winking at his wrists. His tie, dark blue with thin white diagonal stripes, is already loosened. His hair is styled and off his face, showing off his incredible bone structure and his gorgeous eyes. His grin is positively devilish.

I tip my head to one side and smile at him. "I thought you were hungry. Are you going to stand there all night or are you going to eat?"

I spread my legs so my robe falls open exposing my body. He stalks toward me, and without saying a word kneels between my legs. He puts his mouth on my breast, his tongue drawing circles before his lips clamp down on my nipple. My body bucks off the bed at the exquisite sensation that courses through me. He continues licking and sucking while one hand trails down my abdomen to between my legs. He parts the lips of my pussy and glides over my throbbing clitoris, one, two, three times before he leaves two fingers there to apply pressure that has my orgasm building fast and fierce.

"Dean. Oh, Dean."

He only sucks harder at my breast and rubs my clit harder. And I'm coming in a matter of a minute. I grab my pillow and bring it over my face to muffle the scream which rips from my throat.

He moves down my body, his mouth releasing my breast and moving down my torso. His tongue laving, his teeth nipping, as he makes his way.

When his mouth reaches my pussy, I try to close my legs, my body still recovering from the last orgasm to take any more stimulation.

"Open your legs," Dean mumbles. His hands run up and down my thighs, his caress makes me writhe and his command causes my pulse to speed up.

"I don't know if I can take another one," I say dazed.

"You can. Open your legs," he says softly. He starts to pepper kisses up my calves. When he reaches my knees, my legs fall open.

"That's it, baby." His hands run up the inside of my thighs and a shudder courses through my body.

"Dean . . ." I say, not sure whether it's a plea for mercy or for more.

"Yes, baby, tell me what you want," Dean says, his mouth hovering a mere inch from my pussy.

"I want your mouth, I want you." And before I even finish he's on me, his mouth so gentle, so soft, that my legs fall open even farther on their own.

He holds my legs open, eating me slowly, softly. His hands come up to grab my breasts, he kneads them. And just as I start to pant from the building orgasm, he moves his mouth from me, slides up my body and in one smooth move, slides inside, burying himself to the hilt.

While the oral he has given me was soft and almost reverent, his fucking isn't. He's unrestrained. His hands hold my knees up so that I'm folded in half and he pounds into me.

It's amazing. Every single thrust is like the swipe of a flint against stone, and soon a fire is raging inside of me. I match him, thrust for thrust. Soon we are both sweating; the sweat from his hair drips onto my chest and he dips his head to lick it off and captures my nipple at the same time.

His thrusts slow down, but their intensity increases and soon, I'm falling off the edge of the world.

My orgasm leaves me senseless. I cannot hear, or see, or breathe. All I can do is feel. My entire body, every single nerve ending, is on fire. And I never want this to stop. I never want Dean to leave my body. I didn't even know sex could be like this. I didn't know any of this was possible.

And as Dean chases his orgasm, he grabs my headboard and uses it for leverage as he thrusts home. Each thrust is punctuated by a word.

"This. Is. A. Fucking. Dream. I. Don't. Ever. Want. To. Wake. Up. From." And then he collapses on top of me, for a second letting me bear his full weight, and it feels incredible.

I wrap my tired arms around him, and he rolls to his side bringing me with him. My hair is a tangled mess and we are coated in sweat.

I have never been more content than I am now.

Dean is breathing hard next to me. When he catches his breath, he swings his legs off the bed and reaches out a hand to grab me.

"Come on, let's get ready for bed. I'm fucking exhausted."

I get up to join him. As we stand in the shower and then at the sink brushing our teeth, I know with a certainty I've only ever had about being a mother that I want this for the rest of my life.

unlocked

two weeks later

"YOU SHOULD COME WITH US."

I look up from my phone, wistful but unmoved. "I've got to get this house on the market. And you should probably tell your sister about us before I just show up to her surprise engagement."

She rolls her big, golden eyes and goes back to packing.

"Oh shit, it's him." I stand.

Milly stops and walks over to me. "Who?"

"The PI I hired to look into Jean-Luc."

I've been so sucked into this brand new happy life I've found myself living, I'd forgotten all about him.

"What have you got?" I ask as soon as we've said hello. I don't want to draw this out any longer.

Milly sits down next to me and puts the phone on speaker so she can hear, too.

"There's no billionaire French count with a son named Jean-Luc."

"What?" we speak at the same time.

"That kid's a fraud. He's French and his name is Jean-Luc, but nothing else you told me is true. He's an actor and waited tables in Sedona until 2009. His family in France are all dead save one sister and she's far from rich."

My head spins and I close my eyes to try and focus. But I can't. Milly's grip on my hand tightens but she doesn't say a word.

"Wait...so if he's not the money, and my mother didn't get money from an insurance policy, where is the money from?"

"No clue. But if you can get me a bank statement or something, I have a good forensics guy that might be able to tell you."

"Thanks, Nick. I'll be in touch."

Milly and I look at each other, silent and wide-eyed for a full minute after the call ends.

"Will you come with me?" I turn to Milly.

She doesn't ask where we're going, she just slips her hand into my outstretched one. "Yes."

I still don't have the code to the alarm, but at this point I don't care. If the police come, I'll explain. My name is on the deed, and that's all I need. I'm not waiting another day to get in there and find out what she doesn't want me to see. My stomach roils but I start my car and call the first locksmith that comes up on my google search.

I'm reeling. I grab the keys to my Porsche and head to Milly's place. I'm terrified of what I might find, what she'll bear witness to, but this is an errand I don't want to run by myself.

dean

deceit

"GO AHEAD AND OPEN IT." I nod to the locksmith when he hesitates.

"Are you sure it's okay? I mean, your ID says you live in New York."

I sigh and cross my arms over my chest. "This is my house. If you're not going to open it, leave. I'll call someone else. There are plenty of people who would be happy to make $500 for two minutes of work."

Next to me, Milly is silent, grim-faced. The weight of her anxiety has been pressing hard on me all day, and finally, my threadbare patience snaps.

"Fuck it, I'm in a rush." I mutter and pull out my phone.

His face flushes, and he gives us a dirty look. "Whatever, it's not my business. But if this goes left, I'll make sure the police know that I tried to stop you."

I scowl at him.

He gets to work and I check my mental inventory of the things I need to do once we're inside. I have no idea what I'm looking for, I just want to get in and out of this house as fast as I can.

"There you go." He steps aside, sweating and still scowling.

"Here." I hand him my credit card and he peers at it and grumbles, "Same name, at least."

"Man, just hurry up and run it." I step inside and enter the four-digit code on the alarm key pad.

The house is damp and musty with grief. Dust motes make flurries in the sunbeams pouring through the partially open blinds.

I turn a full circle turn in the foyer and shake my head in amazement that this house used to be my home.

Everything is as it was, the dust covered furniture exactly she'd left it when she moved out.

I step back out and wait for him to finish his business.

"Here you go." He hands me my credit card and then whips up his phone, aims the camera at me and takes a picture.

"Are you serious right now?" I ask, stepping toward him. "You can't just take my picture."

"I'm not taking any chances. If I hear this place got robbed, I'll be taking this to the police." He backs away from me, arms up like he's about to start kung fu fighting.

I burst out laughing and stay where I am. "What about me looks like a criminal to you?"

He smirks. "As if all criminals look like Voldemort." He tucks his phone away and then plasters a friendly smile on his face. "Thank you for choosing Easy Open. You'll get a link to leave a review, you can ignore it." His smarmy smile feels more like a middle finger.

"If you don't leave, I'll be filing a complaint," Milly snaps. He takes one look at her scowl, turns heel, and speed walks down the driveway.

"Let's go." I link our fingers as we step inside and close the door.

The furniture is draped. Cobwebs cling to corners and criss-cross the room. The air in here is oppressive. I'd forgotten how sad I'd been in this place.

"Come, let's see what we can find and get out of here."

"Okay." Milly nods and we move together to the little desk where my mother used to sit to pay bills.

We've been searching for an hour before we find the file folder labeled bank statements.

It's empty.

"Wait, that drawer, its bottom is too shallow. Maybe it's a false one?" Milly says.

I realize with a start that it's the first time she's spoken since we got here.

I'm grateful she was paying attention.

I move out of her way. She crouches down and reaches into the drawer and presses it with her palm. "Oh yeah, it's loose." She grunts and reaches further in.

"I got it." She yanks and pulls out a thin piece of composite board.

I peer inside and my heart falls to my stomach.

I hoped I wouldn't find anything, I prayed that however she got the money, I'd never know.

I pull out the glossy white envelope with gold writing that reads "The Fauquier Bank."

Whatever was inside was going to change my life forever.

My hands shake as I pry open the prongs holding it shut, and pour the contents out onto the desk.

It only holds three things.

A checkbook, some sort of bank record, and a bundle of pictures.

My entire body breaks into gooseflesh as I look through the stack of photos. They're long distance lens shots of my father with hers outside their house. They're arguing, the pictures are frame by frame of it and then stop when Mr. Hassan turns to go back inside.

There are pictures of them coming out of an office building, arguing again, and then getting into separate cars.

What in the world was my mother doing with these?

I flip open the checkbook. There's a name and a code that simply says "SWISS". The sole transaction on this statement was dated December 2, 2008 in the amount of 240 million dollars.

That was the day before my father disappeared.

"What the fuck?" Milly shouts and then covers her mouth.

"I don't know. How could she have this money?"

"Maybe because she and your dad stole it?"

I blink, surprised by the hardness of her voice and the razor-sharp edge of accusation in her words.

"How?"

"I don't know. But we need to tell the FBI."

Alarm brings me to my feet. "Wait. We don't know what this means."

"Exactly, so we need to give it to them. Maybe they'll stop hunting my dad and actually start trying to figure what happened to him."

I grab her hand. "Let me talk to my mom, first. What if we're wrong?"

"Then, she'll be fine. But if we're right, every second we wait, my dad is out there on the run for a crime he didn't commit."

———

We've been lost in our own thoughts since yesterday and have barely spoken. I know I should let her call the FBI, but she's my mom.

I need to be sure before I set something in motion I won't be able to stop. And I want to know the truth before the rest of the world does.

"I hope we can get this resolved soon. I hate not telling my mom the truth." Millys says.

I'm dropping Milly, her mom, and Anthony off at the airport and her mom and Anthony went inside to give us a private moment.

"Thank you for giving me this time," I say.

She looks so solemn, so sad. "Of course. I love you. I'm sorry this is happening." She kisses me and then turns to join the others.

I jump into my car, pull out my phone, and look at the picture I took yesterday. The bank name, account number, and routing number on the note are the same as the bank name, account number, and routing number on this checkbook. I took Milly home and went back to the house by myself. But then, I couldn't bring myself to go inside.

I sat there for an hour, stunned at what I'd found. I couldn't make any sense of it. My mother has the money the whole world thinks Omar Hassan stole.

She is the reason my father is dead.

She's the reason Mr. Hassan is gone.

My stomach heaves at the terrible thought that flashes in my mind. *"What if he's dead, too?"*

The love of my life has lived without her father for all of these years and my *mother* made that happen.

I sit there until the sun starts to set and then I force myself to do what I know I must.

I book a flight to Marseille and go home to pack.

I need to do this face to face.

I can't believe that less than forty-eight hours ago, I felt like I had everything I ever wanted.

And now, I'm about to lose it all.

before the storm

WE ARRIVED in Paris this morning. Anthony, my mother, and I all flew in and went to the hotel Simon reserved for us.

It's incredible, sumptuously decorated and with a butler assigned to each room. Lilly arrived before us and is already lounging by the pool. I wish Dean had been able to come, but it will be a fun trip anyway, all of us are sharing the same suite. It'll be like a sleepover.

Simon's brother, Kyle, and his nephew, Henry, are staying in the rooms on either side of us. Simon and Addie are in the hotel, too, but on a different floor so that Addie doesn't see us.

Tomorrow, we're heading to Versailles to witness Simon's very thoughtful and romantic proposal.

It's wonderful for all of us to be together again. It's so different from our the last time we were together. Addie and my mother walked on eggshells around each other and ended up having an epic argument. Now, they've resolved their issues and I hope this trip will be very different.

We're getting ready to head down to the suite Kyle and Henry are sharing, where we've all agreed to meet for dinner. This will be Anthony's first time meeting Henry, who is just a month past his first birthday. He's been talking about his cousin Henry nonstop.

Lilly's been in a great mood, too. In fact, this is the happiest I've seen her in years. And I can't wait to get a chance to talk to her and find out what's behind it.

Just then my phone pings with a text. When I look at the screen I see it's from Dean. An involuntary smile comes to my face before I remember that he's going to see his mother.

I'll never understand her determination to keep us apart, but I've accepted it.

Dean is in denial, but it's clear to me that she and his father stole that money and she's let my father take the blame all these years. I hope he doesn't expect me to just let that go.

Dread starts to line my I put my phone away and walk out into our suite's sitting room where Lilly, my mom, and Anthony are waiting.

"It's about time. I was just about to send Anthony in for you." Lilly stands up and pokes a finger in my ribs.

"Cut it out." I swat her hand playfully and grab Anthony's hand.

"Were you and lover boy arguing about how would hang up first?" Lilly laughs.

"Grow up," I snap.

"Lillian, stop teasing your sister. Millicent, you're going to make us late. We don't want Simon's brother to have a bad impression of us."

My mother looks nervous and I feel bad for delaying us. She has been on tenterhooks since we arrived. When I talked to her about it in the taxi she said she was just excited about Simon proposing. And nervous that Addie, who in general hates surprises, wouldn't react well.

"Sorry, Mom. Let's go." I smile at her. I grab her hand to give it a quick squeeze before I grab my purse.

———

Dinner was amazing. My mother, though, was agitated and distracted all night. She excused herself and went back to the room before the second course was served. She declined my offer to walk her back down to our room. I let her go and tried to enjoy the beautiful evening Simon planned for us.

Our chaperone for the evening is Simon's brother, Kyle. They could be twins, they look so much alike. His hair, longer on top than Simon's, is a gorgeous mop of silky chocolate corkscrew curls. He's got a very easygoing personality. He laughs a lot and has been the life of the party all evening. He's rakishly charming and irreverently funny. And he loves Addie. It's obvious from the way he talks about her that they are very close.

I'm so glad she has her own little family here. Tomorrow is going to be such a special day, and I'm grateful Simon wanted to share it with us.

Cara and Louis are the happiest wedding planning couple ever. Their wedding is in six months and they are so relaxed about the whole thing that I wonder if maybe they are on drugs. It's not a small affair they are having, either.

Lilly, Anthony, and I get back to our suite with Lilly carrying a sleeping Anthony to my room for me.

I walk over to my mother's room to check on her. When I open the door, I find it empty. I step back out into the suite's sitting room and look around.

Lilly and Anthony are already in my room when I call out, "Mom?" It's odd she would leave the room without saying anything. But, maybe she wanted some fresh air.

Lilly walks out of the room, looking around. "Is Mom not here?" She sounds as surprised as I feel.

"Nope," I say and plop down on the couch, kicking my shoes off.

"That's so weird. Should we be worried?" Lilly asks as she takes a seat next to me.

"I don't know," I answer honestly.

Our mother speaks no French, but I can't imagine that would stop her from roaming. She's always liked to do that.

"Maybe she just went on a walk to clear her head," I posit, not entirely convinced of this myself.

I decided to shake off my bad thoughts and focus on getting some sleep. I've been worried about Dean, watching my phone and praying he'll call.

I hate the turmoil he's going through, but I realized I couldn't hold his hand through it. Because all I wanted from him was to turn over what we'd found so at the very least, we could clear my father's name.

"I'm going to go down to the bar and get a drink," Lilly says suddenly.

"Okay, I'm going to wait here and try to get some reading in. I'm sure Mom will be back soon. I'll go to bed when she gets back." We smile at each other.

"Glad you're reading again. I know it was one of your favorite things to do when we were kids. Glad you're getting back to it."

With a, "I'll see you later" she's off. I check my phone. Dean hasn't called.

"It's okay. Whatever happens, you're never losing him again." I pray I'm right, pray his mother doesn't find a way to drive a wedge between us, and grab my Kindle.

chaos

SIMON'S PROPOSAL was a fairytale brought to life. Addie was uncharacteristically emotional, but we all were. There wasn't a dry eye in the room. Then, we had an amazing dinner at a legendary restaurant in Versailles.

We had all just gone to sleep when my mother's phone rang. She never silences her phone and keeps the volume on her ringer turned up as loud as it will go.

Therefore, when it starts to ring right after midnight, I hear it in the room I'm sharing with Anthony. But that's not what gets me out of my bed and racing into the suite's living room, crossing it in three strides and opening my mother's door without knocking. It's the yelling that does it.

I barge in and find her moving around like a tornado. Her hair is a mess and her clothes are askew. She's yelling to whoever is on the other end of the phone. Lilly is standing there watching her eyes wide and hand clasped over her mouth.

"I'm on my way back. He has a lawyer. You can't talk to him without his lawyer present. I'm calling him now."

She's throwing clothes into her suitcase, frantically packing her things. When she's done screaming demands into the phone, she throws it down and runs into her bathroom.

"Mom, what in the world is going on?" I follow her and see her scooping toiletries haphazardly into her little travel sized bag.

She turns around and without stopping, runs back into her room, yelling back at me over her shoulder. "Your father turned himself in. They have him. They are on their way back to DC right now. I'm going to meet him."

My heart hammers against my chest, my scalp prickles with the nerve impulses speeding through my body as I try to process what she's saying. I shake my head to free myself from my stupor and look at her.

She is moving like a dervish throwing her clothes on. I have to grab her shoulders to make her stop.

"Mom, stop. Please. Tell me what's going on," I say forcefully.

She shakes herself free. "Are you deaf, Milly? I just told you. Your father's in FBI custody. I need to get to him."

While she turns back to her bed, I look up at Lilly for help, but she has left the room.

How can any of this be happening? Why is my mother so . . . excited? Because that's what she is. She doesn't seem nervous, or scared, or shocked. She seems joyfully excited.

I run to stand in between my mother and her suitcase.

"Mom, is this it? Did he give you the signal?" I demand.

She looks at me like I don't have the sense I was born with and purses her lips while she rolls her eyes.

"Of course, Milly. How else would I know?" And then my mother, all five feet two inches of her, puts her hand on my arm and shoves me out of the way to continue packing. "You're wasting time asking questions. If you want answers, come with me. I'm leaving now."

My head is spinning. I run back to my room to call Addie. I let her know what has happened, worrying how she will react to the news. But she only offers to help us pack. So, I start packing our things and prepare to travel with my mother.

Less than two hours later, we are at the airport, buying our plane tickets to DC. Addie decided to come with us in the end. And for my mother and my sisters, it is so reminiscent of the last time our father threw our family into chaos. But this time, my mother seems focused and not the least bit unnerved.

I'm not as scared as I was before, because no matter what happens, I'm going home to Dean. It's only as we are buckling ourselves into airplane seats I realize in the craziness of this day I didn't speak to him once and have no idea where he is.

I check on Anthony who is already asleep again, and then close my own eyes, knowing when I open them again, I'll be on my way to see one of the two men I love most in this world.

clear blue nothing

IT'S total pandemonium when I land in Provence, the airport that services my mother's vacation home of Marseille. I'm tired, peed off, and hungry.

But then I turn on my phone and see Milly's text asking about my mother. I start to text her back when a CNN news alert pops up on my screen. "Omar Hassan of Enron infamy in FBI custody. Being escorted back to the United States."

My phone clatters to the floor. I even look down, but don't pick it up until someone taps me on the shoulder to tell me I've dropped my phone.

I scoop it up and walk back to the ticket counter. My first thought is that I have to get to Milly. I know she is supposed to be traveling to London today, but I doubt she will be anywhere but the United States.

It's almost noon here, and I hope that if I leave now I can be back by late afternoon.

My hopes are dashed when I'm told the last flight to DC has already left for the day. My mind dashes to London, maybe Milly is still there and I can go there instead. She will need me, and I need to show her what I found.

I dial her number and she picks up right away. "Dean, oh my God. Where are you? I've been calling you since we landed. Have you seen the news?" She is speaking in a rapid and hushed tone.

My heart races. How the hell am I going to explain being in France without telling her everything over the phone?

Shit.

"Milly, I'm sorry. I was on a plane. My phone was off. I just landed and saw your text."

"Dean, can you—" She starts to cut me off but I keep talking.

"Milly, please listen. I'm in France. I can't get a flight home until tomorrow morning."

"What?" Her hushed tone disappears and I hear rustling. It sounds like she's moving.

"It's a long story. And I'll tell you when I get home. But I'm here to see my mother, and then I'll be back."

"I thought you were in Sedona to see your mother." She sounds exasperated and tired. And I feel guilty for adding to whatever stress she must be under right now.

"She wasn't there, and I really needed to talk to her. Have you seen your dad yet?" I ask quickly.

"No, we haven't. We are at Langley now, waiting to see him."

I lean back in my seat in surprise. "Langley? That's the CIA building, isn't it?"

"Well, that's where they took him. We are all here waiting to see what's going on. But the only thing we do know, because we've spoken to his lawyer, is that he's not under arrest." The exasperation is gone from her voice and all that is left is the exhaustion.

I'm just as tired, but I know that what she's saying makes no sense. "How can he not be under arrest? The FBI has been looking for him for more than a decade."

"I don't know yet. But my mother… My mother knows things . . ." She trails off and I hear the struggle she's having to keep her voice steady.

"Who is there with you?" I ask, deciding that asking any more questions at this point would be counterproductive.

"My mother and my sisters," she responds.

"Where is Ant Man?" I ask her right away, worried about how my little guy is faring in all this craziness.

"He's with Rabea. We dropped him off when we got here. He was so exhausted. We didn't talk about much in front of him because he hears everything. I didn't want to scare him."

She yawns at the end of her sentence and I decide that's my cue to let her go and figure out what the fuck I'm going to do with myself.

"Okay, baby. Listen, I'm sorry I wasn't there when you got back. But I'll be there tomorrow afternoon, and we'll talk then, okay?"

"Okay, Dean." Her voice is thick with tears and I've never felt more useless or treacherous in my life. I don't know how to tell her what I've found.

"I love you. I will be there tomorrow. And we'll do this together." I try to sound sure of myself, even though I'm not sure Milly will *want* anything to do with me once I tell her everything.

"I love you, too. Please hurry, I need you," she whispers, sounding so defeated and scared.

"And I need you. So, take care of yourself until I can get there."

No one has ever needed me, not *just* for me. I won't let her down. I don't owe my mother a thing. And I'm not going to let her come between Milly and me again.

I walk out into the bright, blue sunshine of the Cote d'Azur, but I might as well be in Siberia for how cold I am on the inside.

All of the beauty of my surroundings is completely lost to me as I hop into a waiting cab and give them my mother's address. Marseille is about fifteen miles from the airport, so I have thirty minutes to sit back and think while we zoom past the coastline.

I don't know how today will end, but I know that when I

walk out of her house, I'm also going to be walking out of her life. The woman who gave birth to me isn't anything close to being my mother.

———

MARSEILLE

We pull up outside my mother's white stucco, red tile roofed beach house. I can smell the salt of the Mediterranean Sea in the breeze. The dichotomy between the beauty around me and the pain and ugliness whirling around inside of me is so startling, I have to catch my breath before I get out of the cab.

I pay the man, hop out, and walk up the steep stone steps that lead to my mother's front door. I can hear an upbeat pop song playing in the house, and I steel myself. That my mother is enjoying herself seems unfathomable to me. But I'm going to get to the bottom of everything today.

I knock loudly. I can hear my mother's voice shout something in French. I can't make it out, and I don't try. I just knock again. In the middle of my second knock, the door flies open and a young woman, no older than seventeen, opens the door.

"*Bonjour, monsieur. Puis-je vous aider?*" *Hello, sir. Can I help you?*

"*Oui, je cherche* Madame Orleans." I tell her I'm looking for my mother and her eyes grow suspicious.

She opens her mouth to ask me another question when my mother appears like an apparition behind her.

"Dean!" She looks like she has seen a ghost as she stares at me. "What in the world are you doing here?" she asks me, but somehow, I know it's not genuine surprise.

The girl ducks out of the doorway and scampers up the stairs right behind her.

My mother stands there staring at me. I take her in. Her blond hair is caught in a chignon at the base of her neck. She's dressed in a white billowy sundress, her skin is perfectly golden, and she's barefoot. She looks totally at peace.

I step past her and into her house. I've only been here once before, a long time ago. I see they have renovated the space. The whole downstairs is one huge room that incorporates a dining room, living room, and a library. At the opposite end of the entrance of the house is a wall of glass doors that open to a veranda.

I look at my mother who is watching me. The way a mouse might watch a lion. She looks petrified. She should be.

"Can we go out there and talk?" I ask as I nod toward the veranda.

"Well, Jean-Luc will be back any moment, so . . ." she hedges, looking around like she's planning an escape route.

"Well, then it will be better if we are outside when he does so that he doesn't overhear what we are about to discuss. Unless of course he already knows about your treachery."

She blanches but doesn't say a word. She simply starts walking. She gives me a wide berth when she passes me. Yet, she looks back over her shoulder at me when she steps outside. Her eyes lock with mine, and for the first time I see honest, naked regret in my mother's eyes.

"So, you know," she says as I sit down on one of the wooden lounge chairs they have on the terrace.

"What do I know, Mother?" I ask her slowly and calmly. My tone is at odds with the way I feel. I'm afraid. I have no idea what she's going to say next.

"Ed called me, asking me all sorts of questions. He said he ran into you, and you mentioned your father's life insurance policy."

She looks out over the balcony, staring at the ocean view this beautiful home comes with. She takes a deep inhale and releases it on an unsteady breath.

"I figured I'd be hearing from you. And here you are." She

looks at me— her lips pursed, the fear gone fròm her eyes—total calm in its place.

"Yes, here I am." Our eyes linger for a long moment, but I don't see anything in hers I recognize. I break our gaze and open my carry-on, pulling out the envelope I found in the false bottom of her drawer.

She jumps up and reaches for it. I only narrowly manage to keep it out of her grasp.

"Where did you get this? Did you break into my house?" she screams and reaches for it again.

I stand up to put some distance between us and raise my voice to match hers. "Mother, sit down. Now."

She glares at me, defiantly and with something akin to hatred in her eyes.

"You are such a shit. Just like your father. He ruined my life when he forced me to have you. I never ever wanted children. He knew this, so he tricked me," she screams at me, but sits down.

I feel like I've been kicked in the stomach with a steel-toe boot. This was always my suspicion, but to have it hurled at me so violently nearly cuts me off at the knees.

"Who is Jean-Luc, really?"

"He's really my husband. And he helped me move on when your father died."

I give her a disbelieving look. "And before that?"

"It's your father's fault." She has the audacity to feign wide-eyed innocence and swoon onto her luxurious chaise lounge. "I discovered, purely by chance, that he was putting huge amounts into an account, straight from the company's accounts. I thought he was embezzling money so he could leave me."

"He *was* leaving you," I snarl, the truth lunging out of me like a caged tiger.

"And I was happy to see him go. But I wasn't going to be left high and dry. So, on that last trip he made to Zurich the week before everything happened, Jean-Luc followed him. He took some pictures, while I went to Switzerland to open a bank account. And then, we hired a hacker who moved all the money from his account to Omar's and then to ours where the trail disappeared." She says it like she's talking about a day at the grocery store.

My fury is on a tight leash only because I need to hear everything before I react.

"And then what?"

"Then your father came to me and confessed about the money and told me that he was in trouble."

"What kind of trouble?"

"He'd been laundering money for some arms dealing, human trafficking assholes. He needed the money back or they were going to kill him."

"And he knew you had it?"

"No, he thought Omar had stolen it."

"And you let him?"

"I never liked that smug man. I figured they'd look into it and see he didn't have it and let him go."

I snort. "Yeah right. As if you even cared."

"Believe what you want. I don't know why he tried to be a hero."

"What do you mean?"

"He offered to go and meet with the cartel guys for your dad, pay them off with all the money he could liquidate, and beg for mercy. And then he never came back. I was afraid they'd killed him and maybe they'd kill us, too. So I didn't do anything and your dad, well, he made his choices, too." She shrugs one of her dainty shoulders, like what she just said is of little consequence.

I sit back down, unable to hold myself up anymore. "You're a monster. How could you?"

She rolls her eyes in exasperation. "Your father was miserable and in over his head. You were leaving for college and didn't need him anymore. I certainly didn't need him anymore. And I had Jean-Luc. We've all turned out okay."

She leans back on her chair, staring out at the sea. A view paid for with people's freedom, their family's well-being, my father's life.

And she looks content.

My blood is rushing in my ears, and it drowns out the sounds of the city that has been our companion during this conversation.

Bits of her diatribe come back to me.

She *wanted* my father to kill himself. She never wanted children. She didn't care about anyone but herself. Milly was just collateral damage in her eyes.

When my mind trips over Milly's name, all of my senses come rushing back to life.

That's where I need to be. I don't know what to do with the information I've just received, except that I need to tell Milly.

She needs to tell the FBI.

I need to make sure she has evidence.

I swallow the bile that rises up as I look at this woman sitting next to me. I wonder, absently, what happened to make her this way. Not that it matters.

"I've got to go." I stand up to leave the veranda. She merely glances at me, and then looks back to the sea.

"I suppose you're going to the police or something noble like that?" Her voice is full of disdain and acrimony.

I shake my head and look back at her. I can't find it in me to respond. I wouldn't know where to begin. And if I start screaming, I might never stop, and I need to get to Milly.

And so, without another word to my mother and knowing this is the last time I will see her, at least voluntarily, I turn and leave.

Something has broken in my soul. That piece of it that no matter what they do to you, allows you to believe your parents love you. It falls off, hits the ground, and shatters into a million pieces. In its place is a fissure I know won't ever be filled again. I'm an orphan. I have no parents. I'm lost in my loneliness.

I'm in a cab on my way back to the airport area to find a hotel for the night when I kick myself.

I'm a rich man. Not rich enough to own my own private plane, at least not yet. But, I can certainly afford to charter one.

I lean forward and ask the cab driver to head directly to the airport.

I need to put as much distance between myself and my mother as I can.

Our memory is a powerful thing. And so, I use it to recall Milly. Her name, as it moves through my mind, the name helps me to remember the way it feels to be loved. Then I remember I haven't really been alone since I was sixteen years old. Because that's when Millicent Hassan crawled into my heart, staked her claim on it, and never let go.

I remember if I can make it onto that plane, survive the flight, that the arms waiting for me are strong, loving, and all mine.

I use my memories of our first kiss, of the first time I saw her again, of the last time I saw her to help me put one foot in front of the other to get on that plane so I can get back to her.

And then I figure out what the fuck I'm going to do.

I open my phone and call Val. "I need your help."

sacrifice

Langley, VA

We've been at the CIA headquarters now for more than twenty-four hours. My mother is beside herself. She has screamed, begged, cajoled, all to no avail. We haven't been able to see my father.

Until now.

They have taken us back one by one. We haven't been allowed to talk to each other after our meeting with him. I agreed to go last.

They said once we are all done, we will be able to see each other and leave.

It's all so strange. His lawyer says he's not under arrest, but he can't leave with us. Addie is in with him now, while I'm sitting here in this brightly lit room with comfortable chairs—an attempt to make it seem welcoming—by myself, coming out of my skin with anxiety.

Because I know Anthony is safe with Rabea, the only other

thought that permeates my brain besides this disaster with my father is Dean.

I haven't heard from him again. I'm confused and worried. He sounded distracted when we talked. I hate that we're not together right now. I really do need him. But I can also sense that he needs me. I haven't ever been a particularly romantic person. But my relationship with Dean seems to transcend all of the definitions I ever placed on my heart.

I don't know how to define what he means to me other than by its vastness. And then I can only say that the depth and breadth of my love for him is fathomless. He's a part of me. We have always been able to see past the exterior. See past what everyone else sees when they look at us, and just see the human heart beating in time to our self-doubt, our worry, and our brilliance.

I know without a doubt that as long as he draws breaths, Dean is the only person I want to navigate through this messy journey we call life with.

I turn my phone over again and call him one more time, it goes straight to voicemail. I don't bother leaving a message. It would be the same as the others I've left today.

I'm just slipping my phone back in my purse when the door opens and Agent Walker walks in.

She was with the group that brought my father in. I saw her briefly when we arrived, but I haven't seen her again since.

"Ms. Dennis, I'm here to take you to your father. Your sister, Adelaide, is done and is in a room with your mother and Lillian. When you're done with your father, we will take you to them, and you will be escorted out of the building."

She's a striking woman, beautiful skin a shade darker than my mother's milk chocolate complexion. Her eyes, mouth, nose, and cheekbones all work in perfect harmony to make her look like a Nubian goddess. Those eyes, though, are completely devoid of any warmth as she speaks with me.

I simply nod, and we start to walk out of the room.

"Agent Walker, why are you here?" I ask as we enter the hallway.

"I'm on the task force that has been looking for your father," she responds shortly.

"Yes, but you're with the FBI. Why are you at the CIA head-quarters?"

She stops walking and puts a hand on my arm to stop my progress. She looks at me, and for the first time since our brief acquaintance I see her smile.

"I could tell you, but then I'd have to kill you." And then she winks at me and starts to walk again.

I wish I could muster some amusement at her response. "That's really helpful," I mumble.

"Don't worry, Ms. Dennis. Your father will tell you every-thing he can. I'm sure you'll understand perfectly then."

When we reach the end of the hallway, she turns to me once more. "Are you ready?"

I nod, but I know nothing could ever make me feel ready for what's about to happen.

She nods back and then opens the door. She steps back, making room for me to enter. I walk through the door, and for the first time since I was seventeen years old I see my father.

"Milly?" my father asks. He's standing as tall and straight as ever in the middle of the room. His hair is almost completely white now, but otherwise he looks exactly as I remember. His glittering amber eyes, the eyes he gave all three of his children, are red-rimmed, yet sharp as he watches me.

I just stare at him. My breaths short, my chest heaving, my eyes burning, and my throat clogged with unreleased sobs.

"Are you going to hit me?" he asks seriously.

"No," I huff out in surprise. "Why would I?"

"Because Lilly did. I understand. I just want to be prepared."

"I'm not going to hit you, Daddy." I can't believe I'm looking at him, sharing the same space with him.

"Can I...can I hug you, baby?"

I've been waiting to hear his voice for so long. To feel his arms around me…and I'm overwhelmed by how much we've all been through.

I can only nod. When he's a few feet away, he holds his hands out to me. I stare at them. I know these hands so well, distinctive for the heavy spray of freckles that cover them and his arms, yet no other place on his body.

I reach my hand out slowly because I'm so afraid if I move too fast all of this will end. That somehow this is a trick.

But our fingers touch, and I know he's real. His hand grasps mine, and it's so familiar and so comforting. My father's touch.

"Daddy?" I whisper. I look at our joined hands and then up at his face. Tears stream down his cheeks. My trembling hand reaches up to brush his tears away, and he does the same for me. I feel the stubble on his unshaved jaw and I'm transported to my childhood and his Saturday morning snuggles. The ones he gave us before he shaved.

He pulls me into him. I wrap my arms around his waist, lay my head on his chest, and take a deep, fortifying breath. I try to calm myself down so that I can speak. He just holds me, stroking my hair and not saying a word.

I pull away from him after a few minutes because I'm desperate to see his face again.

He pulls back, too, but keeps his grasp on my hand and pulls me to the table near the front of the room. Two chairs sit opposite one another. It looks like an interrogation room I've seen on TV. There is one window, and I wonder if anyone is watching. I ask this aloud and he says, "No, I don't think so, but at this point I also don't care."

He sits down across from me and grasps both of my hands. He looks me in the eyes. "I never thought I would have this chance. To sit and talk to you. To hear your voice. I'm so sorry, baby. I've missed your whole life. Please, tell me everything."

I stare at him for a second, and then I snort in laughter. "Uh, Dad, no. You need to tell *me* everything, first."

The ghost of a smile, so much like Lilly's when she's chagrined, spreads across his face.

"Yes, of course, my dear. I owe you so many explanations. Let me start from the beginning. I didn't know anything was wrong until two weeks before the shit hit the fan."

I lean away and back. "How is that possible?"

He sighs. "Nick was a very, very good accountant. He may have left that career behind to grow the company. But he knew how to hide things in ways that no one would notice they were missing. He came to me, told me he'd been laundering money for a global arms dealer for years. He was looking for a way out, he wanted me to help him turn himself in to the FBI. He was hoping he'd get immunity from prosecution if he turned on them. We were working on it. I was scared shitless and tried to help him, but kept my distance and documented everything he told me, as he told me."

I nod. "So, you had no idea."

"None at all. None. I was our sales guy, I traveled and brought in business and investors and sold our ideas. I was the window dressing, he was the entire window."

He runs a hand over his head. "I was in a daze, scared, shocked. I couldn't believe he'd been doing that right under my nose. I didn't trust myself or anyone else."

"We contacted the FBI, and the day before we were to turn ourselves in, he disappeared. The day before he came to my house, frantic because the money was gone. And he thought I'd taken it. He threw a bank statement in my face that showed a wire from my account to it. I don't know where he got them from. But he was crazed. Accusing me of colluding with his wife. And then, he was gone."

"Dean said he told them he'd be back in a week."

"He lied to them. And to all of us. I got a call telling me Nick had been kidnapped and that they'd exchange him for a hard drive cache he'd hidden in a safe at our office. I did what they said. When I got there, Nick was nowhere to be seen. The last thing I remember from that day is a blinding pain in the back of my head."

"Was that the same day the bankruptcy was announced?"

"I think. I lost a few days. But I know that the FBI raided our offices, discovered that the money on our earnings statements were completely made up and thought I was the culprit because that's how Nick had made it look."

"Oh my God. What?"

"The business was a money laundering Ponzi scheme."

I'm too stunned to speak.

"When I came to, like I said, I'd lost days. They showed me the news report of Nick's death. They killed him, they said. Made it look like a heart attack. Swore to do the same to me, but only after they killed everyone I loved." His eyes are haunted as he speaks.

My heart is in my throat, fear prickles down my spine. We'd been in greater danger than we could have imagined.

"So…why didn't they?"

"I convinced them I could help them set up a scheme that would make their money back quickly and exponentially."

"You did that?"

"Yes, but I never planned on being gone this long. I thought… I could stay, work for them doing whatever they needed of me - contracts, funneling funds, creating identities, whatever and then in a few years I'd have enough evidence to turn them in."

"What happened?"

"I spent the first eight years in a cell, I only left to exercise and eat."

"Oh my God."

"I never stopped planning to escape. It took me a long time to earn their trust. But I held on and did what I needed to because I knew you were safe. I became indispensable, befriended leadership. Had a few who even called me brother. They believed me when I said I preferred a life of crime to my life with you all. Three years ago, I started traveling for them by myself."

"Three years?" I ask, shocked that it's been so long.

He nods. "I know. I wanted to run. But I knew they were testing me. And so, I did what I could to keep an eye on you all and kept gathering my evidence. I finally got everything I needed to put those bastards away for good."

"So, the FBI didn't know any of this?"

He looks so grave I feel my hands turn cold with fear. "No. It was risky. But I traveled to Paris under one of my assumed passports and met your mother the first night you all were there." My eyes widen as I remember my mother leaving dinner and then not being in our room when we got back.

"It was the first time I'd been able to touch her in so long. I know I've caused you all so much pain, but I had to protect you."

"And the FBI had no clue that you needed rescuing, and not finding?"

"No, these guys had them chasing their tails. They would have arrested me if I didn't have hard proof of everything I just told you and they're going to let me go. As soon as it's safe."

My jaw is on the floor. I cannot believe what I'm hearing.

"So, the money? Where is it?"

He breaks our eye contact for the first time since we started talking. "I couldn't trace the owner of the account where the money was deposited into. So, I found a hacker who could, and he finally did it. Those Swiss bank accounts are almost impossible to penetrate." He gives me a wry smile and reaches up to touch the chain dangling around my neck.

"You're wearing your pendant and Dean's ring," he says quietly as he fingers both. "You remember what I told you Sankofa required of you, Millicent?"

"I do, Daddy," I respond quietly.

He looks up at me and his eyes, so like my own, are full of pride.

"Always remember who you are. When you need to, use the past as your prologue and write a story of your life that shows you haven't forgotten where you came from," I recite verbatim, the charge my father recited to me when he gave me the necklace.

"My father stands up to round the table and comes to stand in front of me, resting both hands on my shoulders.

"I need to tell you the rest of it. I haven't told anyone else, not even your mother. I wanted to tell you first."

I listen as he speaks. When he's done, my ears are ringing and my heart is hammering in my chest. My head spins with the ramifications of what he has told me.

How am I going to tell Dean?

breaking chains

"ARE you sure you want to do this? If you hand it over, what happens next will be completely out of your control."

"I'm one hundred percent sure, Val. I'm not going to help her get away with it."

I'm in Paris at Interpol's office waiting for the contact Val had there to see me.

"I'm proud of you. But I'm so sorry you had to do this."

"Me too."

"You're going to have to give them your phone and they'll keep it as long as it takes to extract the recording."

"That's fine. It's the least I can do."

"Have you talked to Milly?"

"No, but I want to before all hell breaks loose."

I shiver at the reminder that I've still got to explain this to her and that between me and the light at the end of this tunnel is a yawning darkness with unseen dangers.

"Don't worry, Dean. She loves you. You're as much of a victim in this as she is."

"I know. I just hate that my mother had a hand in her misery." It's an understatement, but I don't know that I'll ever have the words to articulate the depth of my regret. At the same time, relief is already tickling the edges of my heavy heart. I'm doing the right thing. Finally, I'm setting the record straight. My father is dead, what people think of him doesn't matter. But Mr. Hassan is very much alive and he deserves for everyone to know the truth.

When I leave the office more than six hours later, I'm exhausted, my emotions are a painful blur. I don't know what the future holds, but knowing the truth has cleared a path forward.

FORGIVENESS

"On my way."

I breathe a sigh of relief when Milly's text finally pops up.

I've been pacing a hole into my carpet waiting to hear from her. I wanted to join her in Virginia, but she asked me to wait for her to come to me.

She asked for a day, and I gave it to her. But my mother's arrest made the news at the time that we were apart.

I don't know if she'd seen it, but she was distant and short on the phone and my greatest fear has been stalking my thoughts ever since.

She's seen her father and he would have told her that he didn't have the money.

I have so many questions, but more than anything, I miss my woman, so much. This is the longest we've been apart since I found her again and I've never wished for wings before layovers kept me from reaching her.

If I've learned anything in the past few days it's that this Milly, the woman I have gotten to know again, is at her core the same woman I knew back when we were kids. She still sees to the heart of me. She still forces me to lay myself open and be absolutely honest with her.

The way I love her scares me because it's so big and vital that I don't know if I'd ever find happiness again if I lost her. I'll tell her what I know and if she can't look at me when I'm done, I'll find a way . . .

No, fuck that. I will tie her ass up and keep her that way until she sees reason.

I ran my hands through my hair for the hundredth time since she called to say she was on her way.

The die is cast. I can't do anything but wait.

I take a quick shot of Patron and continue to pace.

Ten minutes later, I almost jump out of my skin when the elevator that only stops on my floor dings. I walk over so that I'm standing there when it opens.

Milly walks in carrying a sleeping Anthony. He's draped over her like a monkey, legs wrapped around her waist and arms around her shoulders.

She smiles at me over his head and motions for me to take him.

"He wouldn't let me come here without him. Said he had missed you. So, I brought him. I hope it's okay," she says as soon as he's in my arms.

He's such a bundle of energy, and so incredibly clever. But right now, he's fast asleep and when I take him from his mother, he snuggles his soft head into my neck.

"Of course, it is. I'll put him down in the spare room. Make yourself at home." And I take my precious cargo and tuck him into the bed in my guest room.

I come back out to find Milly staring out of the window of my Rivers Wilde penthouse suite. I've recently leased it until I can find something to buy, but it has spectacular views of the city.

I walk to stand behind her and put my hands on her shoulders. Relief courses through me when she leans back into me.

Her jeans can't disguise her generous ass, and I can't control the erection that immediately develops to press into her back.

"Miss me, did you?" She smiles at me over her shoulder and grinds that ass, the one I love and can't stop looking at, into me.

"I always miss you, Milly, but this week has felt like a special kind of hell without you." I drop kisses on the shell of her ear, under her jaw, and down her neck, breathing in her sweet rose scent.

"Mmmm, baby, me, too," she murmurs.

She turns around and steps up on her toes to press a hot kiss to my mouth. And that's all it takes. It's like all of our longing erupts at that moment. The next thing I know, I have her hoisted up, legs wrapped around my waist.

I'm walking her to the waist high counter in my kitchen. We are lost in our kiss, it's angry, desperate, loving, sexy, hot. Her tongue parries with mine. She sucks at it, licks the inside of my mouth, nips my lips, kisses me like she needs me to know that she's on fire.

And I kiss her so she knows my heart is on fire for her. So she knows I know who these lips belong to. I say I'm sorry with this kiss. I say I love you with it. I say I would fucking burn the earth to ashes to keep you with me, and I say please don't ever leave me.

She reaches between us and pulls my sweatpants down. My cock, eternally ready for her body, jumps out and bobs between us.

I unbutton her jeans and break our kiss just long enough to pull off her shoes and her jeans and her panties all the way down her legs.

"Dean, please, now," she demands. My woman does not beg, she knows she never has to, and I comply.

I slide home, she's wet and warm. It feels so good; I know my eyes roll into the back of my head. My lips find hers again as I make love to her. On the counter, with my heart in my throat and my love on my lips as I kiss her with everything I have.

Because everything I have, everything I am, is hers.

She groans, a sound that might as well be the song of the siren calling Odysseus, because I start to chase it, to move so she makes this sound endlessly.

She lays down on the counter, and I lift her blouse so that her magnificent breasts are in my line of sight. I bend down over her and suck her beautiful, dark brown nipples until I feel her coming.

And when we come, we come together. The ferocious wave of pleasure that moves between us is a centrifugal force. I don't know where it begins, but I know I never want it to end.

I kiss her as I pull out of her, and she captures my mouth in a searing, quick kiss and mumbles, "I love you," as she releases me.

I reach around the counter for a paper towel and wipe up the mess we've made.

"Can I just get a T-shirt or something," she says as she sits up on the counter. She pulls her shirt all the way off and she sits there naked. She looks like she has been well-fucked, her beautiful lips tipped up in a smile of satisfaction as she eyes me.

"Of course. Let me get one from my room. I walk down the hall, snag one of my Stanford T-shirts, and rush back. She slips it on, slides off the counter, and walks to the bathroom without a word.

I'm sitting on the couch when she comes out a few minutes later and plops down next to me.

"Dean, I need to tell you a few things," she starts.

I stop her. "Milly, can I go first? I have so much to explain about where I've been and what I've learned," I implore.

She looks pained but nods. "Okay, go ahead."

I tell her about the last seventy-two hours. My conversation with Ed, my trip to Sedona, my visit with my mother, and what I think it all means.

When I'm done, she looks at me with an expression I cannot discern in her eyes. So, I keep talking.

"I know it's a lot. I don't know how you can reconcile spending your life with the son of the people who did this to your family, but I had to tell you, even if it meant you wouldn't be able to—"

She cuts me off when she leaps off the couch, stands in front of me, and eyes stricken says, "Are you fucking breaking up with me?"

I'm so relieved that I laugh. I thought she was going to be the one breaking up with me. Her eyes look like they are lit with fire burning within her. And Milly never curses and I feel like an ass all over agin.

"Red, no. I just—"

"You just what? Please, don't even finish that sentence. You *cannot* finish that sentence."

She pins me with a glare that makes me grateful I just finished having sex because my balls might not be capable of descending far enough to ever do it again. She starts to stride back and forth in front of me.

"I know about your mom. I saw the news. That money wouldn't have saved him from these assholes that have had him all these years. What your father did was terrible, and your mother..." She shudders. "But *you* didn't do it. Unless you're about to tell me you were in on their scheme?" She stops to look at me.

"No, of course not."

She drops to her knees in front of me. "You are the greatest love of my life. We met, and my soul said, 'that's him, Milly.'"

I reach out to grab her by the biceps and pull her up into my lap. She smiles at me as she sits.

"I'm not letting you go for anything, Dean. Not for anything. I can figure everything else in the world out, but I cannot figure out how to live without you." She picks up my hand and presses a kiss to my knuckles.

She kisses each one. "Please don't, Dean, because you are me.

I've just found my whole self again. And if you try to take away a piece of it, I won't let it go easily."

Relief courses through me like a river freed from the dam holding it back. My arms go around her.

"Red, you and Ant Man, you guys are my lighthouse. I couldn't find my way without your light and without your love."

I reach around her and unclasp the chain around her neck. I slip the little heart shaped pendant off to reach the promise ring I gave her. I clasp the chain back around her neck.

I reach for her right hand and slip the ring onto the third finger. The same finger I put it on fifteen years ago.

I make her promises.

But this time, I'm a man in charge of my own life. It will take an act of God to stop me from keeping them.

Milly accepts my ring, I know I finally have someone willing to keep the promises they have made to me, too.

I don't know where we are going, but I remember where we've come from. And I know that this love, this happiness is a choice. Our adventure, the grand experiment of blending a family, healing old wounds, loving without limitation, reservation, or condition, is just starting.

epilogue

Coventry, England

maya hassan

LIFE IS GOOD. We are all in Coventry for Louis and Cara's wedding. Cara is beautiful, and Louis is almost hysterical in his happiness. Everyone is happy.

And I'm here with my husband. He's back with me, and we've moved home to Houston. We are getting our second chance at life and love, and we are taking full advantage of it.

The only fly in our ointment is that Dean's mother is also back in Houston, and we've had to stop frequenting our favorite breakfast place because she's a waitress there.

The first time I saw her, I couldn't keep my jaw from hitting the roof. This is a woman who hadn't worked a day in her adult life, but I guess she had no choice.

The statute of limitations for blackmail is five years, so she couldn't be prosecuted for her crimes, but the hacker who found her account in the first place also managed to take the money in the account and move it to my husband's. Dean has cut her off, and without him to support her, she's had to get a job.

I look at the sleeping child in my lap: Henry, Addie and

308

Simon's nephew, is one and a half now. He calls me Grandma, and I love it. He calls Omar, Pops, just like Anthony does.

I gaze out onto the dance floor where my five other heartbeats are dancing.

Milly and Dean are wrapped in each other's arms, dancing slowly—even slower than the song "Amazing" by Luther Vandross requires. I love seeing them together. Every time Milly walks into the room, Dean's eyes light up like he's seeing her for the very first time. Like he can't believe how beautiful she is. I'm so glad she finally has this.

Anthony is dancing with Louis' mother, even though his head only reaches her middle. They have been dancing all night, as Louis' dad sits and watches.

Lilly is dancing with her father, her head resting on his shoulder.

I look at Omar's face and see his eyes are closed as his head rests on the top of Lilly's. Lilly's eyes, though, are wide open. She's staring across the room at Louis' brother, Harry. He's sitting, sullen, at a table by himself. His jaw is clenched so tightly, I am sure he is pulverizing his teeth.

When we arrived here for the wedding, they clearly recognized each other and for a few seconds looked elated to see one another. Then the elation, at least on Harry's face, was replaced by an expression of horror. And they haven't spoken again since.

Lilly refuses to divulge what's going on. I haven't pressed her, but only because I know that's the worst way to get her to talk. I'll get to the bottom of it soon.

Addie is dancing with Kyle, Simon's brother, and they are laughing hysterically at something. They are clearly very close.

Addie's own wedding is in six months, and they have decided to get married in Houston. Addie asked her dad to walk her down the aisle just last week. They have had the hardest time in terms of their reunion, but they have worked hard to find peace with each other.

My life has been the most unexpected adventure. Over the

last decade, I have wanted to give in to my fear and my doubt, but love, real love, is stronger than all of those things.

And I believe in fairytales; I know we've got some work to do, but I'm chasing my own Happily Ever After. I'm so close I can taste it. I kiss the top of Henry's little head and survey my family.

Oh yes, I can taste it. And it's delicious.

milly

When the song ends, Dean and I slip off the dance floor. Anthony is still dancing with Louis' mother, and I want to take the opportunity to get Dean alone.

I've been waiting for the perfect moment to tell him what I found out this afternoon. I didn't want to distract from Cara and Louis' day, but I can't hold it in any longer. I turn to him as he starts to lead me back to our table.

"You want to go for a walk? Get some fresh air?"

He smiles. "Great minds think alike; I was just about to ask you the same thing."

We walk past our table where my mother sits with Henry asleep on her lap with my dad and Lilly on either side of her. Lilly looks forlorn. And I don't know why. I need to get her alone so we can talk.

I put that aside and focus on Dean. He cuts a dashing figure in his tux. I admire the view while I trail behind him as we make our way through the crowd on our way outside.

We walk in a companionable silence until we are at the lake which is at the center of Louis' parents' property. Dean sits down on the bench and pulls me onto his lap.

"You having a good time, Red?" he asks, smiling up at me. Even in the dark with the moon and the fairy lights strung in the trees around us as our only light, I can see so much love in his eyes.

"I'm having the best time." I smile and place a quick peck on his lips.

He reaches into his pocket and pulls out a worn piece of paper. He doesn't say anything as he hands it over to me, but he's got the biggest smile on his face.

"What's this?" I ask, my curiosity peaked.

I take it from him and unfold it. He pulls his phone from the inside pocket on his suit and turns on the flashlight feature. He shines it on the paper in my hand, and I see that it's my list.

"I found this, tucked away in a kitchen drawer. I saw you'd crossed everything off, but I thought it was missing something. So, I pulled it out and put it in my pocket. I wanted to wait for the right time to talk about it."

My stomach sinks a little, and I feel myself getting annoyed.

"It's not really for you to decide whether it's complete or not," I snap as I fold it back up and start to move off of his lap.

"Hey, Red, don't be upset. You're right. It's not for me to decide, but I thought I could ask you to add one more thing and see if you thought it was a good idea," he says, not looking the least bit contrite.

"I mean, I guess. But, I have to tell you, I asked you to come out here so I could tell you something. And this isn't the romantic conversation I envisioned us having."

I stop, trying to get up, but stiffen my spine so I'm not leaning on him anymore.

"You wanted to tell me something?" He looks very pleased with himself, his smile only widens.

"Yes, I do. And it's something amazing," I clip. But just saying that completely erases my annoyance because I remember the happy news I have to share.

"Okay, well then go ahead," he says, his smile incandescent and huge.

"Are you ready?" I ask him. He only nods, and I can see his Adam's apple bobbing in his throat as he swallows hard. I cup his face, look into those beautiful green eyes, and tell him.

"I'm pregnant." I see his eyes widen, and then I see them fill with tears he doesn't shed. I feel my own tears prick the back of my eyes as his smile softens, but his eyes radiate true joy at me.

His hand drifts to the small swell that barely there and nothing has ever felt so right. "Our baby." His eyes never leave mine, and I'm rendered breathless by the love I see in them. I bring my lips to his, and whisper against them, "It's really early, but I got the call from my doctor this afternoon. I'm just a little over nine weeks along, if I've done the math right."

He closes his eyes. "Milly, I brought you out here to ask you to marry me. I was going to ask you to add Become Dean's Wife to your list."

I suck in my breath at this declaration. And my cup of happiness and love overflows. I press my forehead to his.

He opens his eyes and keeps talking. "I thought I would wait until your divorce papers are filed next week. But all day, I felt like today was the day. And that I should just do it." He lifts me off his lap, places me on my feet, and stands.

"Will you sit, please," he asks and I do. I sit back on the bench and am grateful for the support because my knees have gone weak.

He drops to one knee in front of me. "Millicent, I won't ask you to make me the happiest man alive because you've already done that. But I will ask you to give me the chance to return the favor. And I'm asking you to let me do it for the rest of my life."

He grabs my left hand, reaches into his pocket, and pulls out a tiny blue box.

"I want you to wear my ring, and I want you to be my wife. I want us to raise our family together. I want to get the chance to show you just how much I love you. You are my champion, my hero. Your strength inspires me. I know every day you show me something new and amazing about yourself. I know your beauty has so many splendid facets, I could look at you forever and never see them all. Please, do me the honor of letting me pledge my life to you."

He pops the box open and inside is a gold band with three emerald cut diamonds nestled next to each other.

My eyes travel from the ring to his face and back again. I'm so overwhelmed by his proposal I can only stare at him.

How did I get so lucky?

This magnificent, sensitive, honest, and beautiful man loves me in a way I didn't know I could be loved.

I nod and he slips the ring on my finger. And when he leans in to kiss me, I remember our first kiss.

"When you look at me like that, I know nothing could ever truly keep us apart. Even when our graves claim us, they won't hold us because we'll always find each other. You're the one."

I whisper, "Still and always."

A Gift for you:

Straight to the Heart is a completely free, gorgeous ebook that includes the reading order for all of my books and gives you a deep dive look at each character I've written - and a couple you'll meet this year - click here.

acknowledgments

Notes of Gratitude

There are so many people to thank, but my loyal readers are always number one. Thank you for continuing to show up even when you're not sure exactly what you're going to get. I write for you and always will.

To all my friends and colleagues in the book community - your support, advice, and encouragement has been the wind beneath my wings. Thank you.

To my parents and sisters and their families - thank you for believing in me and loving me so fiercely.

Last but most especially, to my husband and children who are my fertile ground, my safety net, my heart and soul food…I would be lost without you. Thank you for making my life meaningful and beautiful. Love you all forever, across time and without limit.

about the author

Dylan Allen is a Texas girl with a serious case of wanderlust.

A self-proclaimed happily ever junkie, she loves creating stories where her characters chase their own happy endings.

When she isn't writing or reading, eating, or cooking, she and her family are planning their next adventure.

I love talking to you guys! Feel free to send me an email at Dylan@dylanallenbooks.com

Are you on Facebook? If you are, then PLEASE join my private reader group, Dylan's Day Dreamer.

It's where I spend most of my time online. My Day Dreamers get exclusive giveaways, sneak peaks, glimpses into my every day, and lots of other fun bookish things! It's fantastic and my favorite place on the internet.

Click here to join and make sure you introduce yourself.

You can find me on the following social media platforms:

also by dylan allen

Also By Dylan Allen

RIVERS WILDE SERIES

The Legacy

Book one of the Rivers Wilde Series. An opposites attract, enemies to lovers stand-alone that kicks off this brand new series.

The Legend

This is a second chance at love story. Remington Wilde has loved one woman in his life and even though timing and family manipulations keep pulling them apart, it's a love worth fighting for.

The Jezebel

Regan Wilde and Stone Rivers were born enemies. But love has other ideas.

The Gathering

A delicious holiday novella with points of view from all six main characters including a scene from Tina and Tyson Wilde's point of view for the first time

The Daredevil: A Rivers Wilde/1001 Nights Novella

Tyson Wilde laughs in the face of danger and has yet to face a challenge he's not up to. Until Dina Lu walks into his life and threatens to turn it upside down.

The Mastermind: A Rivers Wilde/1001 Nights Novella

He lives under a golden spotlight. She's shackled to a past that must stay hidden. A fire-burning, second-chance romance novella.

THE SYMBOLS SERIES.

Then Came You

Set in London this is a workplace romance that features two people who are trying to outrun their pasts and protect their cynical hearts from more pain. But when their lives collide and their hearts and bodies yearn for each other, they'll have to decide if they are brave enough to fight for their love.

Still The One

This second chance romance features high school sweethearts who were torn apart by tragedy and treachery. Years later, when they realize that their feelings haven't changed, they embark on a mission to unravel the mystery surrounding her father's disappearance. But what they discover about their past might make a future together impossible.

STANDALONES

The Sun and Her Star

A friends to lovers, second chance at story. Angsty, emotional, sexy, and unforgettable. Graham and Apollo are two people who find each other just when they need to. What starts as a deep, abiding friendship grows into the kind of love that can move mountains. This story is a reader favorite.

Thicker Than Water

A friends to lovers and workplace romance that follows the love story between an undocumented writer and the movie executive who changes her life. This story is hopeful, honest, and achingly relevant. Go in with an open mind and prepare to fall in love.

The Sound of Temptation

A second chance forbidden romance that follows star-crossed lovers, a talented musician and the artist who becomes his muse. It spans nearly ten years and is a turbulent, exhilarating, heart pounding, and deeply intimate love story you will never forget.

Find all of them here.

If you've read my books and haven't already, please leave a review. Nothing fancy, but a line or two helps so much!

I love to hear from readers! Stay in touch with me everywhere using this link.

Made in the USA
Middletown, DE
26 June 2024